INGO

INGO

Helen Dunmore

HarperCollins*PublishersLtd*

Ingo

© 2006 by Helen Dunmore. All rights reserved.

Published by HarperCollins Publishers Ltd

First Canadian Edition

HarperCollins books may be purchased for educational, business,
or sales promotional use through our Special Markets Department.

HarperCollins Publishers Ltd
2 Bloor Street East, 20th Floor
Toronto, Ontario, Canada
M4W 1A8

www.harpercollins.ca

Library and Archives Canada Cataloguing in Publication

Dunmore, Helen, 1952-
    Ingo / Helen Dunmore. — 1st Canadian ed.

ISBN-13: 978-0-00-200618-7
ISBN-10: 0-00-200618-9

    I. Title.

PZ7.D9219In 2006   j823'.914   C2005-905531-6

HC 9 8 7 6 5 4 3 2 1

Printed and bound in the United States

FOR TESS

CHAPTER ONE

You'll find the mermaid of Zennor inside Zennor Church, if you know where to look. She's carved from old, hard, dark wood. The church is dark, too, so you have to bend down to see her clearly. You can trace the shape of her tail with your finger.

Someone slashed across her with a knife a long time ago. A sharp, angry knife. I touched the slash mark very gently, so I wouldn't hurt the mermaid any more.

"Why did they do that to her, Dad? Why did they hurt her?"

"I don't know, Sapphy. People do cruel things sometimes, when they're angry."

And then Dad told me the mermaid's story. I was only little, but I remember every word.

"The Zennor mermaid fell in love with a human," said Dad, "but she was a Mer creature and so she couldn't come to live with him up in the dry air. It would have killed her. But she couldn't forget him, and she couldn't

1

live without him. She couldn't even sleep for thinking about him. All she wanted was to be with him."

"Would she have died in the air?" I asked.

"Yes. Mer people can't live away from the water. Anyway, the man couldn't forget her either. The sight of the mermaid burned in his mind, day and night. And the mermaid felt just the same. When the tide was high, she would swim up into the cove, then up the stream, as close as she could to the church, to hear him singing in the choir."

"I thought it was mermaids that sang, Dad."

"In this story it was the man who sang. In the end the mermaid swam up the stream one last time and he couldn't bear to see her go. He swam away with her, and he was never seen again. He became one of the Mer people."

"What was his name, Dad?"

"Mathew Trewhella," said Dad, looking down at me.

"But Dad, that's your name! How come he's got the same name as you?"

"It's just by chance, Sapphy. It all happened hundreds of years ago. You know how the same names keep on going in Cornwall."

"What was the mermaid called, Dad?"

"She was called Morveren. People said she was the Mer King's daughter, but I don't believe that's true."

"Why not?"

"Because the Mer don't have kings."

Dad sounded so sure about this that I didn't ask him how he knew. When you're little, you think your mum and dad know everything. I wasn't surprised that Dad knew so much about the Mer.

I stroked the wooden mermaid again, and wished I could see her in real life, swimming up the stream with her beautiful shining tail. And then another thought hit me.

"But Dad, what about all the people the man left behind? What about his family?"

"He never saw them again," said Dad.

"Not even his mum or his dad?"

"No. None of them. He belonged to the Mer."

I tried to imagine what it would be like never to see Dad again, or Mum. The thought was enough to make my heart beat fast with terror. I couldn't live without them, I knew I couldn't.

I looked up at Dad. His face looked faraway and a bit unhappy. I didn't like it. I wanted to bring him back to me, now.

"Can't catch me!" I shouted, and I ran off clattering up the stone aisle of the church to the door. The door was heavy and the fastening was stiff but I wrestled it open.

"You can't catch me!" I yelled back over my shoulder, and I ran out through the porch, down the stone steps and into the sunshine of the lane. I heard the church door bang and there was Dad, leaping down the steps after me. The faraway look had gone from his face.

"Look out, Sapphy, I'm coming to get you!"

That was a long time ago. Dad never talked about the Mer again, and nor did I. But the story lodged deep inside my mind like an underwater rock that can tear a ship open in bad weather. I wished I'd never seen the Zennor mermaid. She was beautiful, but she scared me.

It's Midsummer Eve now, and when it gets dark they'll light the Midsummer Fire on Carrack Down. We go up there every Midsummer Eve. I love it when they throw the wreath of flowers into the flames, and the wreath flares up so that for a few seconds you watch flowers made out of fire. The bonfire blazes and everyone drinks and dances and laughs and talks. Midsummer Night is so short that dawn arrives before the party's over.

Dad's up there now, helping build the fire. They pile furze and brushwood until the bonfire stands taller than me or Conor. Conor's my brother; he's two years older than me.

"Come on, Saph! I'm going on up to see how big the bonfire is now."

I run after Conor. This is how it usually is. Conor ahead, and me hurrying behind, trying to keep up with him.

"Wait for me, Con!"

We wait for the sun to set and for the crowd to gather, and then it's time to light the Midsummer Fire. The first star shines out. Geoff Treyarnon thrusts his flaming torch into the dry heart of the bonfire. The fire blazes up and everyone links hands and begins to dance around it, faster and faster. The flames leap higher than the people and we have to jump back.

Conor and I join the ring around the fire. Mum and Dad dance too, holding hands. It makes me so happy to see them like this, dancing and smiling at each other. If only it was always like this. No quarrels, no loud voices...

The flames jump higher and higher and everyone yells and laughs. Conor drinks a bottle of ginger beer, but I don't like the taste. I wrap myself in a rug and sit and watch until the flames blur into red and orange and gold. My eyes sting and I shut them, just for a minute. The fire melts into velvety blackness. There are stars in the blackness and I want to count them one by one, but they're dancing too fast...

I must have fallen asleep. Suddenly Dad's here, swooping down out of the night to pick me up.

"All right, Sapphy? Hold on tight now and I'll carry you down the hill."

I'm too big to be carried, but it's Midsummer Night and Dad says that's the one night when all the rules can be broken. He picks me up, still wrapped in the rug with my feet poking out. I look back over his shoulder. The fire has flattened down into a heap of red ash. People are still sitting around it drinking, but the dancing's over.

The path that leads down to our cottage is rough and steep, but Dad won't let me drop. My dad is strong. He takes his boat out in most weathers and he can swim more than three miles. He has a medal for life-saving.

Mum and Conor are walking ahead of us on the path down. They're talking, but I can't hear the words. I put my arms round Dad's neck and hold on tight, partly because the path is rough and partly because I love him. His strength makes me feel so safe.

Dad begins to sing. He sings O Peggy Gordon and his voice rises up loud and sweet into the summer night.

> *I wish I was away in Ingo*
> *Far across the briny sea,*
> *Sailing over deepest waters…*

I love it when Dad sings. He has a great voice and people used to say that he should be in the church choir, but Dad only laughs at that.

"I'd rather sing in the open air," he says. It's true that when he's working in our garden people lean against our wall to listen to him. Dad likes singing in the pub as well.

Mum, Dad, me and Conor. All of us going home safe on a summer night.

I always think that our family is made up of two halves. There is Conor and Mum, who are calm and sensible and always do what they say they're going to do. And there's me and Dad. We flare up like the Midsummer Bonfire, lose our tempers and say things we should never say. Sometimes we don't know what we're going to do until we've done it. And I sometimes tell lies when I need to, which Conor never does. Conor tells you the truth straight out. You just have to get used to it.

But it doesn't matter that we're a family of two halves, as long as we stick together.

We come to the steepest part of the path, and Dad has to put me down. Westward over the sea there is still a bit of light, like the ghost of a sunset or maybe the ghost of the moon rising. The sea stretches out dark in the distance. I'm glad that Dad's stopped here, because I love to watch the sea.

Dad has stopped singing too. He stands there still and silent, staring way out to sea. He looks as if he's searching for something. A boat maybe. But there won't be any boats out tonight. Not on Midsummer Night.

Even though Dad's standing next to me, I feel as if he's forgotten me. He's far away.

"Dad," I say at last. I feel uneasy. "Dad?" But Dad doesn't answer. I'm tired and cold now and my legs are shivery. I just want to be at home, all four of us safe inside our cottage, with the door shut. I want to be in bed, falling into sleep.

"Dad, let's catch up with Mum and Conor. They're way ahead of us. *Da–ad—*"

But Dad holds up his hand. "Hush," he says. "Listen."

I listen. I hear an owl hunting. I hear the deep noise of the sea, like breathing. On a calm night you have to listen for it, but it's there all the time. You would only hear silence if the world ended and the sea stopped moving. As soon as this thought comes into my mind the uneasy feeling gets stronger. I don't like this. I'm afraid.

"Listen," says Dad again. The way he says it makes my skin prickle all over with fear.

"What, Dad?" I say sharply. "What are you listening to?"

"Can't you hear it?"

"*What?*"

But Dad still won't answer. He stares out to sea a little longer and then he shakes himself as if he needs to wake up.

"Time to go, Sapphy."

It's too dark for me to see Dad's face clearly, but his voice is normal again. He swings me back up into his arms. "Let's be getting you home."

By the time we reach our cottage, Mum has already sent Conor upstairs to bed.

"Go on up now, Sapphy," says Dad. He stretches and yawns, but his eyes are brilliant and wide awake. I notice that he's left the door ajar, as if he's planning to go back outside. The front door to our cottage comes straight into our living room, and then you go through the back to the kitchen. Mum's in the kitchen, clattering plates.

"I'm away down to the shore," Dad calls to her. "I can't settle to sleep yet."

Mum emerges from the kitchen, blinking with tiredness.

"What? At this time of night?"

"It's a wonderful night," says Dad. "The longest day and the shortest night. Think of it, Jennie, we won't get another night like this for a whole year."

"You'll break your neck on the rocks one of these nights," says Mum.

But we all know he won't. Dad knows his way too well.

This is how you get down to our cove. The track runs by our cottage. You follow it to the end, and then there's a path where bracken and brambles and foxgloves grow up so high that you wouldn't find the way unless you knew it. Push them aside, and there's the path. When I was little I used to pretend it was magic. You go down the path, and suddenly you come out on to a grassy shelf above the cove. You might think you're nearly there, but you're not, not at all. You have to scramble over the lip of the cliff and then climb down over a jumble of huge black rocks.

The rocks are slippery with weed. Sometimes you have to stretch yourself down for the next foothold. Sometimes you have to jump. Sometimes you fall. Conor and I have both got scars on our legs from falling on the rocks.

Down and down, and then you can squeeze between the two boulders that guard the way to the cove. It's damp and dank in the shadow of the boulders, and it smells of fish and weed. Conor and I find long-legged spider crabs there, and lengths of rope, and fish skeletons, and pieces of driftwood.

After you pass through the boulders there are more rocks to climb across. But you can see the beach now. You're nearly there.

The beach. Our beach, made of flat, white sand. The best beach in the world.

You jump down on to it. You're there! But the beach only exists at mid to low tide. At high tide it disappears completely, and the whole cove is full of the sea.

But when the beach is there, you can swim, climb on the rocks and dive, picnic and sunbathe, make a fire of driftwood and cook on it, explore the rock pools, watch the gulls screaming round their nests... Conor and I go there nearly every day in summer, when the tide's right.

Sometimes we explore the caves at the back of our beach. They're all dark and slimy, and they echo when you call. *Hello... lo... lo... Can you hear me... hear me... hear me...*

The air's clammy, and there's a sound of water dripping. You can't tell where it's coming from. You can wriggle your way down narrow passages, but not too far in case you get stuck and the tide comes in and drowns you. Imagine being stuck in a slimy tunnel of rock while the cold sea curls round your toes and then your legs, and you know all the time what's going to happen, no matter how much you struggle.

"Keep a sharp lookout when you're in those caves," Dad always tells us. "Don't forget the time. The tide comes in fast, and you could get cut off."

You have to watch the tide. When the water reaches a black rock that me and Conor call the Time Rock, it's time to go. Back over the sand, scramble over the stones, squeeze between the boulders and then up the rocks, as fast as you can. No good thinking you can swim for safety.

If you tried to swim around the headland you'd be caught by the rip and carried away.

Dad keeps his boat on the other side of the rocks, where it's deep water. When the weather's bad the waves could smash the boat against the rocks, so Dad has a winch to haul the *Peggy Gordon* up above the tide line. Dad's always out in the *Peggy Gordon*, fishing or checking the crab pots, or else taking photographs. He takes photos and changes the images on his computer and he writes text on them; then they get framed and he sells them to tourists.

So when Dad says he is going down to the cove, there's no reason to worry. Dad would never break his neck on those rocks, and it will be dawn before long. I used to be scared when he was out in his boat and the weather turned bad, but he always came home safe. He knows every wrinkle of the coast. *I know every pool of salt water and every creature in it*, he says, and it doesn't sound like boasting, because it's the truth.

But tonight, Mum's worried.

"Don't go, Mathew," she says. "It's much too late. Let's get to bed."

"Why don't you come with me?" he answers. I can tell he really wants her to come. "Why don't you leave these children for once and come with me?"

He says 'these children' as if it's strangers he's talking about, not me and Conor. As if I'm not even in the room. I hate it. I feel cold again, and scared.

"How can I leave Sapphire in the middle of the night?" asks Mum.

"What's going to happen? You'll be all right, won't you, Sapphy, if me and Mum take a walk together down to the cove? Conor's only upstairs."

I look at Mum, then back to Dad.

"Yes," I say, in a voice that means no. Mum's got to understand that I mean no...

"She's too young," says Mum. "It's all right, Sapphy, don't look so scared. I'm not leaving you."

Dad flashes with anger. "Are we never going to have a life of our own again?" he asks fiercely. "They're not babies any more. Come down to the sea with me, Jennie."

But Mum shakes her head. I feel guilty now as well as scared. I hate it when Dad's angry, and it's my fault this time.

"I'll go on my own then," says Dad. His face is hard. He turns away. "Don't bother to wait up for me, Jennie."

"Mathew!" says Mum, but the door swings wide and Dad's vanished into the night. The door bangs.

"Go on up to bed now, Sapphy," says Mum, in a tired, quiet voice.

I go up to bed. There are two bedrooms in our cottage. Mum and Dad sleep in one, and I sleep in the other. Conor has the best deal of all. There's a ladder up from my bedroom that goes into the loft, where Conor sleeps. Dad made him a window in one end. When Conor wants to be alone he can pull up the ladder and no one can get him.

I get undressed, thinking sleepily about the bonfire, and about Mum and Dad arguing, then I put it all out of my mind. I roll into bed and snuggle down deep under the duvet and sleep comes up over me like a tide.

I don't know anything yet.

I don't know that this is the last night of me and Conor, Mum and Dad, all safe together. I don't know that the two halves of my family are starting to rip apart while I sleep.

But I dream about the mermaid of Zennor. I dream that I'm tracing the deep knife cut that slashes across her body. I'm trying to rub it out, so that the mermaid will be whole and well again. I dream that she opens her wooden eyes and smiles at me.

CHAPTER TWO

ext morning I wake up late to the smell of cooking. Dad's in the kitchen, frying mushrooms in the big black pan. He's whistling softly through his teeth. Mum's banging knives into the drawer.

"He didn't come home until eight this morning," Conor whispers to me.

The atmosphere in the kitchen is thick with anger. Conor and I retreat into the living room with a bowl of cereal each. As we eat, they start to quarrel again. Their voices grow loud. "Are you crazy, Mathew, taking that boat out at night alone when you'd been drinking?"

"I didn't take the boat out."

"Don't lie to me. I can smell the sea on you. Look at the wet on your clothes. It wasn't enough to risk your neck climbing down those rocks in the dark, you had to take the boat out too. I haven't slept a wink. Are you out of your mind?"

Dad's voice crashes back. "I know what I'm doing. I'm in

14

no danger. Are you going to stay on land for the rest of your life, Jennie? If you'd only come with me—"

His voice breaks off. He's angry with Mum, too, just as much as she's angry with him. But why? Dad knows Mum hates the sea. She never goes out in the boat, and for once I'm glad of it. It makes me shiver to think of them both away out there on the sea, on the dark water. So far away that even if I called as loud as I could, they'd never hear me.

"*You* know why I won't come," says Mum. "I've got good reason to keep away from the sea." Her voice is full of meaning. We're so used to the idea that Mum hates the sea and won't go near it that we don't ask why, but suddenly I want to know more.

"Conor, why won't Mum ever go out in the *Peggy Gordon*?" I whisper. It's always, always been Dad who takes me and Conor out on the sea, and Mum who stays at home. Conor shrugs, but suddenly I see in his face that he knows something I don't.

"Conor! You've got to tell me. Just because I'm the youngest, no one ever tells me anything."

"They didn't exactly tell me, either."

"But you do know something."

"I heard them talking one day," says Conor reluctantly. "Mum was saying that she was going to cook a saddle of hare for Sunday dinner."

"Hare! Yuck! I'm not eating that."

"Yeah, that's exactly what Dad said. He said it was bad luck to eat a hare. So Mum said she didn't care, she wasn't

superstitious. Dad said she was the most superstitious person he'd ever met in his life. And Mum said, *Only over one
thing, Mathew. And I've got a good reason to fear the sea."*

"What did she mean? What good reason?"

"I asked Dad later. I said they were talking so loud I
couldn't help overhearing. He wasn't going to tell me, and
then he did. He said a fortune-teller had told Mum's fortune once, and after that she'd never gone out on the sea
again. It was years ago, but she never has. Not once."

"What do you think the fortune-teller said?"

"Dad wouldn't tell me. It must have been something
really bad, though."

"Maybe the fortune-teller said that Mum would die by
drowning."

"Don't be stupid, Saph. A fortune-teller wouldn't ever
say that to someone. *You're going to drown, that'll be ten pounds
please."*

"But she must have told Mum something terrible. Mum
wouldn't stop going in boats for the rest of her life otherwise—"

"Saph, please don't go on about it or I'll wish I hadn't
told you. And don't let them know you know. Dad said
not to tell you in case you got scared."

Mum and Dad's voices rise again. Why do they have to
argue so much? I hardly ever quarrel with Conor.

"I'm going in to make some toast," says Conor. "That'll
stop them."

"I'll come with you."

Mum and Dad are standing by the stove. They go quiet

when they see us, but the air prickles with all the bad things they've said. Sometimes I think that if adult quarrels had a smell, they would smell like burned food. Dad's mushrooms are shrivelled up and black. He sees me looking at them, and he picks up the pan and scrapes the burned mushrooms into the pig bin.

What a waste. I love mushrooms.

The next night Conor and I bike up to see his friend Jack. We stay longer than we mean to, because Jack's Labrador bitch has three puppies. We haven't played with them before, because they've been too little, but now they're seven weeks old. Jack lets us hold one each. My puppy is plump and wriggly and she sniffs my fingers, licks them, and makes a hopeful whining sound in the back of her throat. She is so beautiful. Conor and I have always wanted a dog, but we haven't managed it yet.

"You are the most beautiful puppy in the whole world," I whisper to her, holding her close to my face. She has a funny little folded-down left ear, and soft, inquisitive brown eyes. If I could choose one of the puppies, it would be her. She wrinkles her nose, does a tiny puppy sneeze, and then snuggles in under my chin. I feel as if she's chosen me already.

Poppy, the pups' mother, she knows us, so she doesn't mind us playing with them. She stays near, though, looking pleased and proud and watchful. Every time a pup tries to sneak away to explore, Poppy fetches it back and drops it in the basket. I love the way Poppy makes her mouth soft to pick up the pups by the scruff of their neck.

We forget all about the time. When we remember, it's getting late and we have to rush.

"Come on, Saph. Mum's going to kill me if we're any later!"

Conor's up ahead, racing. My bike's too small for me and I have to pedal like crazy, but it still won't go fast. When Conor gets a new one, I'll have his old one. Dad says maybe at Christmas Conor will get his new bike.

"Wait for me!" I yell, but Conor's away in the distance. At the last bend he waits for me to catch up.

"You are *so slow,*" he grumbles, as we bike the final downhill stretch side by side.

"I'm just as fast as you are, it's only my bike that's slow," I say. "If I had *your* bike..." Conor's already told me he'll paint his old bike for me when he gets a new one, and I can keep the lights. He'll paint it any colour I like.

We reach the gate where the track goes down past our cottage. Ours isn't the only cottage here, but our neighbours are set far apart. At night we can see the lights from the other cottages' windows, shining out against the dark hillside. Our cottage is closest to the sea.

"Look, there's Mum. What's she doing?" asks Conor suddenly.

Mum has climbed to the top of the stile opposite our cottage. She's standing there, outlined against the light of the sunset. She strains forward, as if she's looking for something.

"Something's wrong," says Conor. He drops his bike on the side of the track and starts to run. I drop mine too, but its handlebars get tangled up with Conor's bike. I stop to sort out the bikes and prop them against the wall. I want to run to Mum, but I also don't want to. I hang back. I have a cold feeling in my heart that tells me that Conor is right. Something is wrong. Something has happened.

This is when the long night begins. The longest night of my life so far, even though it's summer and the nights are short.

None of us goes to bed. At first we all sit together in the kitchen, round the table, waiting. Sometimes I start to fall asleep. My head lolls and then I lurch out of sleep just before I tip off my chair. Mum doesn't notice, and she doesn't send me to bed. She watches the door as if any moment it will open, and Dad will be back.

"Dad often takes the boat out this late," Conor keeps saying stubbornly, as the clock moves on. Ten o'clock. Eleven o'clock.

"Not like this," says Mum. Her lips barely move. I know that she's right, and so does Conor. Something's wrong. When Dad goes fishing he usually goes with Badge or Pete. He does go on his own sometimes, but he never, ever just disappears without telling us where he's going. We help him load up the boat and often we watch him go out on the tide.

But this time Dad has said nothing. He was working in the garden all afternoon. Mum heard him singing. She went to lie down for half an hour, because she was so tired from not sleeping the night before. She must have fallen asleep. When she woke the sun was low. She called to Dad, but no one answered. She went down the track and called again but everything was still. Our neighbour, Mary Thomas, came out.

"Is something wrong, Jennie?" she asked. "I heard you calling for Mathew."

"No, nothing's wrong," said Mum. "It's just I don't know where he is. Maybe he's working on the boat. I'll go down to the mooring and check."

Imagine Mum going all the way down to the cove, so near to the sea. She must have been scared, but she did it. She slipped on a rock as she climbed down, and cut her hand on mussel shells and got blood all over her jeans. She went down as far as she dared, until she could see that there was no boat tied up at the mooring place. The tide was high, just on the turn. Mum called and called again even though she was

sure by now that Dad wasn't there. She couldn't stop herself calling.

"I had a feeling that Mathew was nearby. He was trying to get to me, but he couldn't."

Mum doesn't tell us all this as we sit around the kitchen table. Much later that night, when she's told us to go upstairs and get some sleep, we sit on the stairs and listen to her talking to Mary Thomas, telling her all the things she hasn't told us – about calling Dad, and thinking he was nearby, but he couldn't get to her.

Dawn comes, and Dad's still not back. Mary Thomas is with Mum in the kitchen. Conor and I are still sitting on the stairs, waiting and listening. I must have fallen asleep, because suddenly I wake up with Conor's arm round me. I'm stiff all over. My head hurts and the heavy frightened feeling inside is stronger than ever.

Mum said Dad would be back in the morning. But it's morning now, and he's not here. There's a murmur of voices through the closed kitchen door, and we strain to make out what Mum's saying.

"I don't know what to do now, Mary!" she says, and we can hear the fear and panic in her voice. I wait for Mary to tell her to relax and calm down, because Dad's been out in that boat a million times and no harm has ever come to him. But Mary doesn't. Morning light creeps into our cottage, and Mary says, "Maybe we should call the coastguard now, Jennie."

"Come on Saph," says Conor. He stands up, and his face suddenly looks much older. We push through the kitchen doorway, and Mum stares at us as if she's forgotten who we are. She looks awful.

Mary says to Conor, "I was saying to your mum, Conor, that maybe it's time to call the coastguard now. It's not like your father to go off like this and leave your mother worrying. There's enough light to search by. If he's out there fishing, there's no harm done if the coastguard happens by. I'll get the phone for you now, Jennie."

Mum phones, and everything begins. Once it starts you can't stop it. I'm still clinging to the hope that the police and the coastguard will say we're being stupid to bother them. *Take it easy, your dad'll be fine. Wait a while and he'll turn up.* But they don't.

The coastguard Jeep comes bouncing down the track. People talk into radios and mobiles. The police crowd into the kitchen, filling it with their uniforms.

Neighbours knock on the door. Mary goes out to talk to them, quietly, so that none of us will hear her telling the story over and over again. There are mugs of tea on the kitchen table, some empty, some half full. People start bringing sandwiches and cakes and biscuits until there's so much food I think it'll never get eaten I can't eat anything. I try to swallow a biscuit and I choke, and Mum holds a glass of water to my mouth while I sip and splutter. Mum's face is creased with fear and lack of sleep.

The old life of me and Dad and Mum and Conor has stopped like a clock. Another life has begun. I can hear it ticking: your dad has *gone,* your dad has *gone,* your dad has *gone.*

The sun shines brightly, and it's getting warm. Conor stays downstairs with Mum but I go up to my bedroom and wrap the duvet tight around me and shut my eyes and try to bring Dad back. I shut out all the sounds of people in the kitchen below, and concentrate. If you love someone so much, how can he not hear you when you call to him?

"Dad," I say, "Dad. *Please.* Please come home. Can you

hear me, Dad? It's me, Sapphy. I won't let Mum be angry with you if you just come home."

Nobody. Nothing. All I can hear is the rushing sound of my own blood, because the duvet is wrapped around my ears.

"Dad, *please...*"

I sit up, cold all over, and strain my ears for the two things I want to hear more than anything else in the world. One is the beating of Dad's heart, as I heard it when he was carrying me down from the Midsummer Fire. The other is his voice rising up in the summer air, singing *O Peggy Gordon*.

O Peggy Gordon, you are my darling,
Come sit you down upon my knee...

My name's not Peggy, I used to say when I was little. *Come and sit on my knee anyway*, Dad always answered, and he'd cup his hands under my elbows and swoop me up to sit on his lap and I would bounce and laugh and he would laugh back and bounce me higher and higher until Mum told him to stop before I was sick. But she wasn't ever angry then. She was laughing too.

If only time would go back, like the tide. Back and back, past yesterday, past the night before. Back when the bonfire wasn't lit, back to when none of this had happened. And then we could all start again...

The coastguard search up and down the coast, but they find nothing. All that day they search, all the next day and the one after. A helicopter comes down from the air-sea rescue. It flies low and hammers the air, searching coves and cliffs.

After two days Conor explains to me that they are now scaling down the search. He tells me what that means. It means that if Dad is in the sea, or on the cliffs, they don't believe that they'll find him safe any more. Too much time has passed. The helicopter stops flying, and there are only neighbours in our kitchen now, instead of police and coastguards and volunteer searchers. And then the neighbours go back to their own lives, except for Mary.

A few days later Mum says she thinks it's better if we both go back to school. It isn't doing us any good, staying in the cottage and waiting, always waiting.

Five weeks later a climber on the cliffs miles down the coast sees something. It's the hull of the *Peggy Gordon*, wedged upside down between the rocks. He reads the name on it. The coastguards go down, and a team of divers searches the area. There is no sign of Dad. Finally, they pull the boat off the rocks and tow it into shore, so they can examine it thoroughly and find out what caused the accident. But the boat doesn't give a single clue.

Mum says to us, "We have to accept it now. Your Dad had an accident."

"No!" says Conor, slamming his fists on the table. "No, no, no. Dad wouldn't lose the *Peggy Gordon* like that, on a calm night. That's not what happened." He bangs out of the house and gets his bike and disappears. I think he goes up to Jack's. Anyway he comes home late, and when he creeps into my room to climb up his loft ladder, I'm already half asleep.

"Conor?"

"*Ssh.*"

"It's all right. Mum's asleep. She's been—"

"Crying?"

"No. Just sitting, not looking at anything. I hate it when she does that."

"I know."

"Conor, where's Dad?"

I'm still half asleep, or I'd never ask that question. How can Conor know, when nobody knows? The question just slips out. But Conor doesn't get angry. He tiptoes over and kneels by my bed.

"I don't know what happened, Saph. But he's not drowned. I'm sure of it. We'd *know* if he was drowned. We'd feel it. We'd feel a difference, if he was dead."

"Yes," I say. Relief floods me. "You're right. I don't feel as if he's dead either."

Conor nods. "We're going to find Dad, Saph. However long it takes. But you mustn't tell Mum. Swear and promise."

"Swear and promise," I answer, and I spit on my right palm and Conor spits on his, and we slap our palms together. After that I sleep.

They hold a memorial service for Dad in the church. Mum explains that we can't have a proper funeral, because Dad's body hasn't been found. *It hasn't been found because there isn't a body to find. Dad isn't dead*, I think to myself, and I know Conor is thinking the same thing.

Everyone comes to the memorial service in dark clothes, with sad faces.

"Oh Jennie, Jennie dear," they say, and they put their arms round Mum. Some women kiss me, even though I don't want them to. Conor stands there frowning, with his arms folded so no one will dare to kiss him. Conor's angry because everybody's flocking to the memorial service like sheep, believing that Dad's dead, even though no one has found his body. Most people think that Conor is being brave, for Mum's sake.

"You're the man of the house now, Conor," says Alice Trewhidden in her creaky old voice. "Your mother's lucky that she's got a son to take care of her." Alice only likes boys, not girls. In fact girls practically don't exist in Alice's eyes.

"Conor has his own life to live, Alice," says Granny Carne sharply. I didn't see Granny Carne arrive, but suddenly she's there, tall and strong and wild-looking. People fall back a little, to give her room, out of respect. Everyone shows respect to Granny Carne, as if she's a queen. "Conor has his own choices to make," Granny Carne goes on. "None of us can make them for him."

Grumpy, sharp-tongued Alice Trewhidden says nothing back. She just mumbles under her breath and shuffles off sideways like a crab to find the best seat. She's not exactly scared of Granny Carne, but she doesn't want to cross her. Nobody does.

I'm surprised that Granny Carne has come to the memorial service. I've never seen her inside the church before. Everybody else looks surprised too. Heads bob round to look at her as she comes in, and murmurs fly around the cool, echoing space.

Look who's here!

Who?

Granny Carne. Can't remember the last time we saw her inside the church.

"I never seen her inside this church in my life, and that's going back many years," mutters Alice Trewhidden.

Granny Carne doesn't go far inside the church today. She stands by the open door at the back, watching and listening. Maybe she hears all the mutters and murmurs, but she takes no notice. She wears her usual shabby old earth-coloured clothes, but her poppy-red scarf is the brightest thing in the church.

Granny Carne is tall and forbidding. People are still pushing their way into the crowded church, and they glance sideways at her as they come in, and a lot of them nod respectfully, just the same way as they nod to the vicar. The thought of Granny Carne being like the vicar makes my lips twitch.

Granny Carne catches me looking at her. The faintest smile crosses her face. Suddenly I feel a flicker of hope and courage in the dark sadness of the church.

Who is Granny Carne? Why is she different from everyone else?

I remember asking Dad that, when I was about seven. We were sitting on the beach on a day of flat calm, and Dad was skimming stones on the water with a flick of his wrist. Just Dad and me, on our own. The stones hopped on the silky smooth water. One jump, two, four, six jumps—

"Dad, who is Granny Carne? Why do they call her that when she's not anyone's real granny?"

"Some say she's a witch," answered Dad.

"I know," I said. I'd heard that in the playground. "But there aren't real witches now, are there?"

"Who knows?" said Dad. "She has power in her, that's for sure. If you want to put a label on it, you could call it witchcraft. Or you could call it magic."

"Does she do spells, Dad?"

"Out of a great big spell book, do you mean?"

"Or she might know them off by heart."

"She might. She has earth magic in her. That's why she's so strong, old as she is."

"How old is she, Dad?"

Dad shrugged. "She's always been as old as she is now. If you ask her how old she is she'll say she's as old as her tongue and a little bit older than her teeth. Maybe she's been old for ever."

"Are you scared of her, Dad?"

"No, I'm not scared. There are two sorts of magic, Sapphy. I'd say that Granny Carne's magic is mostly benign."

"What does that mean?"

"That her magic does good, rather than harm. Most of the time."

"Not all the time?"

"Magic's wild. You can't put a harness on it, or make it do what you want. Even the best magic can be dangerous."

I remember being very surprised that Dad talked about magic as if it was a real thing. I knew that most grownups didn't believe it was.

"Always show respect to Granny Carne, Sapphy," said Dad. "If you do that, and you don't cross her, she'll be a good friend to you. She's always been a good friend to me. Never whisper about her behind her back, like ignorant people do. You think she doesn't know, but she does."

Benign. Dad thought that Granny Carne's magic was benign. I didn't even know what the word meant then, but much later I looked it up in a dictionary. *Characterised by goodness, kindness*, it said. I thought about good magic, and wondered what Granny Carne's magic was really like.

And here she is at Dad's memorial service, dressed in earth colours and red like flame, not in best black like all the others crowding into the church. Her face is deep brown from wind and sun, and her eyes are yellow amber, like an owl's.

Is there such a thing as owl magic? Maybe Granny Carne is really an owl, changed to a human and sailing high above the church and then swooping down on us. Owls are strong and powerful and wise, but they can tear you with their claws. *Mostly benign*, Dad said. Her owl-eyes are piercing and full of light, as if they can see everything you try to hide.

People have come to the church from miles around, in their dark clothes. Mum and Conor and I sit in the front pew. No one except the vicar can see our faces.

The choir sings, but no one has a voice as good as Dad's. I remember what Dad said about wanting to sing in the open air, instead of inside the church, in the choir. If Dad was here, he wouldn't stay. He'd slip out of the open back door. He'd wink at Granny Carne as he went. I nearly laugh when I think of Dad escaping from his own memorial service, but I stop myself.

Oh hear us when we cry to thee
For those in peril on the sea…

They sing this hymn because it's the hymn for sailors and fishermen, and they believe that Dad has drowned.

And ever let us cry to thee
For those in peril on the sea…

Mum doesn't sing. She stares straight ahead as the song swells louder. Her lips are pressed so tightly together that there's no colour in them. If you didn't know Mum was sad, you'd think she was furiously angry. She often looks like that since Dad went. It's such a slow, gloomy, droning hymn. Dad would hate it. He likes music to have life in it.

I close my eyes, and shut my ears to the church hymn. I strain to listen to a different music. Yes, I can almost believe that I hear Dad's voice:

> *I wish I was away in Ingo*
> *Far across the briny sea,*
> *Sailing over deepest waters...*

Maybe that's where Dad has gone, sailing over deepest waters. He's away in Ingo, wherever Ingo is. That's where we'll find him. If I can just catch one note of his voice, I'll be able to follow it. I'll follow a single thread of his voice, to where Dad is.

The hymn ends. People cough and rustle as they sit down, cramming themselves into the tight pews. Fat Bridget Demelza is spilling over the edge of the pew and into the aisle. I turn to Conor and whisper, "We'll find him, won't we, Conor?"

"Yes," whispers back Conor. "Don't worry, Saph. Let them get on with their memorial service if it makes them happy. It doesn't mean Dad's dead. I know we'll find him."

We'll find Dad in Ingo, I tell myself. In Ingo, however long it takes. We'll find Dad, however hard it is.

No, I am not going to cry. I tip my head back so the

tears that are swelling in my eyes will not fall. They run down the back of my throat and into my mouth, tasting of salt. I swallow them. Dad's still alive. He wouldn't want me to cry.

CHAPTER THREE

t seems like a hundred years since the day of Dad's memorial service. But really it's a year and a month and a day. Three hundred and ninety-six days

Sometimes when I first wake up I don't remember. I think I can hear Dad downstairs, or in the bathroom. Everything's normal. And then it sweeps over me like a dark cloud.

In the daytime I make myself forget. It doesn't always work, even when I'm doing things I love, like swimming or eating chocolate cake, or designing stuff on the school computers. The thought of Dad is always in my mind somewhere, like a bruise. It's the same for Conor. We don't talk about Dad in front of Mum, because she gets upset. We hate her getting upset. She's a lot better than she was. She eats proper meals now, and she doesn't get up in the night and drink cups of tea and walk about downstairs for hours.

We never, ever tell Mum that we think one day we'll find Dad again. She wouldn't believe us anyway.

I used to run to the phone every time it rang.

Yes? Hello? Who is it?

Each time it wasn't Dad's voice I felt as if all the lights had been switched off. When the postman came I'd try to get to the door first, and grab the letters with my heart pounding. But it was never Dad's handwriting on the envelopes. Even when somebody knocked at the door my hopes would spring up again. But why would Dad knock at the door of his own house?

I don't do those things any more. The phone ringing is just the phone ringing, the postman's probably bringing another bill, and a knock on the door means a neighbour.

You know how the sea grinds down stones into sand, over years and years and years? Nobody ever sees it, it happens so slowly. And then at last the sand is so fine you can sift it in your fingers. Losing Dad is like being worn away by a force that's so powerful nothing could resist it. We are like stones, being changed into something completely different.

If you looked casually at me and Mum and Conor now, you might think we were the same people as we were a year ago, except that we're a year older. But we are not the same people. We've changed where no one can see it, inside our minds and our feelings. I didn't want us to change, but I can't stop it.

"Where's Conor? Have you seen him?" Mum's rushing round, getting ready for work. She's always rushing these days, but at least that means that she never just sits, staring into space…

Mum's on the evening shift this week, at the restaurant where she works in St Pirans. She leaves at four, and she'll be back after midnight.

Mum stops in front of the living-room mirror to pin up her hair and put on her lipstick. She never used to wear lipstick every day…

"Sapphire! Are you listening to me?" Mum snaps. I jump. Mum snaps quite a lot these days. She doesn't mean it, it's because she's always tired. She works in one of the expensive new restaurants down by the harbour. The tips are good, but the hours are long in the summer season. Mum got a twenty pound note from one party last week. Twenty pounds! Imagine having so much money you can give away a twenty pound tip on top of paying for your meal. But then there are also mean people, who spend a hundred pounds on one dinner, and think a pound tip is enough—

"Sapphire! *Will you please stop daydreaming!*"

"Sorry, Mum."

"For the third time, where's Conor?"

"Gone up to Jack's." I have no idea where Conor is, but I want Mum to go off to work happy.

"I *told* him to be back by three," says Mum. "I don't like leaving you here on your own, Sapphy. Yes, I know you'll be all right, but I feel safer if Conor's here. Oh dear, these school holidays, they go on for ever."

"But they've only just started, Mum!"

"It's all right for the teachers. *They* get the whole holiday off work, to be with their own kids. They don't have to go to work all summer and worry themselves half to death about leaving their children on their own—"

"Mum, we're not little kids. We're really sensible, and anyway, Conor'll be back in a minute. But Mum, I wouldn't ever be on my own if we had a dog—"

"Sapphire, *please don't start that dog business again.* Oh no, now I've messed up my lipstick."

"I think you look nicer without lipstick."

"The customers don't," mumbles Mum as she wipes off the smudged lipstick and puts on more." Look at the rings under my eyes, Sapphy, I need a bit of colour... Now, if Conor's not back by five, call me on my mobile."

It is so unfair. Jack's got three dogs and we haven't even got one. His mum said we could have Sadie, my favourite puppy, the one with the folding-down ear, but Mum wouldn't let us. We kept telling Mum we'd look after Sadie and take her for walks and do everything, but Mum said what would happen when she was at work and we were at school?

Sadie is so beautiful. She's over a year old now, but Jack's family hasn't sold her to anyone else. Her coat is pale biscuity gold and she has huge soft brown eyes that look at you as if she knows all about you. And she understands when you tell her things. I take Sadie out for walks whenever I can. It's a little bit like having a dog of my own, when I'm out with her. She comes to heel immediately when I say, "Heel, Sadie!" People who go past in cars probably do think she's my dog.

Sadie is so affectionate, but she's not clingy. In fact she

has a perfect character. She always gets so excited when she sees me. Dogs can tell if you really love them. If Jack's mum and dad ever sold Sadie to someone else, I don't think she'd be happy. I know she'd miss me as much as I'd miss her—

"Sapphire, *listen*," says Mum. "There's a pepperoni pizza in the freezer, and Mary's lettuce, and those spring onions."

I nod. I hate spring onions. Why does anyone bother to grow them?

"You'll be all right, won't you?" says Mum, frowning anxiously. She hates leaving me alone, and she'll worry about it while she's at work. She's got to work, because we need the money. Dad didn't have any life insurance.

I hate Mum worrying.

"Mum, we'll be fine."

Mum gives me a quick rushing-out-of-the-door kiss, and she's gone. I listen to the car starting then Mum toots the horn and I remember I've got to open the gate at the end of the track for her. I run outside, untie the orange twine from the gate post and swing the gate wide. Mum accelerates through, waving at me with a bright smile that doesn't fool me for a second.

Back into the cottage. It's too warm inside, and so I leave the door open. I wonder where Conor is?

He'll be up at Jack's, on Jack's computer, or playing with the dogs.

But Conor usually tells me where he's going. He doesn't just *disappear*.

No. Don't think about that word. I'll make our tea. We'll have it early and then we can watch loads of TV. I get out the pizza and put it on a baking sheet. I wash Mary's lettuce, shake it dry, and carefully cut the roots off the spring onions for Conor. We haven't grown any vegetables ourselves this year. Dad did all the gardening, and usually he grew everything: onions and potatoes and beans and peas and carrots and all our salad stuff. I used to help him. But now our garden is tangled and overgrown and weedy, and I don't know where to start clearing it. Dad would hate the way it looks.

But then I remember something. Deep in the weeds there are three gooseberry bushes. I wonder if any of the gooseberries are ripe yet?

They are. They are fat and juicy and when I hold them up to the light I can see the dark seeds inside the yellow skin. I run into the kitchen, get the colander, and start picking. We'll have gooseberries with sugar and cream. There's half a carton of clotted cream in the fridge, which Mum brought back from work yesterday.

I pick and pick. Brambles scratch my legs and gooseberry thorns jab at my hands, but I don't mind. I've got nearly a whole colander full now. There'll be plenty for tomorrow as well, so Mum will be pleased. Conor's going to love them—

Conor. Where is he? Worry stabs through me again. I look at my watch and it's twenty-five past five. Mum said to call her if he wasn't back by five, but I can't do that. She'd be so scared. She might have an accident from driving back here too fast. And she'd lose a whole night's pay.

I look around. Everything's still. Way in the distance I can see Alice Trewhidden watering the geraniums by her front door. Even from a distance you can see the crabbed way that Alice moves. She has to peer up close at things before she can see them. No good asking her if she's seen Conor.

I could ask Mary.

No, I won't. Conor hasn't *disappeared*. He's late back, that's all. If I ask Mary, it will make Conor's absence seem serious, like the night when Dad—

No. *Don't think about it.* I never, ever want to visit that awful night again.

I could phone Jack's house. Maybe a bit later. But what if his mum answers and says, *No, Conor's not been up here today. Is everything all right, Sapphire?*

I go back inside and put the colander of gooseberries on the kitchen table. I'll top and tail them later.

The cottage seems quieter than ever. I can't settle anywhere. I turn the TV on and then quickly turn it off, in case it stops me hearing Conor's bike. Suddenly I think that maybe Conor is up in his bedroom, asleep.

"Conor?" I call. "Conor?"

Maybe he can't hear me because he's got the duvet over his head. I run up to my room and climb the loft ladder to Conor's room, almost sure by now that he'll be curled up under the duvet.

The bed is empty. The duvet is on the floor. I wonder if he's left me a note on his pillow, the way people do in books, but of course he hasn't. I end up searching all round the loft, as if Conor might have left a clue some-where. I even bend down to peer out of the little window that Dad made. I remember him making it, after he'd boarded the loft for Conor. He let me sit on the floor and watch and pass his tools to him—

No. Sapphire, you are not allowed to think about things like that. They only make you—

They only make your eyes hurt. And Dad's not dead. You know that. He's just—

Stop making that stupid baby noise this minute.

Conor's window. It looks straight out to sea. The sea is striped blue and purple and aquamarine in the late after-noon light. It's very calm, although the swell is rolling in under the surface of the water. There's a fishing boat near the horizon.

It's much too hot and stuffy in Conor's loft. If only I was down at the cove, walking into the water, feeling the delicious coldness of it move up my body. I'd walk in as deep as I could and the buoyancy of the water would lift me off my feet, and I'd be swimming. I would swim right out into the middle of the bay and lie on my back and stare up into the clear sky... Or maybe I'd dive down, deep, deep into the water, and open my eyes and see the ridges of sand that the tide makes on the sea floor, and the tiny shells. I'd see the red and orange weed that clings on to the rocks and sways to and fro as the tide comes in. I could watch the crabs scuttling when they felt my shadow over them, and the fish in little shoals, spurting this way and that. I could cup my hands into a little cave for the fish to swim in and out...

I'm falling into a dream, even though I'm wide awake. The sea feels stronger and more real than Conor's loft room. The white walls seem to sway like water. The sea's all around me, whispering to me in a voice that ebbs and flows like the tide. I want to follow its voice. I want to wade out into the water, far from everything on land. The sea is pulling at me, like a strong current that wraps itself around your legs and lifts you off your feet.

If only I was down at the cove. I must get there. I must go now, this minute.

CHAPTER FOUR

've never climbed down the rocks so fast, even though they're wet and slippy. The sea's only just been here, but now the tide's turned and it's falling, dragging me with it.

I jump down on to the sand. Another minute and I'll be in the sea. I kick off my sandals. My toes are in the water, then my ankles, my knees...

The sea is dazzling. I lift my hand to shade my eyes, and as I do, I see him. It's Conor, far away, sitting on the rocks at the mouth of the cove. I recognise him at once, even though he's turned away from me. His hair is slick with water. He's been swimming! But we never swim here alone, because we know how dangerous it can be. Why did Conor come without me?

Cold. I'm cold. I look down. Already the water is up to my waist. My hands trail in the water. That's so strange. I didn't think I had waded so deep. And I'm still wearing my shorts and T-shirt. The tide is falling fast and it's pulling more and more strongly, as if it wants me to come with it. It's like a magnet. If I didn't dig my feet into the sand, the tide would carry me away with it.

But what's Conor doing, sitting on the rocks at the mouth of the cove, where the water's deep? He must have swum out there.

He hasn't seen me yet. He's still got his back to me. I open my mouth to call him. But suddenly Conor turns his head as if he's…

…As if he's talking to someone.

I push hard against the tug of the water. I'm not going to let it pull me in deeper. I'm not going to call to Conor. I turn round and the tide sucks my legs hungrily as I force my way back into shallow water. The sea doesn't want to let me go, but it has to. Its power is broken.

Knee-deep in the water, I wade towards the left side of the cove. I'll be able to see Conor better from there. I don't want to attract his attention now. In fact I'm hoping that he won't see me. From over here, I should be able to get a good view of the rock.

And now I can see them clearly. No, Conor's not alone. There's a second head outlined against the edge of the rock. A sleek, dark head. It turns, so I see the profile and the long wet hair. It's a girl. Her hair is long, right down her back, like mine. And now I realise that what I thought was part of the rock is part of the girl's body. She must be wearing a wetsuit. She and Conor are close together, talking like old friends who've got so much to say that they don't notice anything or anyone else.

They haven't seen me. Conor hasn't even looked up. What are they talking about? They're much too far away for me to hear their voices.

I've never seen her before, I'm sure of it. But I know everyone who lives round here. Who can she be?

Maybe she's a tourist. Not many tourists come down to the cove, because it's so hard to find. Maybe this girl asked Conor to help her find the way down, and then they got talking, and went swimming together... without me.

No, I don't want them to see me. Conor will think I've been following him and spying on him. He didn't want me here, or he'd have told me he was going down to the cove. We always swim together, not just because it's dangerous to swim alone, but because we like being together.

I wade right out of the water. It pulls at my heels, but feebly now, as if it knows it's not going to win. My wet shorts and T-shirt stick clammily to my skin. Maybe I should go back to the cottage and change? No, I don't want to leave Conor, right out there. It isn't safe.

I wander up and down the tide line, feeling cold even though the air is still warm. I pick up shells and tiny white pieces of driftwood, and let them drop again, and every few minutes I glance out to the rocks at the mouth of the cove. *They* are still there, Conor and the strange girl who doesn't live round here, still sitting close together. And they haven't noticed me at all. They only notice each other.

And then suddenly, the next time I look, the girl has vanished, and Conor is alone. He's standing right on the edge of the rock, staring down into the deep water. But where has the girl gone? He looks down at the water and his body flexes, as if he's about to dive in. A wave of panic sweeps over me, from nowhere. Before I know what I'm going to do, I've yelled out his name.

"Conor! CONOR!"

He looks up, stares around. I run along the water's edge, waving and calling.

"Conor, it's me! *Conor!*"

He turns and sees me. For a long moment we stare at each other across the water. We are too far away to see each other's expressions. And then, slowly, he raises his hand and waves to me.

"Conor, come back! Tea's ready!"

He waves again, and begins to pick his way carefully back across the wet, slippery rocks at the side of the cove. It would be quicker to dive in and swim across to me, but he doesn't do that. He scrambles all the way back across the rocks that line the edge of the cove, and only jumps into the water when it is shallow. Knee-deep, he splashes towards me. He's frowning – not in an angry way, but just as he frowns when he's doing his toughest maths homework.

"What are *you* doing here, Saph?"

"Looking for you."

"But it's not time for tea yet, is it?"

I look down at my wrist, and then I realise something

terrible. I must have walked into the water with my watch on. My beautiful watch that Dad got for me in Truro. Now I remember my arms trailing in the water. I forgot all about my watch! I can't believe it. The hands point to five past seven, but the second hand isn't moving. I shake my wrist hard. Nothing happens. My watch has stopped.

"Oh, Saph. You went into the water with it on," says Conor, looking at my wet shorts and T-shirt.

"It's broken."

"Maybe it'll be all right if we dry it out. I'll take the back off and see," says Conor. But we both know it won't be all right.

"It's broken, Conor." Thick, painful tears crowd behind my eyes. Dad helped me to choose the watch, but he didn't choose for me. The shop assistant had laid my three favourites out on the counter. A watch with a blue face and gold hands, a silver watch on a silver wristband, and this watch. My watch. Dad waited and didn't say anything while I tried them all on again, for the third time. I held my wrist out to see how each one looked, and then I knew. This one was mine. I loved it. But it was the most expensive of the three. I took it off and put it down.

"I think I like the blue one best," I said. I'd looked at the price labels, and I knew that was the cheapest one. But guess what Dad did then? He picked up the one I liked best and said, "Don't look at the prices, Sapphy. You only have one birthday a year. It wasn't the blue one you liked, it was this one."

"How did you know, Dad?"

"You can't fool me. I know you too well, Sapphy."

He knew me too well, because we were alike. Me and Dad, Mum and Conor. It wasn't that I loved Dad more than Mum, but—

"Don't cry, Saph." Conor puts his arm round my shoulders. "You didn't mean to break it. But listen. You mustn't come down here and swim on your own. You know we promised Mum we wouldn't."

Mustn't come down here and swim— Indignation shocks my tears away. "What about you? Look at you, your hair's all wet. You've been swimming with that girl, haven't you?"

"What girl?"

I stare at him. "What girl? The girl who was sitting on the rock talking to you, of course. The girl with long hair like mine."

Conor looks at me with the elder-brother look I hate. "How could you see her hair, if we were right over on the rocks?"

"I could. I could see her quite clearly."

"The trouble with you, Saph, is that you see one thing and then you imagine something else."

"I *don't*. I don't make up stuff. I used to when I was little, but I don't now."

"If you say so."

"I *don't*, Conor. Not much, anyway. You're only saying that to stop me asking about her."

"All right then. I went swimming after I cleaned out the shed. Maybe I should have told you I was going, but I didn't. Just for once I wanted…"

I feel cold inside from fear of what he's going to say. What did Conor want, that I couldn't give him?

"...I don't know," goes on Conor, as if he's talking to himself. "I wanted some space, I suppose..."

"Oh."

"And then, after I'd been swimming, I sat on the rocks to get dry. End of story."

"But Conor – it was *this morning* that you cleaned out the shed. It's way past seven o'clock in the evening now. Probably past eight. Mum went to work hours ago. You're telling me you've been here swimming for *seven hours?*"

"What?" Conor seizes my wrist and stares at the face of my watch.

"It stopped when I went into the water," I say.

"It can't be that late. You must have been messing about with your watch." He shakes my wrist as if the hands of the watch might suddenly run backwards, to match the time he thinks it is.

"Get *off* me, Conor. It's evening, can't you see that? Look at the sun. Look how low it is."

Conor stares around. He gazes at the mouth of the cave, where the sun is low and golden as it sinks towards the horizon. I watch him realise that I'm telling the truth.

"Maybe I fell asleep," he says slowly. He looks lost, confused, not like my brother Conor at all.

"You *were* talking to someone. I saw her. She must have gone off across the rocks," I say, but this time I say it quietly, not because I want to win an argument with Conor, but to make the truth clear. And this time Conor doesn't answer.

"Who was she?" I ask, not even expecting him to tell me. And he doesn't. Conor's face is pale. Tired out, the way you're tired out after a long day in the sea. He doesn't want to talk. Side by side, we walk back up the sand, towards the rocks, the boulders, the way that leads home. I feel shaky all over. There was a girl there, I know there was. One minute she was sitting on the rocks with Conor, and then she was gone.

In bed that night I lie awake. Conor's upstairs in his loft room. He can't climb down the ladder without me knowing. I'm afraid to fall asleep in case he creeps past me, down the stairs and out of the cottage. But why would Conor want to do that? I can't think of a reason, and yet I can't stop being afraid.

There was no reason for Dad to leave us, either.

I know Conor's not asleep yet, because a minute ago I heard his feet stepping lightly across the floor above me, towards the window. The slap of bare feet, and then silence. He's by his window, looking out towards the sea. I know it for sure. My eyes are stinging with tiredness but I can't let go and drop into sleep. Not yet, not until Mum comes back.

We both promised Mum that we would never go off swimming alone in the cove. It's so quiet and lonely there that if anything happened, there would be no chance of help. We've always kept our promise, until today. It wasn't just Conor who broke it, either. If I hadn't seen him on the rock, I would have gone on walking deeper into the water, with the sea pulling me like a magnet.

How far would the sea have pulled me? Maybe there's sea magic too, the same as Dad once said there was earth magic. Granny Carne's magic was mostly benign, Dad said. But what about the sea's magic? The sea's strong, and wild, and if you make a mistake the sea will make you pay. Sometimes you pay with your life.

Dad used to say that the sea doesn't hate you and it doesn't love you. It's up to you to learn its ways, and keep yourself safe.

But I didn't even think about keeping myself safe today, down at the cove. All I wanted was to go with the tide. I didn't even think of Mum or Conor, because the sea was pulling me so hard.

Is that how Conor felt? Did he forget about all of us, so that hours passed like minutes? He *was* talking to that girl. He *was*. I didn't imagine it. She was wearing a wetsuit, and her hair was long and wet and tangly, hanging over her shoulders and hiding her body. They were laughing and talking. She and Conor didn't look as if they'd just met for the first time.

My watch! Mum will go crazy when she finds out that my watch isn't working any more. She said it was too good for everyday, and I should put it away and only wear it on special occasions.

"*Dad* said I could wear it every day," I argued. In the end Mum agreed.

"But you'd better look after it, Sapphy. You can be so careless."

She sounded like my school report. *Good work is spoiled by carelessness. Sapphire needs to concentrate, and stop daydreaming in class.*

Mum said, "It'll be a miracle if that watch is still on your wrist in six months' time, Sapphy."

"It will be."

"Good. I'm hoping you'll prove me wrong."

Mum *was* wrong. My watch is still on my wrist, and more than a year has passed. Maybe she won't notice that it isn't working any more.

Conor's up there in his loft room, not moving, not sleeping, staring out of the window. All I want to hear is the tread of Conor's bare feet back over the floorboards to his bed. But he stays at the window. I pull my curtain open, and see that the moon is rising. Even ordinary things are starting to look mysterious. The thorn bushes look like bodies that have been bent and bowed. Those white towels on the washing line that I forgot to bring in look like ghosts. It is so bright that you could find the path down to the cove quite easily by moonlight. Sometimes the moon makes a path on the sea and it looks real and solid, as if you could walk out on it to the horizon.

I hear a creak. It's Conor, pushing his window wide. Maybe I should go up to him? No. He'll be angry. He'll think I'm following him around. But I'm not. I'm just looking out for him. Trying to look after him, the way Dad said we had to look after each other.

"As long as you two look out for each other, you'll be safe enough."

I can hear Dad's voice saying those words, exactly as if he was here in the room. If I shut my eyes, it will be almost as if he *were* here...

No. If I'm not careful I'm going to fall asleep, and then Conor could creep down the ladder and out of the house, without me knowing. I sit up in bed and very quietly switch on the little lamp by my bed. As soon as I hear Mum's car up by the gate, I can quickly turn the light off before she opens the gate and drives down the track and sees it.

On my bedside table there is a green and silver notebook which I used to keep my diary in. I've torn out the diary pages, because they were all about things that happened a long time ago when our life was different. Now I write lists.

I pick up my favourite black and silver pencil.

List of things that might have happened to Dad:

1. One of those factory fishing boats came too close inshore. Dad's boat got dragged in its net and he was drowned. They untangled his boat and dropped it overboard so no one would have any evidence, because it's against the law to be fishing where they were fishing.

This is what Josh Tregony says his dad says.

2. There was a freak squall and the boat went down.

This was one of the things they suggested in *The Cornishman*, but everyone remembers that it was flat calm that night.

3. Dad never went in his boat at all. He took her out as far as the mouth of the cove then he let her go on the tide and he swam back and went off another way. He had his own reasons for wanting folk to think he had drowned.

Someone said this in the Miners' Arms. I heard it from Jessie Nanjivey, in my class. She said Badge Thomas said he would ram the teeth of the man who said it right down his throat if he opened his mouth again. The man was from Towednack, Jessie said. No one who knows Dad would ever believe it. He would never let the *Peggy Gordon* go on the tide. He loves her too much.

4. "Was your husband worried about anything? Debts? Problems at work? Did he seem depressed or unlike himself? Had he been drinking?"

These are some of the questions that the police asked Mum. Conor and I guessed what the police were trying to find out, but it was all rubbish. Dad was happy. We were all happy.

5."You remember what happened to that other Mathew? Could be it's the same thing come again."

"You don't really reckon, do you?"

"Well, they do say—"

This was Mrs Pascoe and her cousin Bertha talking in the post office stores. They saw me come in and they bit off the rest of what they'd been going to say. I hung around the birthday-card stand pretending to choose one, but the women just paid for their stuff and went out. They could have been talking about something else, but I don't think so. I could see from their looks that they'd been talking about us, and there's no other Mathew around here except Dad. That other Mathew – what did they mean?

I look down at the list I've written, and cross out three and four straight away. That leaves one, two and five. Josh Tregony's dad told him that a factory fishing trawler did once pull down a small boat off the Scottish coast. The small boat got caught in the nets and dragged down, and the fishermen drowned. So maybe it could happen here. I don't believe the freak squall theory. I remember that night too well, and how flat the sea was. So number two can be crossed out as well.

That leaves one and five. I don't understand five at all, so maybe I'd better leave it on the list for the time being, until I find out more.

Suddenly I hear three sounds at once. The crunch of Mum's tyres on the stony track up by the gate. The creak of a window shutting upstairs. The slap of Conor's feet on the boards as he runs back to bed.

I slam my notebook shut, snap off the light, and dive under my duvet.

CHAPTER FIVE

When I wake the next morning, there's heavy white mist outside my window. I can't even see the garden wall. I push my window open and lean out. There's a mournful lowing sound, like the moo of a cow who has been separated from her calf. It's the foghorn, calling to warn the ships.

So many ships have run aground and broken up on the rocks around here. Dad used to tell me a long list of their names: the *Perth Princess*, the *Andola*, the *Morveren*, the *Lady Guinevere*. Some of the wrecked ships were homeward bound from wars more than two hundred years ago, Dad said. You can still find driftwood from ships that sailed to fight Napoleon and never reached home again. Dad once showed me a piece of driftwood with a hole where a ship's brass nail would have fitted.

I held it up and put my finger over the nail hole. I tried to imagine what it was like when the ship sank. The noise of the wind screaming and the waves pounding. Men would yell out orders on deck, trying to save the ship. But the wind and current were stronger than the power of the men, and the ship was driven on to the black spine of the rocks.

The rocks ripped the hull and water gushed in, on top of the people who were struggling to escape. There was nowhere to go, except into the wild black water.

Boys Conor's age worked on those ships. Maybe they climbed the masts as high as they could, trying to save themselves. They clung to the spars as the ship tossed this way and that like a horse that falls at a jump and breaks its back.

They had no chance. The sea knows how to break up any ship. Those rocks are too far out for people on shore to throw lines and save them. In that raging sea you could never launch a boat for rescue.

The foghorn lows again. *Danger*, it says. *Keep away. Danger.* I hope the ships are listening today.

Mum's up. I can hear her banging around in the kitchen. No sound of Conor.

My heart jumps in fear. Barefoot, I tiptoe to the loft ladder. I grasp its sides and climb up as quietly as a squirrel, high enough to see Conor's bed.

He's there. I can see the back of his head poking out of the top of the duvet. He's fast asleep.

I climb down the ladder, go to the bathroom and then pull on my jeans and a sweatshirt. If I'm quick, I'll get the chance to talk to Mum before Conor wakes up. Maybe I'll be able to tell her what happened yesterday – ask her what we can do—

But as soon as I see Mum, I know I can't say anything about Conor and the sea and the girl, and why it frightens me. In the daytime world, none of it makes sense. Mum won't understand why I'm scared.

"She'll have been one of Conor's friends from school," Mum would say. "Conor can't spend all his time with you, you know, Saph. He's growing up."

Mum's busy, making coffee, ironing a dress for work, and finishing off peeling the potatoes, all at the same time. She's got the radio on and she's humming to a song called *Happy Days*, which is getting played about twice an hour this summer:

> *Happy days babe,*
> *I got them for you,*
> *The morning sunshine*
> *The sweet dark too,*
> *Yeah the sweet dark too…*

It's the kind of song people Mum's age love. Her face has gone soft and dreamy, listening to it. She lifts the iron and the steam sizzles, then she smiles at me.

"Hi, Mum. Wow, is that strawberry tart for us?"

Mum brings leftover stuff back from the restaurant sometimes. But this is something special. A big tart stuffed full of shiny ripe strawberries, glazed with jelly. There's only a quarter taken out of it.

"Have a piece for breakfast if you like, Sapphy."

For breakfast? I stare at Mum. There is something completely different about her this morning, but I can't work out what it is. Quickly, before she changes her mind, I divide the strawberry tart into three pieces and take my own.

"Mm, s'dlishus, Mum."

"Don't talk with your mouth full," says Mum, sounding more like herself. But she still doesn't *look* like herself. What's going on?

And then I see what it is. The tight lines around Mum's mouth have melted away. She's wearing her favourite jeans and her pink top. She looks *happy*. I swallow the mouthful of tart and ask, "Did you get good tips last night, Mum?"

"Mm." Mum shakes her work dress and puts it on a hanger. "All right. Nothing special."

So it's not that.

My heart leaps. Suddenly I know what it is. "Mum, is there news about Dad?"

Mum's face changes. "Sapphire, if there was news about Dad, I'd tell you both straight away. I wouldn't keep it from you. But there isn't. And—"

"What, Mum?"

Mum's face struggles. "Even if there was news – even if they found… something… it wouldn't be good news. You know that, don't you? That's why we had the memorial service."

"You mean you want me to forget about Dad."

"No. I'd never, never ask you to do that. But you're not a baby, Sapphy. You can't keep on living in dreams. It's not good for you, it's holding you back."

She starts ironing again, and the subject of Dad is closed. I wish I hadn't said anything. The lines are back around Mum's mouth. Quietly, I make myself a cup of tea and start on the washing-up from last night. After a while Mum says, "Guess who we had in the restaurant last night, Sapphy."

"Um – dunno," I say dully, but that doesn't stop Mum.

"A party of divers. They're exploring up this way, looking for wrecks. They might call in here at the weekend."

"Oh."

"You wouldn't believe the number of wrecks there are that have never been explored."

"I know. Dad told us about it. There's—"

"Your father never went diving," says Mum. "Now Roger – he's one of the divers – he's gone all over the world. He was telling me about it. They have sonar equipment and everything. He's discovered wreck sites in the West Indies, and off the coast of Spain, and all over. He got interested when he was just a boy. He saw them raising this old Tudor ship called the *Mary Rose*, on TV, and they showed how the divers worked. That got him thinking. He made up his mind he was going to be a diver." The iron hisses as Mum attacks one of Conor's shirts. "He had ambition," she goes on. "He knew what he wanted to do with his life. He didn't mess around."

"Dad didn't mess around!"

Mum turns to me with the iron in her hand.

"I never said he did. I was talking about *Roger*. I wish you wouldn't be so touchy, Sapphy. Anyway, Roger was telling me about how they're planning to explore the coast down here, off the Bawns—"

"You didn't tell him about our cove, did you, Mum?"

"For heaven's sake, Sapphire, it's not your own private cove. That's a public footpath that goes down by there."

"I know, but nobody ever uses it except us and people who live round here. Usually there's no one down there except me and Conor."

"That's the whole trouble with this place," mutters Mum, zizzing her iron down the seams." Nobody *does* come. Well, they're welcome to explore off the cove as far as I'm concerned, and they're welcome here too. It's good to see some different faces. I do wish you'd be more friendly, Sapphy. You're like a – like a sea anemone. If anyone comes close, you shut yourself up tight."

"That's how sea anemones survive," I point out.

"But you do it to me too, Sapphy, and I'm your mum. It's got to be a habit, that's what it is. We're spoiled out here, seeing no one all day long unless we choose. If you lived in town you'd have to learn to get along with all sorts of people. Maybe that'd be a good thing. You can't stay in a little world of your own choosing for ever—"

"Mum, we're not moving!" I burst out. Conor and I have a secret fear that Mum plans to move us all into St Pirans, close to her work, so that she can keep an eye on us. She keeps saying how much we'd enjoy the surfing, and how many nice shops there are, and how good the school is.

"Who said anything about moving?" asks Mum in surprise. Or maybe she's not really surprised. Maybe she's preparing the way, so that the idea of moving becomes something familiar...

But we can't move. What if Dad comes back and we're not here?

"All that's happening is Roger's coming for Sunday dinner," Mum goes on. "I've got my day off then. You'll like him, Sapphy. He's very nice."

"Just him?"

"Well, just him this time," says Mum, bending over the board and guiding the iron very carefully.

"I hope you told *Roger* about how much you love the sea," I mutter, quietly enough that Mum won't hear me. "Maybe you could even go out in his boat?"

The strawberry tart isn't as good as I thought when I took the first bite. The strawberries are mushy and the pastry's soft. In fact, it's disgusting. That must be why they let Mum take it home. I slip the rest of my slice into the bin and cover it with potato peelings.

"My God, Sapphy," says Mum, looking up and seeing my empty plate, "I hope you won't stuff your food like that on Sunday."

"Don't worry, Mum, I'll do my best to impress Roger," I say.

"Roger," says a sleepy voice. "Who's Roger?"

Conor appears, with his duvet wrapped round him.

"Conor, please don't trail your duvet on the floor," says Mum. "How many times have I told you? This kitchen floor gets covered in mud with the two of you traipsing in and out all day long. Sapphy, what time did you go to bed last night?"

"Um – about ten o'clock, wasn't it, Conor?"

"Yeah, 'bout that."

Conor reaches into the fridge, gets out the orange juice and tips the carton to his mouth. He doesn't ever touch the carton with his lips; Conor has perfected the art of tipping a stream of orange juice straight into his mouth, without choking or spilling a drop.

"Get a glass, Conor," says Mum, as she always does.

"Saves washing-up," says Conor, as he always does. "So who is Roger?" he asks again, fitting the carton back into the fridge door.

"A friend," says Mum.

"He's a diver," I say quickly. "He's one of a party of divers who are going to explore wrecks. They're going to dive from our cove, Conor. They think there's a wreck out there, by the Bawns. They're coming on Sunday, aren't they, Mum?"

Conor stands still. I can see thoughts flickering in his eyes but I don't know what they are.

"Oh, OK," he says at last, as if there's nothing more to talk about. As if he doesn't care if twenty Rogers come to our cove and have Sunday dinner in our cottage. I stare at him in disbelief, but he just looks back at me without expression.

"Conor, will you *please* get that duvet off the floor?" says Mum. "I haven't had time to mop it this week – and I'm on the early shift today. What time is it, Sapphy?"

"Um…" I look at my wrist and it still says five past seven. But there's the radio clock winking. Eight fifty-two.

"Nearly five to nine, Mum."

"Oh no, I've got to get going. Conor, we need eggs and potatoes today. A dozen eggs, and mind you check they're not cracked. If Badge can help you bring a sack of potatoes down, thank him and say I'll pay for them tonight. While you're up there, ask if they can set aside two pints extra milk for us on Saturday. Sapphy, put your duvet cover and Conor's in the machine, put them on programme four and don't forget to hang them out on the line. And then if Conor sweeps this floor, you can wash it down. The mop's outside the back door. If the man calls about the MOT, Conor, tell him I'll bring the car in at eight o'clock tomorrow morning, before I go to work.

"Now then, there's plenty of bread for sandwiches. Use up the rest of that chicken, and you can take crisps and a KitKat each. I'll be back at six tonight. Mind you clean your teeth properly, Sapphy. You're seeing the dentist soon."

"Yes, *Ma'am*," says Conor, saluting.

Reluctantly, Mum smiles. "I know, I know. But someone's got to think of everything."

"OK, Mum."

"OK, Mum," I echo.

Suddenly Mum stops in her rush from ironing board to fridge to door. She stands and looks at us, really looks at us.

"Come here, both of you," she says. Conor shuffles forward in his duvet. I hang back.

"Come on, Sapphy. Give me a proper hug."

She reaches out for me. I feel bony and awkward, as if I don't fit into her arms any more. But Mum strokes the back of her hand down my cheek and says, "Your Mum loves you," just as she did when I was little, and suddenly I feel myself relaxing, melting…

"You're good children," says Mum, so quietly I'm not sure I've heard her right. "Stay together, mind. Look after each other."

"We will," I say, and I mean it. I am not letting Conor out of my sight today. "Will you be all right driving, Mum? The mist's so thick."

"It'll be clearer up on the road," says Mum. "There's my good girl. Now, I've got to go, or I'll be late."

I go out with her, to open the gate and shut it again after she's gone through. The mist is not quite so bad once you're out in it. I can see as far as the wall, and the thorn bush looming in the field beyond.

Mum has her fog lamps on and she drives forward cautiously, gripping the wheel. She hates driving in bad weather. The mist blows in from the sea. It's thick and silent and salty, and the damp of it is all over the gate post in silvery beads. Mum's tyres crunch over the rough stones, and through the gateway. She gives a little toot of the horn, and drives on up the track. I swing the gate shut, watch the red rear fog lights disappear into the mist, and then tie the twine securely around the gate again. There won't be many walkers coming down here today, not in these conditions. It's dangerous on the coast path when the mist is down like this. You could walk straight over the edge of a cliff. We won't go down to the cove today.

But for once I don't mind that. It feels safer inside the cottage.

Safer? Why did I say that? The mist swirls, dragging wet fingers across my face. I'm going to go back inside and maybe I'll light a fire if we've got any wood left in the shed. It's cold when the mist is down. I hurry back inside and there's Conor's duvet on the floor.

"Conor! I'm not picking up your dirty washing for you! You can put it in the machine yourself."

But there's no answer. The cottage is silent.

Maybe he's gone up to the farm to get the eggs and potatoes.

No. He'd have had to go past me. Even in the mist he couldn't have gone past without me seeing him.

"Conor?" But this time I don't shout. I am asking the empty, familiar kitchen to tell me where he is. The radio clock winks. The fridge whirrs. They must have seen him go, but they're not telling me.

They don't need to. A cold shiver is creeping over my skin, as cold as the mist. I know where Conor's gone. Down the track, through the bracken and foxgloves, down the path and out on to the grassy lip of cliff above the cove. Everything wet and shining with mist. The rocks hidden, the sea hidden. Down the rocks, between the boulders, on to the rocks. Everything slippery and dangerous—

The sea pulling like a magnet. Pulling Conor as it pulled me.

What's the time? The tide will be going out. I remember how the sea swirled round my legs, urging me deeper and deeper—

Conor, wait. Wait, *wait*. Don't go without me. Wait, Conor, I'm coming.

CHAPTER SIX

ever go down to the cove alone. Are you listening to me, Sapphire? If Conor isn't with you, you don't go.

But Mum —

Sapphy, I want you to promise me that you won't go on your own. Ever. It's for your own safety.

I can swim just as well as Conor.

I know. But you're such a daydreamer, Sapphy. If the tide comes in while you're dreaming, I won't be there to help you. So promise.

Make Conor promise too.

He has already.

All right, Mum. I promise.

Mum's words from years ago drum in my head as I feel my way through the mist, down the track and along the path. Shapes loom out frighteningly, but when I get close, they're only bushes. The mist has already closed up behind me, damp and woolly and smothering. I can't see any of the cottages. I can't see the track, or the gate, or even the gap where the path begins —

I trip and stumble, and scramble up again, rubbing my grazed leg. Pebbles rattle under my feet, wet bracken slaps my legs. I can hear the sea echoing, and the mournful sound of the foghorn.

Danger. Danger. Don't come here.

But I've got to carry on. This is the path to where Conor is. I must follow it. My heart bumps so hard it feels as if it's up in my mouth. Take a deep breath, Sapphire. There's nothing to be scared of. It's only mist.

I creep out on to the grass. I've nearly reached the cliff, but I can't see the edge. The grass is wet and slippery and I'm afraid of falling, so I get down on hands and knees and crawl forward slowly, feeling my way.

Haaaaa says the sea, *haaaaaa*. I creep forward, digging my fingers into tussocks of rough grass. I won't go over the edge, whatever happens.

Here it is. I lie down on my belly, lean over, and look down. Below me, mist swirls. It's coming in from the sea, thicker and thicker. The shapes of boulders loom beneath, like dark heads rearing out of the mist. I can just about find my way down, but the rocks are shining wet. I mustn't slip.

I try to remember where the tide will be. It should be low tide, just on the turn. I'm safe for now.

I let myself down very carefully, over the grassy lip of the cliff, scrabbling for footholds.

You've been down here hundreds of times. It's completely safe. But my heart bangs and sweat prickles under my arms. Climbing down through the mist is like trying to do your best handwriting with your fingers in thick gloves. My left foot brushes a foothold, finds it. I lower my weight gently. No. My foot slips on wet rock and I start to slide. I grab a clump of thrift and cling on. My fingers want to hold on for ever but I won't let them. *Don't be stupid, Sapphire. You won't fall. You can't stay here clinging on to a cliff. No one's going to come and rescue you, and anyway you've got to find Conor.*

I take a deep breath. My feet will know where to go if I can just stop panicking. They know where the next foothold is, and the next, and the next. My feet have been learning the way down for years.

I take another deep breath. Slowly, slowly, I let go of the clump of thrift. My right foot finds its way down to the next ledge like a key finding its place in a lock.

Down the rocks, squeeze between the boulders, over the stones. The dripping of water sounds eerie in the mist. I can hear the waves breaking, far out, but I can't see them. I move as quietly as I can. I don't want anyone to hear me coming.

At last, at last, my feet touch firm, flat sand. I'm down on our beach, safe. My legs are shaking, but I did it! I did it on my own, in the mist, without Conor.

Yeah, you did it on your own, my thoughts jeer at me. But don't get too excited. You haven't found Conor yet, have you?

I'm going to, I tell myself firmly. And maybe – maybe the mist's lifting a little? I can just about see the edge of the tumble of rocks that meets the sand. The cliff I climbed down has vanished back into white woolliness, but I can't get lost. When I want to go home, all I have to do is walk away from the sound of the sea, and I'm bound to come back to the rocks, with the cliff above them.

I step forward cautiously, one foot after another on the hard sand that slopes downward slightly to the water. White, echoey swirls of mist stroke my skin.

"Conor! Conor, where are you? Are you here?" I call softly. I don't dare call too loud. Anything could come out of this mist.

Nobody answers.

"Conor! Conor! Please, if you're here, come out!"

I don't like hide-and-seek when I'm the seeker, and everyone's hiding and waiting and watching, ready to jump out. *Coming, ready or not!* I hate things that jump out on me. But I'm still sure I was right to come down to the cove. I'm sure Conor came this way, and that he's here, close.

But I'm scared to call again. I glance back up the beach, but even the rocks have vanished now. I'm surrounded by white, choking mist. The sound of the sea seems to come from everywhere. *Haaa... Haaa... Haaaa...*

I clench my hands so tight that my nails dig into my palms. You're safe, Sapphire. Don't be such a stupid little baby. It's all right, because as long as the sand slopes downward, then it must be leading towards the sea. I know the shape of this cove as well as I know the shape of my own hand. The sea bed slopes gently for a long way, nearly as far as the mouth of the cove, but then it drops down sharply. When you're swimming you can see the water go suddenly dark, where the deep comes. Conor has tried to dive to the bottom, but neither of us has ever touched it.

I hold my arms out in front of me and step forward, fumbling through the mist.

And that's when I hear the voice. It's far away, over the water, and it's singing.

I wish I was away in Ingo
Far across the briny sea,
Sailing over deepest waters
Where love nor care never trouble me—

Dad? Dad, it's Dad! My body prickles all over as if I'm standing in lightning.

"Dad!" I call, "Dad, where are you? It's me! It's Sapphy! Dad, please come back!"

The singing breaks off, and there is a long silence. I hear the echo of the song in my head. I know that song so well, and the voice singing it…

But do I? Very softly, very far away, the singing starts again. And this time I am not so sure. The singing is beautiful. The voice is so sweet and pure that I can't tell if it's a man's voice, or a woman's, or a child's. It's so sweet that I want the mist to lift me and carry me away to where the voice is.

Come tell to me the very reason
That I am slighted so by thee…

I asked Dad once what the word "slighted" meant. He told me that to slight someone was to put them aside and take no notice of them. To make them feel that you don't want them. In the song, the singer wants to know why that has happened. Why he's been slighted by the one he loves.

Slighted. I don't need to ask what the word means now.

Why have you left us, Dad? Didn't you want us any more? Weren't we good enough for you? Where are you, Dad? If you can hear me, please, please answer…

But I don't say these words aloud. I stand as still as a stone in the mist, trying to catch the echo of the singing. It's Dad's song, but the more I listen the less I can believe that the voice is his. The song is Dad's, but the singer isn't him.

Now something else is happening. The mist is starting to lighten. It's lifting. There's brightness in the air and as the mist swirls again it parts to show a white disc of sun, struggling to come out. I look back and the outline of the rocks appears. There are the caves. There are the boulders. I turn towards the sea. And there, down by the water, perched on one of the high rocks at the side of the cove, is a boy.

He's facing out to sea, away from me. I can only see his head and shoulders. But that dark wet hair… It looks like – it must be—

"Conor!"

The boy turns round. Even from here I can see that he's not Conor, but a stranger. A shiver of fear runs through me. He raises one hand and waves as if he knows me. But I don't know him. I've never seen him in my life. He waves again, and this time he beckons. He wants me to come over.

And suddenly I've got to go to him. My feet are pounding over the hard wet sand towards the rock. There's a pool of water around the base of the rock, and I splash through it. The boy leans over the side of the rock and looks down.

"Can you climb up to me?" he asks.

"Of course I can."

But it's not so easy. The rock is overhung, slimy and covered with seaweed. There are mussels and limpets that hurt my hands. A baby crab scuttles over my fingers and I nearly lose my grip.

The boy doesn't scramble down to help me, as Conor would. Maybe that's because he's wearing a wetsuit – or at least I think he is. I can't see properly from this angle, but it looks as if he's wearing a wetsuit pulled down to the waist.

I grab hold of a spur of rock near the top and haul myself up. And that's when I see him clearly for the first time.

I topple backwards. I nearly fall. I would fall, except that the boy's hand shoots out and grabs mine.

"Careful," he says.

It's a costume. He's wearing a costume. He must be. It can't be real. He can't be—

"You can't be," I say aloud, without meaning to. "It's impossible." I look down at the hand that is still holding on to me. Human fingers, just like mine. Human arms, head, neck, chest... but then...

"I'm asleep, aren't I? You're part of a dream."

He squeezes my fingers tight, and then lets go of them.

"Did that feel real enough? I can pinch you if you like."

"No, no, that's all right. But you can't be a—"

I still can't get the word out. It's not a word I've ever heard outside a story. It doesn't belong to real life. I stare at the dark curve of what I thought was a wetsuit, and the smooth place where flesh like mine joins on to – what? It reminds me of something. It's not like the scaly fish tail you see in a kid's book. It's like the tail of another creature altogether. Powerful, glistening, sleek, made for water and not for land—

"A seal," I whisper. The two halves of what I'm seeing won't join up. I see a boy like Conor, with dark wet hair and brown eyes and suntanned skin. And I see the curving tail of a seal.

He looks as if he's heard every thought I've had. "Seals can't talk," he points out. His teeth are perfectly white and even. *His* mum won't be nagging him about going to the dentist.

Why am I thinking about dentists, when I'm looking at a—

"You thought I was Conor, didn't you? Don't worry, Conor's here somewhere. He's with my sister."

"Your sister?" I bleat. Thoughts and pictures whirl in my head. The girl with the long wet hair. The girl in the wetsuit. *His* sister.

"I know your name," he goes on. His eyes glint with satisfaction. "I know all about you. You're Sapphire. Conor told me about you."

"Oh."

"Don't you want to know mine?"

"Your what?"

"My name," he says.

"Oh. Um, yes, that'd be good."

"My name is Faro," he says with grandeur, as if I must have heard it. But I still can't get my mind working.

"How come you're speaking English?" I blurt out. "I mean, you're not—"

"Not English?"

"Not – um – human."

"*Human?* I should think not," says Faro, as if there aren't many worse things to be. "And how do you know we're speaking English anyway? We might be speaking Mer."

"I can't speak anything except English," I say. This is one thing I am certain about, at least.

"You *think* you can't," says Faro. "But if your mother was here, she wouldn't be able to understand a word we're saying."

"She wouldn't be listening. She'd be too busy yelling at me for coming down here on my own."

"That's true," says Faro, as if he knows Mum well.

"But I thought – I mean, don't mermaids have tails like fish? With scales? I'm sure that's what I've seen in pictures."

Faro raises his eyebrows. "*Mermaids.* That is such a human way of talking. I suppose you're friends with lots of *maids* at school, are you?"

"Well no, we don't call them maids, not any more. That

was in the olden days. The Tudors or the Victorians or something."

"So what makes you think the Mer are living in the olden days?" asks Faro, laying a faint sarcastic emphasis on the last two words.

Of course you're living in the olden days, I want to say. You sit on rocks and you have a golden comb in one hand and a mirror in the other and you sing all day and comb your hair and wait for sailors to come past so you can tempt them into the sea. That's not exactly twenty-first century behaviour, is it?

"So, that's two things you've got wrong," says Faro, almost purring with satisfaction. "One, I'm male, not female, so how could I be a mermaid anyway? Anatomically impossible. Two, all that scaly-tail and hair-combing mermaid and merboy and merman stuff comes from *humans*. It's got nothing to do with the way we live. It's all up in the Air."

"So what do you call yourselves?" I ask curiously.

Faro's eyes darken. His smile disappears. "I can't tell you that," he says. "We don't talk about it to Air people. But you can call us 'the Mer' if you want. That's the word we use when we're talking in the Air. Mer, Meor, Mor, Mare... any of those will do." He shrugs his shoulders as if the whole subject bores him.

The sun is coming out more and more strongly now, burning up the mist. Everything is clear again. And Faro is as clear and solid as the shape of the rock. I glance sideways at his tail. I don't want to stare too much. Now that the mist is burning off, his tail is drying too. It doesn't shine as much. I wonder if he should dip it in the water. There are patches of sand on his skin.

Faro catches me looking and raises his eyebrows again. I feel myself blush.

"Do you think that we *are* speaking Mer? Really?" I ask quickly. I listen to the words as they come out of my mouth. They sound the same as always. They don't seem to make different shapes.

"Not full Mer," says Faro. "But you've got a bit of Mer in you. You must have, or you wouldn't be here. It means we can speak to each other. But if we were speaking full Mer, you'd be able to understand what *he's* saying." And Faro nods at the gull that's riding the air above us, screaming out gull abuse.

"What's he saying?"

"Think of all the swear words you know, and then double them."

I stare up at the gull. It tilts its wings to balance itself more comfortably on the air, and stares back with its cold yellow eye. It opens its beak wide and lets out another volley.

"They don't like people looking at them," says Faro.

"Can you talk to it?"

"Talking's a waste of time, the mood he's in. He doesn't like me talking to you."

"Why not?"

"Gulls are like that. They think it's safer to keep separate. Humans are bad news to most of them."

"Oh."

Faro watches a tiny spider crab haul itself up a strand of bladder wrack.

"Can you hear what he's saying?" he asks.

"No."

"You might be able to – if you weren't in the Air."

"But I can't live out of the air."

"You only think you can't," says Faro. "Listen to that gull. Listen. Really listen."

I strain my ears but all I can catch is the usual cry as the herring gull swoops low, skimming the water, then soars again.

"You were looking for Conor," says Faro, after a pause.

"Yes. Yes, I was," I say slowly, realising that I haven't thought of him since I saw Faro. I can't believe that I forgot I was searching for Conor.

"I told you, he's with my sister. He's quite safe."

"But where are they?"

Faro shifts a little. Out of the water, the tail is strong and smooth, but also a little clumsy. He puts his weight on his arms and moves himself forward again, so that he can look over the edge of the rock.

"They'll be in the water," he says. "Somewhere down there."

I look where he points and I see that the flat sand has gone. The tide is bubbling around our rock. Already the water is deep. How has it come in so quickly, without me noticing?

"How has it come in so quickly?" I repeat aloud.

"It's only the tide," says Faro easily. "It always comes in like this."

"But – it was low tide a few minutes ago."

"Was it?"

"I'll have to swim back to the rocks. I've got to go back now, before it gets too deep."

I'll have to be careful. The incoming tide can be dangerous. It can sweep you against the rocks and bruise you or worse. *Keep in the middle of the cove and swim straight*

  for the shore.

"Where are you going?" asks Faro, as I stand and peer over the edge of the rock to see if it's safe to jump. Jumping's quicker than climbing down – and the water is rising fast—

"I've got to get back. I'll get caught by the tide."

"But your brother's still here," says Faro casually.

My body freezes. Slowly, I turn back to him. How could I have forgotten Conor again? How could I ever think of getting myself home safe, and leaving him behind?

"Where? Where is he?"

"I'll take you to him," says Faro. "Take my hand, Sapphire, and I'll take you to him."

Faro is poised on the edge of the rock now. His strong seal tail hangs above the water and his arms are braced as if he's ready to push off from the rock and plunge in. He faces the mouth of the cove, where the fresh water of the new tide is pouring in. I know in every bone of my body that Faro's not going to take me in, to the safe sand at the back of the cove, where I can climb up and find the path home. He's going to take me out into deep water, beyond the mouth of the cove. But I'm not allowed to go there – it's too dangerous—

"I can't," I say. "I've got to get back."

"Without Conor?" asks Faro, critically. "If I knew that my sister was in the Air, I would never leave her. I would never go home without her."

"Do you mean that Conor's in danger?"

Faro looks at me but says nothing. He's testing me, I know he is. If Conor were really in any danger, how could Faro just sit here on this rock and tell me about it without doing anything to help? People don't act like that.

People. Humans. I glance down at Faro's curved, powerful tail. I can hardly see the place where human flesh ends and Mer flesh begins. One part of Faro seems to melt into another. Faro catches my glance.

"It must be strange to be divided, the way you are," he says, with a tinge of pity in his voice.

"Divided?"

"*You* know," goes on Faro, looking embarrassed, the way you do when you have to point out that someone's got a splodge of ketchup on their chin. "You know, the way you are. *Cleft*." He points at my legs. "Must feel strange, having two of those."

"But it's *you* that's divided, not *me*. You're half-human and half—"

"Half?" snaps Faro. "There you go again, with your Air thinking. I am not *half* of anything. I am wholly Mer." He says it proudly, as if being Mer is like being royal, and he glances down at his tail with satisfaction.

"Conor is with my sister," says Faro. "Now, are you coming?"

I have no choice. No matter how deep the shelf that drops away at the mouth of the cove, no matter how fast the tide pours in, it's only Faro who can take me to Conor. And how can I go back home without Conor?

"I'll come with you," I say.

"Good," says Faro. "But you have to leave your Air thinking here on this rock. We don't swim as you do, half up in the Air." He mimics someone doggy paddling along with their face stuck up out of the water.

"I can't breathe underwater!"

"Don't even think about breathing. Breathing is what you do in the Air. We Mer do things differently. Hold my wrist, just here. Clasp your fingers around me. Tighter than that. When I dive, you dive. Don't try to hold your breath. Don't even think about breathing. You must let it all out, all your breath. Hold my wrist. You won't drown while you're with me."

Faro's wrist feels warm and strong. It feels like that word he says so mockingly: *human*. But I look down at his strong smooth tail. It twitches, as if it already feels the water and wants to be in it.

"When I dive," says Faro again, "you dive."

I hold his wrist tight. I look down at the water which has risen so fast that it's slapping at the rock less than a metre below us. I look at Faro and see that he has shut his eyes. His nostrils are narrowing, closing up like the nostrils of a seal before it dives deep.

I clasp Faro's wrist. I shut my eyes, lean forward, take the deepest breath I can, and push off from the rock. We dive.

CHAPTER SEVEN

We dive. I cling to Faro's wrist because there's nothing else, but it doesn't feel like a human wrist any more. It feels cold and smooth, like a thick stem of oar weed. My hands slip and I dig my fingers into the flesh. I'm too frightened to care if it hurts him.

I open my eyes. We're moving faster than I've ever swum before, rushing down and down in a race of bubbles. Faro's tail is driving us both. There's salt in my nose and I want to cough but I can't cough underwater. Water presses in on me, crushing my chest and making it burn. There's a tight band around my ribs, squeezing in, like iron hands squashing my lungs.

I can't breathe. The water won't let me breathe. It's choking me. The iron band around my chest is red hot now. My fingers tingle and sparks of light shoot across my eyes. The water's rushing up past me and I don't even know which way up we are any more. It's like being wiped out by a wave when you're surfing, but this time there's no way up into the air. No way to cough and gasp and spit the salt away. The weight of the water won't let me.

Terror rushes over me, and wipes me out.

"Conor! Conor!" I scream inside my head. I can't make the words into sound because there's no air to make them with. My eyes are full of darkness. The band round my ribs is a circle of fire. It hurts so much that I think I'm going to die.

Thoughts fly through my head like frightened birds. I'm going to die. Not sometime far away in the future, but now. Here. I see Mum's face, turning to the door, waiting for me. I hear her voice calling me: *Sapphy, Sapphy where are you? It's time to come home!* I try to call back, to say I'm sorry I broke my promise, to beg Mum to come and save me, but my mouth is full of salt and no words come out.

"*Hold on to me,*" someone says, close to my ear. "Don't let go. As long as you hold on to me, you're safe. You're safe with me, Sapphire."

I remember Faro. I open my eyes and he's there, beside me. We're deep, deep under the water and I'm still gripping his wrist as if it's the only thing that holds me to life.

I can't hold my breath any more. I've got to let go. The last of my human breath streams away in bubbles. Little bright pictures rush with the bubbles. Mum ironing in our cottage, the memorial service for Dad with the choir singing, the Midsummer Bonfire flaring up into the sky—

No bubbles of air come from Faro's mouth. He turns

to me with his hair streaming upwards. His nostrils are still closed.

"Let go," he says urgently. "You're safe with me."

He's talking! Faro's talking underwater and I can hear him.

"Let go," says Faro again. "Let go, Sapphire. Leave the Air. Let go, or you'll drown."

His words boom in my ears. *Leave the Air, leave the Air.* Can I do it, like Faro? How can I leave the Air? I'm not Mer, I'm human. My ears are bursting, my chest flares with fire that is licking up my throat now and into my brain. I've got to breathe in. I've got to. But I'm so far down underwater that I'll never get back to the surface in time to breathe.

"Leave the Air," says Faro imperatively. "*Now.*"

I have no choice. Water thrums in my ears. *Let go or die, let go or die.*

I let go. Mum's face fades away as Air leaves me. All the bright pictures in my head fade and disappear as the sea rushes into me. Into my mouth, my nose, my ears, even my eyes. And suddenly it doesn't matter. The sea is in me and I am in the sea. The tight band around my chest loosens. The burning eases. The darkness dissolves into light. I am breathing. I am in the water, but I am breathing. I'm cool and light and free. Why was I so terrified? I'm breathing, deep under the water, and all the pain has gone.

The sea combs out my hair and it flows behind me in the rush of our speed. We dive down, down, like swallows diving in summer sky. My hand is on Faro's wrist, but I don't cling to him any more. My feet are close together, like fins, and my free arm pulls strongly through the water. How fast we're swimming! The sea floor rushes past as if we're freewheeling downhill.

"I'm breathing!" I say in wonder. "I can do it, Faro!"

Faro laughs.

"You're not Mer yet, Sapphire. But I let you in, so you'll be safe here. I'll look after you. You can let go of my wrist if you want."

"I don't want to… not just yet."

"Don't worry. It's all right. I let you in, so you're safe as long as I'm with you."

I lift my hand from his arm, just for a second, then I grab hold of him again. I'm not ready to swim alone down here, in this strange place where the whole world is water.

We rush onwards, side by side. Sunlight strikes down through the water and we swim in and out of pillars of light and shadow. Below us is white sand, gleaming and glittering. The pull of the tide has made deep ridges in it, so it looks like ploughed land.

"Look up," says Faro. I look where he's pointing, and there's a brilliant skin of light way up above us, wobbling and shimmering.

"That's the surface," says Faro. "Air."

"Oh." It looks far away. "Can I get back to it if I want?"

"Yes, of course," says Faro. But there's something in his face – doubt, or maybe fear—

"What's the matter? I can get back, can't I, Faro?"

"If – when you want to go back, you can. But it hurts. You get a pain – here..." Faro puts his free hand on his ribs, exactly where I felt the burning circle of pain when I dived. I feel a shiver run through his body and into the wrist I'm holding.

"But it hurt exactly like that when I dived down with you. And I was going *into* the water, not leaving it."

"That's the way it is for humans. Some of them drown of it."

"*Some* of them?"

"Well – most of them. Nearly all of them. We call and call to them but they can't listen. They can't let go of the Air, and that's why they drown. It's the other way round for us Mer. *You* drown in water. *We* can drown in the Air."

"But you were in the air when I met you. You were all right, you weren't choking or anything."

Faro frowns. "Yes, some of us can go there. There are reasons—" he breaks off.

"What reasons?"

"Never mind. But it hurts when you go through the skin. It's dangerous."

"What skin?"

"Look up there." Faro points at the bright, distant surface. "That's the skin. You have to go through it. That's what hurts. The change is bad every time."

"So when I go back, it'll hurt—"

"No, not for you. You're human, aren't you? You'll be all right, going back to the Air. Anyway, you're here now.

Safe with Faro." Faro smiles, and very gently peels my hand off his wrist. "There. Try again. You really don't need me now. You only think you do, because of your Air thinking."

We're not moving any more. I'm floating free, in deep, deep water. My hair drifts across my face, then drifts away. The sea holds me like a baby. I'm not scared of it any more. I'm rocking, rocking in the hammock of the sea. Faro is right, the sea will look after me. Gently, my hand floats away from his wrist. I cup my hands and scull the water. Faro's right. I am safe.

Suddenly, with a strong flick of the tail, Faro turns a perfect somersault. And again, and again, faster and faster until he's a whirling circle of human body and seal tail.

"You try it, Sapphire!"

"I couldn't do that. I'll just float."

I spread out my arms to the water as if I have never touched the sea before. And I haven't, not like this. I'm not bouncing about on top of the water doing breast-stroke or backstroke or what humans call floating. The skin of the sea has parted and let me in. I'm living in the sea. I'm part of it.

"Let's surf a current," says Faro. "Come on, we'll find a strong one."

All my life I've been trying *not* to find currents. I know there's a rip beyond the headland. That's why we never swim out there, because it's too dangerous. If the rip catches you, it can pull you a mile out to sea. Even if you're a good swimmer you won't be able to swim against it. You'll be swept out, and you'll drown fighting it.

"There's a good current this way," says Faro. "Come on."

"But—"

"This way, Sapphire!"

I see the current before I feel it. There's movement in the water ahead of us, like a twisting, glassy rope. Or like a powerful sea snake coiling itself in and out. The current looks thicker and much more solid than the calm water around it. Once it gets hold of me, I'll never escape. It'll coil itself around me, pull me tight and take me wherever it wants.

Never, never swim out beyond those rocks, Sapphire. That's where the rip runs.

But I can't see anything, Dad.

It's there, believe me. Now promise.

All right, Dad. I promise.

"Let's go!" calls Faro, springing forward eagerly like a surfer trying to catch the perfect wave. His body twists, and vanishes into the snake of the current. But I can't follow. I promised Dad. I can't—

But I can't stay here alone either. What did Faro say? *As long as you're with me, you're safe.*

I dive, and the current swallows me. Just for a second I feel the terrible python pull of it and I'm scared it's going to crush me like a snake would crush me in its coils. And then I'm part of it. No, once you're inside it, the current is nothing like a python. I feel as if I'm in a plane racing down the runway at full power. There's no choice any more. The plane has got to fly, and I've got to fly with it.

And there's Faro, right in the middle of the current.

"Come farther in, Sapphire!" he calls.

Now I see what you have to do. You have to swim until you're where the current's fastest, where you can feel the muscle of it all around you. And then lie there inside it like an arrow, as Faro's lying. The pull is so strong that it doesn't feel like pull at all. I only know how fast I'm going when I look down and see the ridged floor of the sand fall away as we rush into the deep.

"Yeee–hiiiii!" It's Faro yelling, and then it's me too, riding the back of the current as if it's a wild horse, letting it twist me and turn me and spin me until I don't know where we are or where we're going. And I don't care. All that matters is the ride. Faro's standing upright on the current, balanced on the curve of his tail. I try to copy him but my legs won't do what his tail does. I'll try again—

"Rocks coming up! HOLD ON," shouts Faro, and he swipes us sideways with his tail, and out of the current just before it rushes on to the underwater rocks and splits into a million threads of white.

"You didn't look ahead," Faro points out, as we hang suspended in the calm, gasping.

"Can't look – not when going so fast—"

"Hmm. Slow human reactions. Better not get into any

currents without me for the time being. They like to play rough."

"I think I'll keep out of currents altogether."

"Don't be stupid, Sapphire, how're you going to travel without surfing currents? You need to know them, that's all. They follow their own patterns, but you can learn them. Every current has its own path, but sometimes they come close and you can hop from one to another. That's how you make the longest journeys. Once you've learned to current-hop, we can really travel. Elvira's taking Conor to the Lost Islands next—"

He breaks off, as if he's said something he didn't mean to say.

"Who's Elvira?"

"I told you. My sister. She's around here somewhere."

"Can I see her?"

"Maybe. She's talking to the sunfish with Conor. We keep telling the sunfish they can go farther north now that the water's grown warmer, but they won't believe it. They think this isn't their territory. Sunfish are stubborn, and they have long memories. They still remember when it was the Age of Ice here."

"You mean the Ice Age? Faro, they can't possibly remember that. The Ice Age was thousands and thousands of years ago," I say confidently. It's good to know something that Faro doesn't, for once.

"Fish don't keep their memories in their heads like you do."

"Where do they keep them?"

"In the shoal. Obviously the shoal keeps changing as the sunfish get born and die, but the memory stays in the shoal and every sunfish can access it."

Then I catch up with something else that Faro's just said.

"Did you say that *Conor* was talking to the sunfish? It wasn't just Elvira talking to them? You mean that Conor's learned their language?"

"I wouldn't say he's exactly *speaking* it yet. Elvira's trying to teach him."

"Faro, how many times has my brother been here? With… with Elvira?"

"Oh, I don't know," says Faro carelessly. "A few. You do ask a lot of questions, Sapphire. Conor's just the same. It must be a human thing. Come on, let's find another current to surf."

And we do. Current after current after current. Riding and rising and skimming and swooping and falling and starting again. Little playful currents that whisk you in circles. Powerful ones that pull you for miles. And far, far out, way beyond where we are, there are the Great Currents. Faro says he'll take me there one day. But not yet. I need a lot more practice before I can surf the Great Currents. They are too strong and wild for me yet.

"Has Conor surfed them?"

"No."

The strange thing is that I'm no longer anxious about Conor. I've nearly forgotten that the whole reason I'm here is that I had to find him and bring him home.

I haven't *quite* forgotten; it's there somewhere in the back of my mind, like the daytime world when you're in the middle of a dream. But it doesn't seem to matter all that much. Conor's fine. He's safe with Elvira, talking to the sunfish. All that really matters is the rush of the currents, the tingle of flying water – again, again, again. I don't want it ever to stop.

But just as we slide off a tricky little current that Faro says goes too near the Great Currents for safety, I look up. Between me and the skin of the surface a huge shape hangs. A shape that I've known all my life, although this is the first time I've ever seen one.

Wide jaw, gaping. Body as long as a helicopter. Fins, tail— "Faro!" I whisper, afraid it might pick up the vibration of my voice through the water. "Faro, there's a shark!"

Faro flips on his back, stares up. The shark hangs above us. Its jaws are spread wide, waiting for something. Or someone.

CHAPTER EIGHT

know," says Faro. He lies on his back, sculling with his hands, watching the shark. "She's been here a lot this season. This is a good feeding ground for her."

I'm still shivering with shock. How can he be so relaxed? "But Faro, it's a *shark*."

"You don't need to be scared of her. She's a little-feeder."

As if she's heard him, the shark slowly turns her great head. She's seen us.

"She can smell us," says Faro. He's watching the shark carefully, but he still doesn't seem worried.

"What do you mean, Faro? What's a little-feeder?"

"Watch her."

I watch as the shark points her head forward again, jaw wide, and advances very slowly, swinging her whole body from side to side in the way an elephant swings its trunk. With her mouth open like that, she looks as if she's hoovering the sea.

"She's feeding," says Faro. "Everything goes into her mouth. Her throat acts as a sieve. Most of the stuff she eats is so small you can't see it."

"You mean, like plankton?"

"Plankton. Whatever. You Air People have a word for everything, don't you? Especially for things you don't know much about. It takes a long time to get to know a shark. Keep still, Sapphire! Sharks don't like being disturbed. And don't stare too hard. She can sense when she's being watched. Lucky for you she's not a seal-feeder."

"But Faro, sharks that eat seals don't come here. There aren't any dangerous sharks in Cornish waters."

But as I say it, a shiver of memory runs over my skin. There was something about sharks on TV a while ago. A fisherman thought he'd seen a Great White, two miles off Newquay. He claimed that he'd found a half-eaten seal in his net. No other creature but a shark could have torn into a seal like that, he said, and the camera showed how the seal's belly had been ripped away. I'd wished that Dad was there, so I could ask him whether it really could have been a Great White. Dad would have known.

I had forgotten about the Great White shark off Newquay.

Until now.

"When you say 'seal-feeder'," I ask Faro, "does that mean the same as a Great White?"

"How should I know all your Air names? Seal-feeders eat seals. Sometimes they'll hear you and sometimes they won't, so it's best to keep away from them."

"Do they ever hurt you?"

"I told you. You can't predict what a seal-feeder's going to do. They do what they want, so you have to keep out of their way. Sometimes they can't hear that we're Mer. They want to hear that we're seals, because they're hungry or because they feel that way. And they're very fast, not like her up there."

The shark above us swings her head again. The gape of her mouth shines wide. Even though Faro says she's a little-feeder, she's still a shark—

"She heard us," says Faro sharply. "She doesn't like us talking about her. Let's go."

Faro jackknifes into a dive. When we're a long way from the shark, we slow down and I ask him, "Why do we have to be so careful? You said she wouldn't hurt us. You said she only eats little sea creatures like plankton."

"I don't know how you humans ever get anything done, you ask so many questions." Faro does two perfect somersaults, head over tail, head over tail. "She's got cousins all over the place," he says casually, flicking back his hair. "You don't want to offend a shark, Sapphire, not even a little-feeder like her. Sharks may not be very clever, but they've got long, long memories, and they stick together. They're terrible for holding a grudge. You've got to remember that sharks are fish. I told you, fish share their memories. They never forget a place where they can find food, and they never forget an insult."

"I thought she looked very intelligent," I say loudly, and Faro laughs.

"If we meet any more sharks, I'll let you do the talking," he says sarcastically.

"Well, at least I noticed the shark." I feel triumphant. I may have 'slow human reactions', but I saw the shark first. "You didn't see her until I pointed her out, even though she was right above us."

"Oh, didn't I?" asks Faro. He rolls lazily in the water. "Of course, we Mer aren't very observant, compared to Air people like you. You even put air on your backs and come down and peer around."

"Do you mean divers?"

Faro shrugs. "Air people dressed in black, with air on their backs. It's bad to bring Air into Ingo. They shouldn't do it."

"Ingo?" My heart thuds. I have the strangest feeling, as if I know that word better than I know anything else in the world. But it's hazy, distant. There's a part of my mind I can't reach while I'm underwater. "Faro, what is Ingo?"

"Don't you know that? I thought you knew so much. Ingo is where we are. Ingo is everything that doesn't belong to the Air."

"So am I – am I away in Ingo now?"

"Not all that far away," says Faro in a voice that sounds as if he's secretly laughing at me inside himself. "Just on the edge of it, maybe."

"Ingo," I repeat, tasting the sound of it in my mouth. "I'm in Ingo."

"Those – those *divers* – they bring Air with them, so they can go down where they shouldn't come. They poke around where they shouldn't be," goes on Faro. "*Exploring*, they call it. *Spying*, we call it. Trying to get into Ingo without going through the skin. Luckily they don't see much. They don't enter Ingo at all."

"But they dive down here, don't they? How can you say they don't enter Ingo?"

Faro shrugs. "A stone drops into the water. That doesn't mean that the stone is swimming. Divers come into the water, but that doesn't mean they're in Ingo. So, *you* saw the shark first, did you? Look around, Sapphire, and tell me what else you've *noticed*," he challenges.

I peer through the water.

"Well, rocks – over there, look, sharp ones. I wouldn't want to go near them. And there's a fish! Just going out of sight, look, it's a really big one."

"Huge," Faro agrees. "It must be at least as big as this," and he puts his hands a few centimetres apart. "What else have you noticed?"

"Um – is that a current over there? And I think I saw something scuttling down on the sea bed just now – but it's so far down, it's hard to tell—"

"Anything else?"

"I noticed that shark, anyway. And you didn't."

"All right. My turn." A rush of sound pours out of Faro's mouth.

"Faro, I can't understand—"

"I know you can't. I'm not talking to you. I'm asking everyone who is here to come out where you can see them."

The sea around us begins to thicken. Two grey seals slide by, twisting as they go. They turn to circle us, almost touching us. They have big eyes like retriever dogs, and they look as if they're laughing. Their nostrils are closed tight and their whiskers are flattened against their muzzles. But how strong they are, how powerful. Their muscles ripple under their skin as they go by. A dazzling cloud of silver fish flickers in and out of my fingers. I shut my hand but they vanish between my fingers like droplets of mercury.

I look to my left and there's a huge flatfish, as big as our kitchen table, with one popeye goggling at me. One after another a raft of purple jellyfish floats past, tentacles drifting, their jelly skirts bellying in and out, in and out...

"So *that's* how they move," I whisper. Their tentacles are thick and snaky and have suckers all the way down – what if one of them whipped across my leg? They look as if they would sting. I scull backwards, out of range. The jellyfish sail on in a line, like battleships now, making for war.

"Look down there," says Faro, and a giant spider crab appears out of a whirl of sand, and then another. Conor hates spider crabs. I can always frighten him by picking up a dead one on the shore and chasing after him with it, flapping its claws. But I wouldn't touch one of these.

The sand settles and shows an angler fish, almost buried but for the shine of her lure. Dad caught one once when he was deep-sea fishing, and showed it to me. "It lives far out, on the sea bottom. They're adapted to the dark. Just as well, poor creature, it's ugly as sin. It wouldn't want to see itself in the light."

"Look up," says Faro, and I see a soup of plankton shimmering in the light from the surface. And right above us there's another shark, much smaller but the same shape as the other little-feeder. A shoal of tiny grey fish darts to the side, away from the sieving jaws. And that rock there – it's covered with dog whelks, thickly striped. More fish flick past – and here's a herd of sea horses riding the curve of Faro's tail—

"It's not fair. You made them come. All these creatures weren't here when I was looking."

"*Not fair,*" echoes Faro mockingly. "This isn't a game we're playing, Sapphire. All these creatures were here all the time. *You* weren't looking, that's all." More of the liquid language pours from his mouth. Pure Mer, it must be. I wish I could speak that language. The seals nuzzle him and I think they're speaking it too, but I can't understand a word. Tail to tail, Faro and the seals look the same, sleek and shining and strong, with the herd of sea horses dancing around them...

I have a sudden fear that Faro's going to disappear with them, leaving me alone, way out in the ocean, not knowing my way back—

"Faro, I think we should go back now."

"Go back?"

"I've got to go home. It's late."

"Without Conor?"

Faro's face is teasing. Suddenly I have the feeling that he knows something else I don't. That Conor is close, like the seals and the jellyfish and the spider crabs. That if I looked in the right place, I would see him. Now.

I turn. Something flickers, nearly out of sight. I turn again, trying to catch whatever's hiding. *Come out, come out, wherever you are!* Faro turns too, as if he knows exactly where to look. He stares deep into the water. He's watching for something I can't see. I think he's going to call again, and I can't guess what or who might come this time. But he doesn't call.

"What a pity," he says softly, after a while. "We've just missed them."

"Who?"

"Conor and Elvira, of course. They were here, but they've gone."

"Did Conor see me?" I feel as if Faro's punched me. Conor was *here*. He was so close that Faro saw him, and he disappeared again, without me. Conor didn't let me see him. Conor didn't try to find me. He didn't even call to me. But Conor's my *brother*.

"He was with the seals. He missed you," says Faro.

Conor was with the seals. Maybe Conor understands the language that was just sound to me.

"Does Conor speak pure Mer?"

Faro shakes his head." No. Not yet. Nowhere near to it. He's only just beginning. He's like you, Sapphire, he doesn't know anything."

I turn away. I don't want Faro to see how I feel. I don't even *know* how I feel. Faro says that Conor doesn't know anything, but I don't believe it. If Conor's gone this deep, if he can swim with seals and plans to surf to the Lost Islands with Elvira, then he's gone far away from me already. He's learned too much that I don't know. And the worst part is that he's done it all secretly, without telling me or wanting to share it with me.

Conor and I have always been together. We've always done the same things. Conor's a better diver than me, and he can swim faster, but he waits for me. He used to get impatient sometimes when I was little and I couldn't keep up with him. Sometimes I'd cry and yell after him, *Conor, Conor! Wait for me!*

And he'd come back and find me all covered in tears and he'd take my hand and we'd be friends again.

But that was a long time ago. Dad's gone, and Mum's working all the time. If she works a late shift, we sometimes don't see her from after breakfast to the next morning. Conor and me have only got each other. That's why we always look after each other.

But he hasn't waited for me this time.

No, Conor wouldn't do that. He wouldn't go away without even speaking to me. Faro's lying.

But Conor didn't tell me about meeting the Mer, did he? He kept it secret until I saw him with Elvira. And what about Elvira? Where's she taking him? Conor's going in too deep – I'm frightened—

"Conor!" I call, with all my strength, and all the voice I can find. *"Conor!"* Suddenly, the pain is there again, beginning to burn around my ribs. I feel the heavy water on top of me, pressing me down. I can't breathe.

"No, Sapphire!" says Faro urgently. "Don't do it! Don't try to call him! You'll get hurt." He seizes hold of my hand and puts it around his wrist. The burning pain eases, like the tide going out.

"Think like us," says Faro. "Look at me."

I look at his strong, curved seal tail, his human face.

"Think like us. Look at the seals."

The seals come close, touching me with their sleek sides. Their big eyes seem to be telling me something. Seal language is flowing towards me, not made out of words but made out of something else that I'm just on the edge of understanding. I reach out my hand and the seals let me touch them as they play. They want me to go with them. They want us all to roll and play in the deep water.

There's no pain around my ribs now. I'm safe with Faro. Safe with the Mer.

"It's dangerous to think of Air when you're here," says Faro. His face is serious, his voice urgent. "You must never do it. Promise me."

"How can I promise that? I belong to the air. I'm human. I can't just forget about it."

Faro nods, slowly, as if he's weighing things up. "Yes, but—" and then he stops.

"Yes but what?"

"Nothing." Whatever he was going to tell me, he's changed his mind. "It's time to leave now, Sapphire. Can't you feel the tide?"

CHAPTER NINE

ides are powerful. Tides know where they want to be and they take the whole sea world with them, dragging it to and fro. Faro says tides are the moon talking to Ingo. When the moon talks, Ingo has to listen.

We come in on the tide together, me and Faro and the seals. Faro finds a current first, and then we feel the tide folding us into its strong journey. It's strange that the same tide is still rising, even though I seem to have been with Faro for hours.

"Conor and Elvira have already come in on the tide," says Faro. "Conor's left Ingo now."

I feel calm and easy about Conor again. All my fears have drifted away. I can't remember why I cried out for him, or why I felt so desperate. I'm holding Faro's wrist, and I am safe in Ingo.

Faro takes me as far as the mouth of our cove. I don't want him to come any farther, because I know how much his lungs would burn, and how terror would seize him as he went through the skin of the sea, into Air. He says he'll come with me all the way if I want, but I say no. I'm not worried about leaving Faro, because I know I'll be back. The pull of Ingo has got into me, strong as the tide.

"It's all right, Faro, I know where I am now. You don't need to come any farther with me." I can see that he's relieved, although he tries to hide it.

The seals are still with us. It's easy for them to slip from Ingo into Air, because they can live in both. So they'll come all the way with me, swimming in on the tide. I'm still holding Faro's wrist when I see the place where the deep, deep water meets the shelf of sand. He mustn't come any farther. I'm safe to swim in from here.

"It won't hurt you to go through the skin," Faro reminds me. "You're going home this time."

"Don't come any farther in, Faro," I tell him. I feel protective of him now. He's been looking after me deep in Ingo, and I'm going to look after him here, where we're coming close to my own country. The surface of the sea wobbles not far above out heads. The light is sharp and dazzling, and the air will hurt Faro like knives, the way the sea hurt me when I first went down.

There are flickery broken-up shadows of sunlight all over the sea floor and all over Faro. He looks like a boy and a seal and a shadow all at once as he does a last back-flip and his tail swirls around his head. And suddenly there's only a shadow, and Faro's gone. I haven't said goodbye to him. I haven't asked when I'm going to see him again.

I don't need to. I'm sure that I'll see him soon.

The two seals are close to me, one on each side. They want to push me onwards into the shallower water. The tide's pushing me too and there's sand not far below me, almost underfoot now—

"Tell Faro that I'll be back," I say to the seals. They roll and circle round me and I don't know if they understand or not. *Mer*, I think. *Speak Mer to them, not Air*. I open my mouth and the cool sweet underwater rushes into it. *Speak Mer, not Air*. I let the sea flow out of my mouth and make its own words.

"We will," says the seal closest to me in a gravelly voice like the tide sucking over a pebble beach. I feel his breath on my ear, and then he's gone with his partner, and I'm diving up through the skin of the water, into Air.

It doesn't hurt. It's like stepping off a boat after hours out at sea with Dad. The land feels wobbly when you do that, as if it's still going up and down, up and down. You can't get your balance. Dad says it's because you've still got your sea legs, and you have to get your land legs back. In a while you get used to it and the land stops behaving like the sea, and you're back at home.

I'm back in the Air. I wade through the shallow water, up the beach, towards the rocks at the back of the cove, where I have to climb. It's a perfect day now, hot and still, without a trace of mist. The sand is warm underfoot.

I climb the rocks very slowly. My legs are tired. The

rough, dry rock feels so strange under my hands. I've got used to the textures of Ingo. My arms and legs feel much too light, now that there's no water pressing against them.

I clamber up the rocks, through the gap between the boulders, and haul myself up over the grassy lip of the cliff.

Conor.

Conor's sitting there, waiting. He's pale and there are dark shadows under his eyes. He jumps up when he sees me. He looks shocked, as if he can't believe it's really me. He grabs hold of my arm, and drags me on to the grass. He holds me so tight it hurts. For a moment I'm scared. Conor looks furious. I even think for a second that he's going to hit me. But of course he doesn't. He just stares and stares at me, as if he hasn't seen me for years. Our faces are very close. Conor scans mine, searching for something.

"Saph," he says very quietly, as if he can hardly believe it's me. He shakes me gently, the way he does when he's trying to wake me on a school morning.

"Saph, where've you been? I've been waiting and waiting for hours. I thought you were never going to come back."

"Back from where?"

"Where do you think!" he explodes. "Don't try and fake it, Saph! I know where you've been. You've been away nearly twenty-four hours. Mum would've gone crazy if she'd known. But the car wouldn't start, so she stayed overnight in St Pirans after work. She got Mary to come up last night and check if we were OK. I lied for you. I said you were in the bath. And then I came out here to look for you. I've been waiting all night."

I look around. There's Conor's sleeping bag, and his torch, a KitKat wrapper, and a bottle of water. Maybe… maybe it's true…

"Twenty-four hours," I repeat slowly. I remember the other day, when I saw Conor on the rock with the girl, Elvira. Conor thought he'd only just cleaned out the shed, but it was already evening. *He didn't know how much time had passed, because he was away in Ingo. Like me. So time in Ingo is different from time here.*

"If I've really been gone twenty-four hours, then time must move more slowly in Ingo…" I say, thinking aloud.

"Ssh! Don't talk about it here!" hisses Conor.

"Why not? There's no one but us."

Conor glances around, as if the grass might be listening. A herring gull swoops low, screaming over our heads. Everything sounds hollow and noisy, now that I'm back in the Air.

"You don't know who might be listening," he whispers.

"But Faro said that *you* were in Ingo too, at the same time as me. He said you and Elvira were talking to the sunfish."

"I wasn't talking to them. I don't know how. Elvira was."

"But that was only a little while ago. How could you have been there in Ingo, and up here waiting for me on the cliff, at the same time?"

Conor pulls a grass stem out of its sheath and nibbles the sweet end of it, thinking too.

"What Faro tells you," he says at last, "I mean, the things that Faro says, they're true in his mind. But they may not be true in yours."

"Do you mean he's lying?"

"It's not like that in Ingo. Elvira's just the same. There isn't only one thing that's true, and everything else is a lie. And I think maybe time's like that in Ingo, too. It stretches out – then it presses itself together, like this –" and Conor squeezes his hands together, as if he's crushing time.

"Who told you all that? Elvira?" I ask jealously. "Were you there with Elvira, like Faro says, or not?"

"Yes, I was there… but I don't know how long for. I think time in Ingo isn't just different in how fast it goes, but in the whole way it works. You said it was only a little while since I was in Ingo, but I've been back here for ages. Since yesterday. So maybe time there moves quite differently."

"But did you see me? Did you and Elvira see me, and hear me calling, and then hide from me?"

It feels like the most important question I've ever asked Conor. I want him to kill the picture in my mind that shows him and Elvira slipping away together, maybe laughing, not wanting me to see them—

"You came to me," says Conor slowly. "You came into my mind, Saph, but I didn't see you. I was with the seals, and suddenly you were there in my mind. I thought something bad had happened to you. I told Elvira I had to go back and find you."

"What do you mean, I was 'in your mind'?"

"You know how it is in Ingo," says Conor reluctantly. "Everything you usually think about – everything that's up in the Air – it floats away and fades. It doesn't seem real. Even people fade. Even you and Mum started to feel like dreams, when I was in Ingo. But suddenly all that changed. You were really there, in my mind, solid. I stopped feeling easy and dreamy. I was scared. I thought you were in trouble, Saph, and I might not get to you in time."

"But I was there, in Ingo, all the time. Close to you."

"Yes." Conor's face closes in a frown. "But it didn't feel like that. It felt as if you were far away – calling to me – and I was losing you. Like when a mobile breaks up and you keep losing someone's voice. Elvira said—" He breaks off and frowns even more deeply.

"What did she say?"

"She told me not to call you. She said it could be dangerous. She wanted us to go on surfing the currents. There's a group of islands she's going to take me to – but I said I couldn't go with her. I had to come back and find you. She wasn't very…"

He shakes his head, as if trying to shake away the troubled feeling.

"Wasn't very what?"

"She wasn't very happy about it."

Your precious Elvira didn't care what happened to me, did she? I think, but I don't say it.

"I don't understand how it all works," says Conor.

"Me neither."

Conor was there, in Ingo, and so was I, but we never met. Faro and Elvira kept us separate.

But they didn't stop us when we said we wanted to come back.

No, I'm sure Faro doesn't want to hurt me. He looked after me and made sure I was safe in Ingo.

"You look terrible," says Conor. "Lucky Mum's not back. She'd know straight away something had happened."

The KitKat wrapper glints in the sun. My mouth waters.

"Is there any of that KitKat left?"

"No, I ate it. It was a long night."

"I'm sorry." I'm so hungry. Starving. Hungry for food and hungry for sleep. "Can I sleep in your sleeping bag, Con?"

My legs feel like jelly. I can't walk another step. All I want is to dive into Conor's sleeping bag and sleep until tomorrow – or even the next day—

"No, Saph," says Conor urgently, as my legs begin to fold. "We've got to get home. You can sleep in your own bed once we're there."

"Can't I even rest for a bit?"

"No, Saph, not here. It's not—" Conor breaks off what he's saying, and glances around again. A black-headed gull sits quietly on a rock nearby, his head cocked. If he wasn't a gull, you'd think he was listening to us. Conor whispers, "It's too close here."

"Close to what?"

"To Ingo. The tide will be high again soon."

I remember what happens at high tide. The waves come right in, under the cliffs. There are gullies that the sea has been carving for centuries, and blowholes where the water spouts up with a hiss of foam. When it's rough you can hear the sea roaring like a lion beneath you, and feel the thump of the waves through the granite.

Conor's right. Air and Ingo are close, here. This shore is where they touch. Conor and I are standing on the border, between the two countries. I look out to the shining water and think of Ingo. All the colour and creatures and life of Ingo are there, so close I could still touch them – if I just reached out—

Before I know it, I've moved forward, closer to the edge of the cliff.

"Saph!"

The gull opens his beak in a hideous squawk as Conor grabs my arm again and pulls me back.

"Come *on*, Saph! We've got to go home!"

CHAPTER TEN

wake up slowly. I'm in my own room, lying in bed. Sleep doesn't want to let go of me, and my head is fuzzy with dreams. Strange dreams, that seem more real than the daylight. I dreamed of a huge cavern deep, deep under the cliffs where I slept in a bed of silky sea-moss while a warm current fanned my face. The dream was so real that I can still feel the touch of moss, like feathers against my skin.

But I'm lying under my old blue duvet cover. From the look of the light, it's late morning. I can hear Mum downstairs, talking. I prop myself up on my elbow to listen, but I can't hear another voice answering her. She must be on the phone. I can't hear what she's saying, either, but suddenly I guess who she's talking to. It's that diver, Roger. The man who's coming here on Sunday. Mum's voice murmurs on and on, as if she's already known Roger for years and has a million things to tell him. Sometimes she laughs.

Roger the diver. Mum likes him, you can tell that from her voice. But Faro hates divers. What did he say about them? *Air People with air on their backs, bringing Air into Ingo, spying on Ingo.* That's what he thinks they are: spies.

I'm glad Faro hates them. Now that Mum's told me about Roger the diver coming on Sunday, I don't like divers either. I think they should keep out of the way and not come where they aren't wanted.

Mum thinks I should stop waiting and hoping for Dad to return. She says I've got my life to live. I know she's only trying to help me, but it isn't helping. I'm afraid it means that *she's* stopped waiting for Dad. She doesn't think he's coming back, and she's trying to make a life without him.

She can't do that. I won't let her. I've got to make Mum believe that Dad's not dead or disappeared off to somewhere like Australia. I know that's what some people think. They whisper things about Dad, and when Conor or I come close enough to hear they stop whispering, and give us sly little glances that say, *We know something you don't know.*

I roll over in bed and thump my pillow angrily. Josie Sancreed didn't even bother to whisper. She turned round to me in the playground and said out loud, "Everyone thinks your dad drowned, and they feel really sorry for you, but my mum says most likely he's gone off with another woman."

Gone off with another woman. I couldn't believe Josie had said that. The words scraped me like gravel when you fall off your bike. *Gone off. He's gone off because he's found someone better. That's what's happened to Mathew Trewhella. Everybody knows, it's only his family that doesn't believe it.*

I wanted to run away, right out of the playground and all the way home, but I didn't. No one was going to make me run away. Josie stared at me with a stupid little smile, but I could tell she was also a bit scared at what she'd done. Loads of people had heard, so she couldn't pretend she hadn't said it. Katie said, "Shut up, Josie," but the rest of the girls just stared at me too. I think maybe they were embarrassed, or they didn't know what to do, but at the time I thought they were on Josie's side.

I couldn't bear it. I grabbed Josie by the shoulders and shoved her as hard as I could against the playground wall. She fell, and started crying really loudly so all the girls gathered round her and helped her up. "It's my hand, she's hurt my hand," Josie wailed, and suddenly everything was my fault, not Josie's.

What was worse was that Mrs Tehidy saw me push Josie into the wall. She started clucking round Josie, and she put her arm around her and took her in to the office to have her hand seen to.

"I'll talk to *you* later, Sapphire," she said over her shoulder.

Mrs Tehidy hadn't heard what Josie said about Dad. I didn't ever, ever want to hear those words again, so I didn't tell. Katie was going to, but I wouldn't let her. So I was sent to Mr Carthew, and he said, "I'm disappointed in you, Sapphire. Violence doesn't solve anything."

Oh, doesn't it? I thought. As soon as I got out of Mr

Carthew's office, I went to find Josie. Mrs Tehidy had finished washing Josie's hand and she'd put a big plaster on it. Josie was in the girls' toilets telling everyone what I'd done to her. I walked in, and they all stopped talking.

"If you open your mouth about my dad again," I said, "I'll push you into the ditch that's full of nettles, behind the hall."

Josie knew I meant it, and so did everyone else. Some people were on my side, because they'd heard what Josie said to me, but Esther put her arm round Josie and said,

"Stop bullying Josie, Sapphire."

"*She's* the bully," said Katie angrily.

I never get into fights normally, but it's funny, once you start it seems easier. And when Josie looked at me in that scared way, I felt good. Maybe violence doesn't solve anything, but Josie never said another word about Dad. I didn't tell Conor. He'd only get into a fight with Josie's brother Michael. And besides, I didn't feel so good later on, once the hot angry feeling inside me had died down. I went and sat on a tree stump by the school gate. I kept thinking about what Dad would have thought if he'd seen me grabbing hold of Josie like that. And maybe Josie really did hurt her hand. It was quite a big plaster…

Don't think about all that now. Think about something else. But the only thoughts that crowd into my head are thoughts I don't want.

Roger. I turn around and thump the pillow again. I don't

want Roger the Diver at our table, eating our food. Maybe even sitting where Dad used to sit.

Suddenly another thought curls over in my mind like a fresh new wave, washing all the tangle of worries away. *It's all right. I don't even have to be there when Roger comes.*

It's true. I can go off somewhere else, somewhere far away. It won't matter how much Mum calls me, I won't be able to hear her. And she'll never be able to find me. The thought of it makes me smile. I've got somewhere to go now, a place of my own where no one can find me. *Ingo.*

I can hear the sea. Even though I'm lying in bed, the sound of the waves is as close as if I were lying on the beach. I can hear each one break on the beach, then the long *hushhhh* as it goes out again. My window's shut, but the sea sounds as if it's inside my room—

"Sapphire!" Conor's voice makes me jump. He's climbed down the ladder from his loft room without me noticing. And the strange thing is that suddenly I realise I'm not lying on my bed any more. I'm standing beside my window, which isn't shut at all: it's wide open. But I don't know how I got there, or who opened the window. Was it me? My hand is on the windowsill and the noise of the sea is louder than ever. A huge wave topples over and crashes on to the sand in a rush and swirl of foam—

"What are you *doing*?" asks Conor sharply.

"What?"

"Saph, shut that window. *Now*. I've got to talk to you."

Slowly, reluctantly, I push the window shut. But the air

pushes back, hard. The window wants to be open, wide open, so the noise of the sea can come in—

"Shut it, can't you?"

The snap in Conor's voice makes me push hard enough to close the window and fasten the catch.

"Mum's cooking sausages," says Conor. "She's making a late breakfast for you, Saph. Listen, this is what I told Mum about what happened, so you'd better say the same thing. I said you woke up in the night. You had a night-mare and you couldn't get back to sleep for ages, so that's why you're still in bed now. Mum's really worried about you, Saph. She thinks you're ill. She kept creeping up to look at you while you were asleep, and she says you don't look right."

"I feel fine."

"You don't *look* fine. Look in the mirror."

I go over to the dressing table Mum bought for me at an auction in Penzance. On top of the dressing table there's a mirror on a wooden stand. Mum bought it for me after Dad left. She bought some stencils and we painted the stand white and then stencilled shells over it, and painted them sea blue. I painted tiny shells around the frame of the mirror, too.

You have to bend down to peer into the mirror, because of the way the ceiling slopes at the side of my room.

I bend down and stare into the mirror. The glass is old, and when you look into it, it's like looking into another world. The mirror is spotted and tarnished and its light is green, like underwater. My face in the mirror is pale, and my hair hangs over my shoulders like seaweed. The colour of my eyes is swallowed up in huge black pupils. Do I really look like that?

"Mum says you look washed out," says Conor.

But I don't take any notice. His voice sounds distant, as if he's not really in the room with me. I'm watching watery ripples of light pass over my reflection, like waves rippling over sand. They move across the glass in their dream-like rhythm, and I count them as they go. One, two, three, four, five… and now there's the sound of the sea again, soft and sweet this time, like a breath in my ear… closer and closer…

> *Full fathom five*
> *Thy father lies,*
> *Of his bones*
> *Are coral made,*
>
> *These are pearls*
> *That were his eyes,*
> *These are pearls*
> *That were his eyes.*

But who's singing? Why are their voices so clear and strong? I've got to see them. I lean closer, closer—

"Sapphire, stop it! Don't look in the mirror!"

But I can't look away. The singing of the sea is so sweet that I want to go on listening to it for ever. It's pulling me into the mirror, farther in, farther in, into the green underwater depths—

There's a crash. I jump back, and the singing stops. The enchantment shatters. My mirror is just an old second-hand mirror again, lying on the floor, smashed, face down. What happened? And why's my duvet on the floor?

It was Conor. He threw my duvet over the mirror to stop me looking at it. But the weight of the duvet knocked the mirror to the floor. The glass has broken.

"What's going on up there?" shouts Mum from down-stairs.

"Nothing!"

"Nothing!"

"What was that crash?"

"Saph fell off the bed."

"Stop messing about, the pair of you. These sausages'll be done in five minutes."

I kneel down, gently lift my mirror and turn it over. The glass has cracked all over into the shape of a starfish.

"Why did you do that?" I hiss furiously at Conor. "You've broken my mirror and you've broken the—"

"Broken the what?"

"The – the song. They were singing to me."

"Saph, how many times do I have to tell you? It's dangerous. It's too powerful. It's stronger than we are."

"*You* were in Ingo too, Con! You're such a hypocrite. You just don't want me to share it. You want to keep it all for yourself, so you'll be the only one who knows about Ingo. You and *Elvira*."

But to my surprise, Conor refuses to get angry. He kneels down beside me, and starts carefully picking up the shards of glass. He's bending over, and his face is hidden as he says, "It's not like that, Saph."

"Well, what *is* it like then? What am I going to tell Mum about my mirror? She'll kill me."

"I'll tell her I was mucking about and I broke it. Listen, Saph. I'm scared."

He lifts his face and I stare at him. Conor, scared? But Conor is never frightened. *I'm* the one who gets spooked on wild nights when the wind howls around our cottage walls. *I'm* the one who lies straining her ears for the sound of Mum's car coming home, because I'm convinced she's had an accident on her way back from work. Conor is the sensible one, who knows what can happen in real life, and what can't.

He's only pretending to be scared. But then I look at him, and I know that's not true. His face is pale and tense.

"You were gone too long," says Conor, fumbling for the right words. "The first time I was there – in Ingo – their time was almost the same as our time. Maybe, when I got home, it was a little bit later than I thought it would be. You wouldn't really notice it. But each time I go there, time in Ingo eats up more of our time. It's like – it's like Ingo time is more powerful than our human time.

"When you came down to the cove to find me the other day, and you said that I'd been away for seven hours, and it was already evening, I didn't believe you at first. I thought you were making it up to scare me. But then I saw the sun going down in the west.

"And then the very first time you went into Ingo, you

were gone for nearly a day and a night. That's how strong Ingo time was for you. But how long did you think you were away, Saph? I mean, while you were down there? What did it feel like?"

I try to remember, but it's not easy. What did I do in Ingo? Faro and I talked. We dived and swam. We surfed some currents, we saw a shark and jellyfish and spider crabs...

But we didn't eat, or drink, or sleep. And I've never in my life got through more than two or three waking hours without eating or drinking.

"I don't know. When I was there, time seemed to slip away."

"That's what's so scary," says Conor. "If you go to Ingo again, how long do you think you'll be there? How much of our human time will it eat up? It could be days. Weeks. Or even longer."

"That's stupid, Conor. It can't be like that. You're making it sound like that story about Rip Van Winkle. You know, when Rip Van Winkle comes back and a hundred years have passed or something, and all his family and friends are dead. That's not going to happen. I won't ever stay away that long. I'll come back when I want to."

"*But you won't know how long it is!* That's the point. You'll forget about our human time again, once you're in Ingo. You'll *want* to forget. Look how strongly Ingo's calling you now. You think I don't know? You should have seen your face when you were looking into the mirror. But I couldn't hear anything. You're already much deeper into Ingo than I am, Saph. After only one visit. You're changing – you don't understand what Ingo's doing to you—"

"That's not true! *You're* the one that's in deep, Conor. You've been there lots of times and Elvira takes you everywhere. Faro told me."

But Conor shakes his head. "No. We don't go deep. Elvira gets angry with me, because she says I can't get the Air out of my head, even when I'm in Ingo. She keeps saying I'm too human. Getting in deep means living in Ingo time, not ours. But *you* slipped into it straight away. Why? And it's *you* they're calling for, not me. What if next time you're away for weeks – or months? You've got to think about it, Saph. *That's* why I'm scared."

Weeks – or months. The words chime deep inside me, like a bell. Gone for months without a trace, and no one would know where—

"Like Dad," whispers Conor.

"You mean, you think that's what happened to Dad?"

"I don't know."

"Did you ask Elvira?"

"No. I couldn't ask her that."

"Why not?"

"She'd get angry. Would *you* ask Faro? When you were deep in Ingo and you didn't know the way back? Would you want to make him angry? I mean, down there, we depend on them. They're powerful. We can't survive on our own."

I think about it for a while. A shiver goes over my mind.

"Would *you* ask Faro?" Conor repeats.

"Maybe not."

"They're not human," whispers Conor, as if someone

might hear us, even inside my room with the window shut. "You've got to remember that. I keep thinking that Elvira's – well, you know, that she's just a girl – but then suddenly something happens – she does something, or says something – and then I remember."

"What sort of thing do you mean?"

"Well – once Elvira talked about someone drowning. A surfer, up at Gwithian. And I remembered it happening, because everyone talked about it at school. But Elvira heard about it from one of her friends, who'd seen it happen. One of the Mer, I mean. The way Elvira described it made me feel strange. It was a bit the way we'd talk about a horse dying. We'd be sorry, we wouldn't like it, but we wouldn't care in the way we care about – about people. And then I thought, no, of course she doesn't care about the surfer the way we do. When that surfer drowned, it was important, even though we didn't know him. We've all been surfing up there – it could have happened to any of us. But it couldn't happen to Elvira and so she's not – she's not *connected* to it the way we are."

"Faro said they try to help people when they're drowning. They call and call to them."

"Yes, but what do they call? Are they calling to save them, or to—"

"To what?"

"*You know.* To pull them in deeper. You've got to remember they're not human. It's so easy to forget.

"And they don't want us to take too much knowledge of Ingo back into the Air. We might be a danger to them.

Or they'd think we might be. And if they thought we were a danger, I'm not sure what they'd do."

"But Con, they're our friends! Faro and Elvira are our friends, I know they are—"

"But all their calling doesn't save people, does it? They drown."

"That's not their fault—"

"These sausages won't be fit to eat by the time you two get down the stairs!" yells Mum.

I love sausages, but these don't taste too good. Maybe they're overcooked. I cut them up and push the bits under my knife and fork to make it look as if I've eaten more than I have. Mum hates it when we don't eat our food. But she doesn't seem angry this time. She looks worried.

"Have some bread then, Sapphy, if you don't want the sausages. It's not like you not to be hungry."

But the bread tastes funny too. Much too dry, and chalky – it's as if I'm trying to swallow earth.

"Have a drink of water with it," says Mum. "Here you are."

She passes me a fresh glass of water and I start to drink. But even the water doesn't taste good. There's something missing.

Without knowing that I'm going to do it, I reach out to the saltcellar and tip a white stream of salt into my hand. I lick the tip of the index finger on my other hand and dip it in the salt. Then I taste it. It tastes so delicious that I dip my finger again. Salt. That's what I need. No wonder the food didn't taste good, and the water was all wrong. It needs salt.

"Sapphire, for heaven's sake, what are you doing putting salt in your water?"

I drink down a long, refreshing gulp.

"You can't drink salt water! It's bad for you!"

Mum snatches my glass away. Never mind, I'll make some more when she's not looking.

"Mum, what are those little brown fish called that you get on pizzas?"

"Anchovies."

"Have we got any?"

"You wouldn't like them, Sapphy. One or two on top of a pizza taste all right, but they're much too salty to eat on their own."

"But have we got any?"

"I might have a tin in the cupboard somewhere. Now please, try and finish at least one of those sausages. You haven't eaten anything."

Conor is watching me. Mum's watching me. I cut up one of the sausages into small pieces and try to chew it.

"I can't, Mum. It tastes awful."

"Oh dear, you *are* ill. You're so pale. Maybe you've got a stomach bug. But I've *got* to go to work tonight, there's no one to take over my shift. Maybe I could ask Mary to come in and keep an eye on you again—"

"I'm not ill. I'm fine, Mum, *I just don't want to eat these sausages.*"

"Saph, cool it," says Conor warningly. I make a huge effort and swallow the hot, angry words that are rising in my mouth. Of course Mum's got to go to work, but I don't want Mary here to keep an eye on me. I'm not a baby. I don't want Conor spying on me either. Everyone's trying to stop me from doing what I want to do.

Mum goes to the sink to start the washing-up. Normally I do it in the mornings, and Conor washes up in the evenings. Mum's tired. She works so hard. I'll get up in a minute and dry the dishes. Mum ought to be sitting down with a cup of tea.

I watch Mum's back as she scrubs out the frying pan. Everything seems different suddenly: safe. This is my home, the same as it's always been. Mum's radio is on as usual, Mum's wearing her old jeans and a white T-shirt and she's got her hair pulled back in a ponytail. That means she's not going to work until later.

I'm in the kitchen, having a late – well, *very* late – breakfast with my mum and my brother in a normal school holiday. Maybe I *am* hungry, after all. I don't want the sausages, but maybe a piece of toast with Marmite. I'll make a mug of tea for myself as well as one for Mum. When she's finished the washing-up, she'll sit down opposite me at the kitchen table and drink her tea and tell me funny stories about last night's customers. What they said, and how much they drank, and how much money she made in tips. I love hearing about all the weird things that customers do in the restaurant. A customer even snapped his fingers to call Mum over once, but Mum just said to him, "Have you lost your dog?"

"Mum," I begin, but just then Mum turns the cold tap full on and the gush of the water hides my voice from her.

And at that same moment, I hear it again. A sweet sound, sweet but sharp, like a knife that can cut deep inside you. It's like the sound I heard in the mirror, but this time it's shaping itself into words. The song grows louder and louder, and the comfort of Mum's presence fades like a dream, until she doesn't seem important at all.

> *I wish I was away in Ingo*
> *Far across the briny sea,*
> *Sailing over deepest waters*
> *Where love nor care never trouble me...*

"Saph, what is it?" whispers Conor urgently. "What can you hear?"

"Listen, Conor. Can't you hear them?"

Conor listens. I wait for the sound to fill his ears as it's filling mine. I watch his searching, suspicious expression. I can tell that he hears nothing at all.

I wish I was away in Ingo...

"Conor, can you really not hear it?" I feel frightened, as if Conor and Mum are far away and I'm alone. The words are for me. Only for me, not for Mum or Conor. Conor can't hear anything, and Mum goes on calmly washing-up.

"Don't listen to them, Saph," whispers Con. "Close your ears. If you ignore them, they'll go away."

He thinks it's Faro calling me, and maybe Elvira, but I

know it's not them. These are the words Dad used to sing. But he is not the singer. Even Dad, my Dad with his fine voice, couldn't sing so sweetly. The sweetness draws me like a magnet, out of my chair, across the kitchen, through the open door, away from everything I know and into another world—

But Conor's following me. "Where are you going, Saph?"

"I've got to go, Con. They want me to come. They want me to come *now*."

"You mean Faro and Elvira?"

"No, not them," I say. I feel as if I'm speaking in a dream. I can hardly hear my own voice, and Conor's is thin and distant. "They're Mer voices, that's all I know. They're trying to tell me something – I've got to go there again – they want me—"

"I'm not going to let you, Saph," says Conor. He stands in front of me and spreads his arms wide. "You're staying here. I'm not going to lose you as well as Dad."

I can easily get past him. I've got Mer strength in me now. I could walk straight through Conor, as if he were mist instead of flesh and blood. But Conor's gaze is fixed on my face, holding me back.

"I'm not going to let you go, Saph," he repeats, and this time his voice is stronger.

"I'm sorry, Conor. You have to let me go. I know I can find Dad."

"What do you mean?"

"He's there. You were right. He's away in Ingo."

"Don't you understand, Saph? They're trying to make

you think that! They *want* you to think you're following Dad! That's what this is all about." Conor's eyes blaze. "And then I won't have a sister either. And Mum'll lose you as well as Dad. Can't you think of us at all? Can't you think of anything except Ingo, Ingo, *Ingo*?"

"I just want to find Dad, that's all."

"What's the good of trying to find Dad, if we end up losing you as well as him? It's dangerous. You know it is."

"We swore, Conor. We swore and promised. This is our chance. Maybe the only one we'll have."

"All right then," says Conor at last. "You win. I can't watch you all the time. I can't beat you *and* Ingo. But you're not going alone. I'm coming with you."

CHAPTER ELEVEN

"Mum, we're going out for a bit," Conor calls back casually through the open kitchen door. Usually Mum would shout, "OK, see you later. Stay together," but today she comes to the door, wiping her hands on a towel and frowning.

"But Sapphy's not well," she says. "Don't you want to stay at home with me, Saph?"

"I'm fine, Mum! I'm OK now, really," I say as brightly as I can. Mum looks puzzled, and a bit disappointed.

"Come here, love. Let me have a look at you."

Conor drifts away across the garden. I know he'll wait for me. Mum puts her hands on my shoulders. She smells of the rose perfume she only wears on special days. Why is today a special day? *Maybe she's going to meet Roger*, I think. I frown at Mum, and try to pull away from her.

"What's the matter? Sapphire, look at me," says Mum, gripping me tight as if she thinks I'm going to run away.

Slowly, I lift my head. Mum's eyes, close up, search my

face. For once, we're really looking at each other. We're always rushing around these days. Mum's off to work, Conor and I are off to school or else we're going out somewhere, or there are loads of jobs to do. Mum worries about our clothes and our schoolwork and the house and money and everything. Sometimes it feels as if she hardly sees us. All she sees are her worries about us.

I know it's not Mum's fault. She's only one person, trying to do everything that two people used to do. She's got to earn the money and look after us and keep the house. Even though we help as much as we can, she's always rushing.

We don't even have our meals together very often, because Mum's at work nearly every evening and often in the day as well. Mum tells us where she'll be and what time she'll be back and what time we've got to be in by, and she leaves lots of notes and we have her mobile number. But it's a different family from the one we used to have, and sometimes it's not much like a family at all.

We're just three people who live in the same house, I think. *We're not a proper family any more.*

I look down, in case Mum sees the thoughts in my eyes. She'd be so upset. She'd think I'm blaming her for working all the time, and that I don't understand that she has to earn the money, because Dad's gone.

If only I could tell Mum how strange the days are when she's gone off to St Pirans to work, and I know she won't be back until midnight. The days are long and there's no shape to them. Mum gone, Dad gone, the house quiet. Sometimes I go down to the kitchen at night, when Conor's gone to sleep and I can't. If Mum was at home, she'd come up with a glass of water for me and sit on the side of my bed and say, *Don't worry, Sapphy, just relax and you'll soon drop off.* But when Mum's not here, I can't make myself stop worrying.

I listen to the fridge purring. Every so often it gives a click and stops. I wait for it to start purring again and when it does I feel glad, as if the fridge is a friend – which is so completely pathetic that I could never in a million years say that thought aloud to anyone. Certainly not to Mum.

Visitors say that where we live is like paradise. They pay a fortune to come here on holiday. They say we don't know how lucky we are to live here all the time. This is the best summer we've had for years, everyone says so. It's hot and dry and there's sunshine day after day after day. All the verges are brown from the heat. Mum says St Pirans is jam-packed with tourists. The restaurant is full every night, that's why she gets back so late.

If only I could explain to Mum how empty the days are. How scared I get when Conor wants to go out without me, even if it's only up to Jack's for an hour. He always asks if I'll be OK, and I always say, "I'll be fine. I'm going to watch TV." Mum thinks I go and see Katie, or one of my other friends, but I don't. I feel cut off from them, because their lives are going on the same as ever, but mine has completely changed.

It's all right as long as Conor's here. When he's at Jack's he's not that far away. I could get on my bike and find him if I had to. But when he went away to Ingo without me I was so afraid I thought I would die.

I won't stay here on my own, being scared. I won't be the one who is left behind. I'll leave before Conor does, this time. I'll go far away, where I won't need any of them.

"You're all right, Sapphy, aren't you? You'd tell me if anything was wrong, wouldn't you?" Mum asks. She smoothes down my hair. "This hair's like a tangle of seaweed. We need to brush it all out," she says.

"Can you do a henna wax on it, Mum?"

"I'm sorry, Saph. There isn't time today."

I love it when Mum does a henna wax on my hair. It takes a long time. She washes my hair first, and dries it a little, then she massages henna wax all over my hair, and she wraps my head in a hot towel and we sit and chat for half an hour so that the henna has time to work. The henna's not coloured, it's just to make your hair soft and shiny again after you've been swimming in the sea every day.

"Maybe you should have your hair cut. It'd be easier to keep it in good condition if it was short."

"No, Mum!"

"All right, all right. But if you want it long, you've got to look after it. Some of these knots are so bad they'll need to be cut out soon. And look how long it's getting. It's below your waist."

I'm growing it.

Mum lets my hair fall. She looks at her watch.

"I'm sorry, Sapphy. I've got to—"

You've got to go. I know. But I don't say it. I want to keep the soft look on Mum's face.

"Will you do my hair on your day off, Mum?"

"Mm, maybe Sapphy, we'll have to see—"

I forgot. On Mum's day off, on Sunday, *Roger* is coming. Maybe that's why Mum's got to go now. Maybe she's meeting Roger before work, and that's why she's wearing the rose perfume.

"Conor's waiting for me, Mum. Got to go," I say, pulling away from her. But again, she holds me tight. She strokes her hand over my rough, tangly hair again.

"Your hair," she says, "I really ought to do it," and she glances again at her watch. "Come on, Sapphy, we've just got time."

But I don't want Mum doing my hair in a big rush, glancing at her watch. I like it when we've got loads of time, and we sit and chat. Henna hair waxes are one of the best things I do with Mum, just the two of us.

But not now, not while she's really wanting to be in St Pirans, with Roger. I draw myself out of Mum's grasp.

"We'll do it another time, when you're not so busy," I say. For some reason Mum's eyes go shiny, as if she's about to cry. I'm so alarmed by this that I gabble, "Got to go, Mum, see you later, have a good day," and turn and run across the garden, so that for once it's Mum who is left standing at the door, watching me go.

"You didn't tell her anything, did you?" asks Conor.

"No."

"Make sure you don't, Saph. Mum's got enough to

worry about. Besides, she'd think we were crazy. No one is going to believe any of this stuff."

Our trainers scuff up dust and pebbles as we run. The pebbles rattle, and that's when I realise what the sound is that I'm not hearing. There's no sweet sound any more, no singing voice. There's no pull from the sea either. When did it stop? Was it while Mum was talking to me? There's no hurry any more, no pressure. Conor and I might go down to the cove, or we might not.

As we come round the corner of the track, between the tall granite hedges, we see someone standing in the middle of the track. It's Granny Carne.

"What's *she* doing down here?" mutters Conor. And it's true that you don't often see Granny Carne so close to the sea. She belongs up on the Downs, in her cottage near where the Midsummer Bonfire's built. Her cottage is half-buried in the side of the Downs. Half-buried, or maybe half-growing out of the earth. That's why her earth magic is strong, maybe, because she lives so close to it.

"I don't know," I answer. I feel uneasy. Granny Carne's eyes always make me feel as if she knows things about me that I don't even know myself.

Granny Carne stands waiting for us to come up to her. She is tall and straight and full of dignity, like a tree growing from deep earth.

"How's your mother?" Granny Carne asks. Her amber gaze sweeps over our faces.

"She's all right," says Conor.

"Is she? Let's see, it's more than a year since Mathew went now."

The way she says Dad's name reminds me that Granny Carne was his friend. Dad knew – Dad has known Granny Carne ever since he was a boy. He used to say she always seemed just as old as she is now. Granny Carne doesn't change like other people change.

"My dad drowned," says Conor abruptly. "That's what they say."

"But they never found him," says Granny Carne. "Strange. A drowned man usually washes up somewhere, no matter if it takes weeks, or months. Do *you* think your father drowned, Sapphire?"

"I don't know, I—"

I don't know what to say, but strangely, I don't mind Granny Carne's questions. They're not like some people's questions about Dad, which drip with rumour and inquisitiveness. Granny Carne is asking for a reason. Conor draws close to her, as if he wants to ask her for help.

Granny Carne's called *Granny*, but she has no grandchildren. I don't think she ever had children. She lives her wild life alone. She's always lived in her cottage under the Downs. Sometimes people go there, when they need help. They go secretly. They don't even tell their friends or their family. They knock on Granny Carne's door and wait for her to answer. People say Granny Carne has the power to know the future, and sometimes she can look into your future for you. I don't know how she does it, or what it's like. It sounds scary to me.

Dad once told me most people round here have been up to Granny Carne's at some time. When they had need of her.

"What kind of need, Dad?"

"To help you make a decision, maybe. To resolve a question that's troubling you. To see beyond the present."

"How can anyone see beyond the present?"

"They say she can," said Dad. I had the feeling he was hiding something from me.

"Have *you* ever been to see her, Dad?"

"I'm always seeing her."

"You know what I mean. To ask her about the future, like you said."

"I did once."

"What was it about, Dad?"

"Well, it was about that dummy you still had when you were nearly three years old, Sapphire. I wanted to know if you would ever give it up, or if you would be taking it to school with you along with your packed lunch."

"*Dad!*" It was so annoying. But he wouldn't tell me any more, no matter how much I asked.

"Mathew knows this coast like the back of his hand," says Granny Carne. "And the sea was flat that night he disappeared."

She said, *Mathew knows*. Not *Mathew knew*. That means for

Granny Carne, Dad is still in the present tense. Just as he is for me and Conor. And if you're in the present tense, then that means you must be alive. If Granny Carne really can see into the future, maybe she knows he's alive. Maybe she can see that Dad's going to come back.

"So where is he, if he didn't drown?" asks Conor.

"He's away somewhere, I believe."

"Away in Ingo," I say immediately, without knowing that I was going to say it. Granny Carne's amber eyes flash on me. I feel like a mouse or a vole when the eyes of a hunting owl light on it.

"Ingo," she says. "In Ingo, you say? It's strange you should say that, Sapphire, because when I saw you coming down the lane I thought you had a look of Ingo on your face. There's a bit of it on Conor's face too, but not as strong as on you."

She knows, I thought. How can she know? How much does she know?

"What's Ingo?" I ask her.

"I think you know that," says Granny Carne. Now I feel like a vole when the owl's rushing down towards it, talons spread. "Ingo's a place that has many names," says Granny Carne. "You can call it Mer, Mare or Meor. And it has its own Morveren name, but we don't say that name, not while we've got our feet planted on the earth. Earth and Ingo don't mix, even though we live side by side. Earth and Ingo aren't always friends. Do you know the old name of Ingo, Sapphire? The old Morveren name?" Granny Carne asks the question casually, but now the owl is so close I can hear the rush of her wings. She really wants to know how much I know. But what would it mean, if I did know the Morveren name?

"No," I say, reluctantly, because now I wish I did know it. I wish I was truly part of Ingo and knew everything about it.

"But you know who the Morveren are?"

"No. Not really."

"Ah."

I think she's pleased that I don't know. Suddenly her eyes lose their fierce, owl-like glitter, and she's an old woman again. Granny Carne turns, pulls a bramble out of the hedge, and gives me a plump, shiny blackberry. Even from the look of it you can tell it's warm and ripe. But surely it's too early for blackberries to be ripe – it's only the end of July. I walked up the lane yesterday and I didn't see any.

"You have that one, Sapphire, and I'll find another for Conor." She searches the hedge and brings out another ripe berry. I hold my blackberry. I want to eat it, but at the same time I don't.

"Eat it, Sapphire," says Granny Carne. I put the blackberry into my mouth. It tastes of earth and sunshine and spicy fruit. It reminds me of fields, woods, the farm, the puppies, Mum cooking apple and blackberry pie, autumn, wood smoke, lighting the fire, kicking through fallen leaves with Conor when we were little…

"There'll be plenty of fruit this year, with all the sun we've had," says Granny Carne. "Now, Conor, tell me. Were you thinking of swimming today, down at the cove?"

"Maybe," says Conor. It doesn't sound rude. He smiles across at her and I think that Conor and Granny Carne look a bit alike. Both of them have strong brown skins that love the sun, and shiny dark eyes.

"I wouldn't go today," says Granny Carne. "There's a strong current running. *You* might be able to swim against it, but not Sapphire. It would carry her away. She should keep inland today."

"But I want to go," I say.

"I know you do. Believe me, Sapphire, I know how much you want to go. I can feel it in you." Granny Carne reaches forward and grasps my wrist. Her hand is strong and warm. "I can feel it running in you. But we lost the first Mathew – and then your father – and now who knows what's going to happen? The story's not ended yet. There's a pattern, and it's got to work itself out. Ingo's growing strong. We'll have fish from the sea swimming up the stream to my cottage next. But that's not right. If Ingo breaks its bounds, then Earth will break its bounds. Ingo should stay in its place, and then I can stay in mine."

She stands tall and stern. Her voice is a voice I have never heard from her before. Deep and powerful and not caring about anything but saying what it wants to say.

If Ingo breaks its bounds. I don't understand what she means. The sea comes in to the high tide mark, but no farther. The cove fills with water, and then it empties again. That's what has always happened, so how can it change?

Granny Carne is standing between me and the sea. She's stopping me from getting to it. She's planted in my way like a tree, or a rock. Suddenly I'm sure that if I can only get to the other side of Granny Carne, I'll hear the sea singing again. Her body is blocking out the music of Ingo. I know it, and she knows it too. She's standing there on purpose.

"You'll have heard about the other Mathew Trewhella," Granny Carne goes on. "The first one. He was a fine man. Handsome as a prince, and he sang in the church choir. People used to say that he had a voice like an angel. You know the nonsense people talk. One person says it and then they're all repeating it. But it's true that he had a fine voice. Your father's voice is the only one I've known that ever matched the first Mathew Trewhella's."

I feel as if an electric current's flowing through Granny Carne's hand and into my wrist. It's the same story, the story Dad told me when we were in the church, years ago. The mermaid, the wooden mermaid they slashed with a knife. Here she is again.

Granny Carne won't let go of me. Her voice rises louder. "But of course the story got told wrong over the years," she goes on. "Stories get mixed up as they're passed from mouth to mouth, down the years. It wasn't just one mermaid that enchanted Mathew Trewhella. He fell in love with Ingo. It was Ingo that captured him. Mer... Mare... Meor... Ingo... That's what took Mathew from his friends and family. And he's never returned in all this time."

Why are you telling me all this? I think fiercely, trying to resist the current of Granny Carne's story. *You're trying to stop me from going to Ingo. You're trying to frighten me.*

"You mean – are you talking about the Mathew Trewhella in the old story?" asks Conor in a strange, doubting voice.

"Yes, the first Mathew Trewhella. I'm going back a way, now." Granny Carne's face is stern. She looks as if the things she's remembering aren't easy or peaceful.

Conor asks no more questions. He takes hold of my other hand, which is something he never does, and keeps it in a firm grip. And then he touches Granny Carne's arm, so that the three of us are joined together in a circle. Earthed. The lane smells of dust and blackberries. I don't want to get to the other side of Granny Carne any more. I only want to stay here, safe with her and Conor, with the sun warm on us.

Granny Carne's brown face creases into a smile. She likes Conor, I know that. And Conor likes her. Like, *like* – do I really mean that? No, it's not that Conor *likes* Granny Carne. It's that Conor is *like* Granny Carne.

But how can that be? Granny Carne's as old as the hills. Conor's my brother. She's tall and wrinkled and strange, and when Dad said she was full of earth magic, it wasn't hard to believe him. Conor's just a normal boy. But all the same, they are two of a kind.

The circle holds. It seems like a long, long time that we stand there, the three of us, but probably it's only a few seconds. And then a dog barks. I glance up quickly, because it sounds like Sadie. What's Sadie doing down here?

Yes, it *is* Sadie! She races down the track towards me, and skids to a halt on her front paws, looking pleased with herself. I run to her, kneel down, put my arms round her neck and rub my cheek against her face. She's quivering all over with excitement, and her coat is hot from the sun.

"Sadie, what are you *doing* down here? Did you come all on your own? You bad girl, stravaiging over the country-side, you'll get hit by a car..."

But Sadie doesn't care. She's panting from her long run and wriggling all over with the pleasure of finding us. She's done it all on her own, clever Sadie, finding our scent in the middle of all the other smells of cows and foxes and chickens and cars. The world of smells is like a library with a million books in it, for Sadie.

"Good girl, clever girl, now take it easy, you've been rac-ing much too fast in this hot sun." I give her one last hug and then stand up, slipping my hand through her collar in case she runs off again. She presses against my legs, looking up with her intelligent brown eyes and giving short, sharp little barks.

"We must take her home," says Conor.

Suddenly I realise that Conor and I are alone with Sadie. Granny Carne's gone. When did she go? Conor shrugs. "You know what she's like."

"Sadie, come on Sadie girl, let's go on up to the cottage and I'll find something for a lead, and then we're going for a long walk, all the way back home. They'll be worrying about you. They'll be wondering where you are."

Sadie bows her head consideringly. She loves the word "walk", but it's still the end of her freedom, and she knows it.

"And we'll get you a bowl of water. It's uphill all the way back, you're going to need a drink."

We walk on up to our cottage, Sadie close at my side and Conor behind.

I'm so hungry. Why ever didn't I eat those sausages? If Conor calls Jack to tell him we've got Sadie, we can eat before we walk her up to the farm. What food have we got? I bring up a mental picture of the fridge's contents. There's bolognese sauce, and half a tub of chocolate and pecan ice cream, a bag of peaches Mum brought back—

Suddenly Sadie stops dead. Her rear legs are stiff, her body quivers. Her head goes up, pointing towards the sea. She whines, deep in her throat, then lets out a volley of barks.

"What is it, Sadie? What can you hear?"

"Whatever it is, she doesn't like it," says Conor. "Hold on to her."

I grasp her collar with both hands. She's rigid, trembling. She's not trying to escape, she's flattening herself against me. She's scared.

"It's all right, Sadie, come on, girl. Come on in the house."

Sadie shivers and backs away, pulling me with her. She whines and stares at me as if asking why I'm not hearing what she hears.

I can't hear anything. I'm not going to hear anything. I put my hands over my ears. Stop it, stop it. I'm not listening. I can't hear anything. *Chocolate and pecan ice cream, spag bol, choco-late and pecan ice cream, spag bol, CHOCOLATE AND PEC—"*

"Saph, why've you got your hands over your ears?"

"Quick, Con, Sadie's going crazy. Open the door, let's get her in the house."

We're in. Sadie races around the kitchen, her claws skittering on the tiles. Suddenly she's just a dog going wild and I'm just a girl trying to stop her. Calm down, Sapphire, and stop imagining things. You're home.

CHAPTER TWELVE

I hate saying goodbye to Sadie. I kneel down beside her and she pushes her head against me. Her funny folding-down right ear has grown straighter as she's grown older, but if you look closely you can see it's not the same as her left ear. I stroke her ears gently, the way she likes it.

"It's a blessing you two found her," says Jack's mum. "Jack won't be back till late and I've got people arriving for bed and breakfast, so I couldn't have gone looking for her."

Sadie whines, and presses against me again. She doesn't want me to leave. Jack's mum bends down to pat her, but Sadie takes no notice.

"You'd think she was yours, the way she carries on. Or else you were hers. Sometimes I think dogs know who they ought to belong to," says Jack's mum.

"We should get back," Conor says quickly. "Come on, Saph."

"Why did you drag me away like that?" I complain as we set off for home. "Jack's mum was being really nice. She's made loads of scones for the bed and breakfast people too. I saw them on the table. If we'd stayed, she might have given us a cream tea."

"We need to get home. You shouldn't be outside. It's not safe."

"What do you mean?"

"It's calling you, isn't it?"

"What's calling me?" I know the answer, but I'm going to make Conor say it.

"You know." He looks around and lowers his voice. "Ingo. Saph, were you listening to what Granny Carne said?"

"Of course I was."

"All that stuff about the first Mathew Trewhella. Granny Carne was talking as if she knew him."

"Well, maybe she did," I answer vaguely. I'm still thinking about Sadie. Maybe she is meant to be my dog. Maybe it's really going to happen one day. Mum's going to change her mind—

"Wake up, Saph! How can Granny Carne have known someone who lived hundreds of years ago? It's all crazy."

"Then why are you so bothered about it?"

"I can't believe you're so thick sometimes, Saph. What I want to know is *why* Granny Carne was talking about the first Mathew Trewhella. And why Ingo's growing strong. If it's all got something to do with Dad then we've got to find out more."

I hear the echo of Dad's voice, in the dark church long

ago. I remember my own fingers tracing the outline of the wooden mermaid's tail. I feel the gashes cut into the carving.

"The mermaid enchanted him," says Conor. "She pulled him out of the church choir, down the lane and down the stream that runs to Pendour Cove. He never came back. People said that years later you could stand on Zennor Head and hear him sing his Mer children to sleep."

"It's only a story," I say. "It can't have really happened like that. And Granny Carne can't possibly have known the first Mathew Trewhella."

"But you heard what she said," says Conor. "About his singing and everything. Just as if she'd heard him herself. Do you remember how Dad always used to say Granny Carne had never been any younger than she is now? Never any younger, and never any different. Maybe she *does* remember."

"You mean you think she's hundreds of years old?"

"I don't know. It sounds impossible when you say it like that. But when you're with her, don't you feel it?"

"Feel what?"

"Her power," says Conor slowly. "That's why I want to know why she's talking to us. I think she wants us to do something."

"Or not do something," I mutter, remembering how Granny Carne's force barred the way to the sea.

"What?"

"Nothing," I say.

It's dark inside our cottage, after the brightness of the

day. Conor goes around shutting the windows, locking the back door that we never normally lock. I watch him without saying anything. I'm trying to remember everything I can about the story Dad told me, long ago, about the man who vanished with a mermaid, and who had the same name as him.

"Conor," I say at last, "time doesn't work like that. One person can't live for hundreds of years."

"I don't know... time in Ingo isn't like time here, is it? Maybe there are all kinds of time, living alongside each other, but usually we only experience one of them. Granny Carne might be living in her own time, and it might be quite different from ours. Think of the way oak trees live for a thousand years."

"Earth time," I say, not really knowing why I say it.

"Yes. If she's got earth magic, then she could be living in earth time. And Faro and Elvira are living in Ingo time. So what are we living in?"

"I don't know. Real time? Human time?"

"They're all real. But human time; yeah, could be. So let's say there's earth time and Ingo time and human time, that's three kinds of time already, and there could be more."

"Ant time, butterfly time, planet time, cream-tea time—"

"I'm not messing around, Saph. Wait a minute. Look at Ingo time. I don't think Ingo time is fixed against ours. It's not like one year of Ingo time equals five years of human time, or whatever. It's more complicated than that. Sometimes Ingo time seems to run at nearly the same pace as ours, but sometimes it's quite different... almost like water flowing faster or more slowly, depending on whether it's running downhill or along a flat surface – yes, maybe that's it, something to do with the angle of Ingo time to human time—"

I switch off. Conor will carry on like this for hours once he gets going. That's why he's so good at maths.

Josie Sancreed's jeering face comes into my mind. "I wonder what they *really* said when that first Mathew Trewhella disappeared," I say. Were there people like Josie living then? Probably.

"I bet they said he'd gone off with another woman," says Conor. His face is hard. "Just like they say about Dad."

So Conor knows.

"Did you hear about what Josie said to me, Conor?"

"It's what everyone says behind our backs. Josie said it to your face, that's the only difference."

"But Dad hasn't gone off with another woman! He hasn't gone off with anyone. He would never do that to us."

"Maybe not."

"You *know* he hasn't, Conor," I say angrily. Conor has got to believe in Dad. We're a *family*. Me and Conor and Dad and Mum.

Me and Conor and Mum.

"I don't know anything any more," says Conor. He shrugs. "Sorry, Saph. Everything's upside down and inside out today."

It's so rare for Conor to have doubts about anything that I don't know what to say. Conor's my big brother, the one who knows things. If *he* doesn't know where he is, then where am I?

"It'll be OK," I say doubtfully. "Maybe Granny Carne just likes telling old stories because she's old."

"She told us about that first Mathew Trewhella for a reason," says Conor, in the same way as he's always explained things to me, like who is in which gang at school, and why. I knew how the playground worked before I even went to school, because of Conor. "Don't get scared, Saph, but I think Granny Carne believes we're in danger."

"How could we be in danger?"

"He never came back, did he? The Mathew Trewhella in the story, I mean. Maybe Dad won't ever come back either."

"Conor, *don't.*"

Conor turns and grips my wrists hard. "They got Mathew Trewhella, didn't they? I know what it's like, Saph. You're out there in Ingo, and they make you feel that everything back here on land is nothing. Even the people you love don't count. You can't even remember them clearly."

"I didn't forget you and Mum!"

"Didn't you?"

"You just got a bit cloudy and far away."

"I know. And so you go on, deeper and deeper into Ingo, until you don't care about anything else—"

"Did you feel like that?"

"Of course I did! I would've stayed. I'd probably still be there now. It was the first time I'd got so close to the seals. Elvira said she was going to take me to the Lost Islands. But I heard you calling. I didn't even *want* to hear it. I tried to pretend I hadn't heard you. Can you believe it, Saph, me trying to pretend I couldn't hear my own sister when she might've needed me? But you kept on calling and I was afraid something bad was happening to you, and you were calling to me for help. And so I had to come back.

But when I got up on to the shore, there was no one there. You'd totally disappeared. I waited for you for hours and hours, thinking you weren't ever going to come back. I went up to the cottage, I searched everywhere, I came back down here – I even went back into the sea again to look for you. But I couldn't get into Ingo again. Not without Elvira. I dived and dived but nothing happened. The water wouldn't let me in. It pushed me up like a rubber ball every time I dived. The water was laughing at me."

"But – but it wasn't more than a few minutes after I called you that I came back. It can't have been longer."

"Believe me, it was. You were so deep in Ingo that it felt like minutes. But it was *hours*, Saph."

I'm almost scared of Conor now. He looks like he did after Shadow had to be put down, the summer before last. Shadow was fifteen, which is old for a cat. We all loved Shadow, but Conor *really* loved him. I think of Conor searching along the shore, searching the cottage, trying to find me, running back to the cove, frantic, afraid that something terrible had happened to me.

"I'm sorry, Conor. I really didn't know. I didn't think I'd been away so long."

"It's all happening again, that's what scares me," says Conor in a low voice. "First, the olden-days Mathew Trewhella disappears. OK, it's only a story that's supposed to have happened a long time ago. But then Dad disappears. And then I can't find you. I really thought I was never going to be able to find you again.

"I'll tell you something, Saph, I won't go there again. *Whatever* Elvira says, I'm not going to Ingo again. It's too dangerous.

"Granny Carne doesn't want us to go. She's stopping us. I can feel it. You know when you try to push two magnets together, and they won't? It's like that.

"But Elvira wants me to go. And she didn't want me to come back either. Do you know what she said? *That can't have been your sister's voice. These currents make strange echoes. I didn't hear anything.* But I knew I'd heard you. How could I be wrong about my own sister's voice?"

I hate the pain and confusion in my brother's voice. I hate the idea that Elvira wanted to keep him away from me.

"Conor, listen. You won't go up to Jack's again today, will you? You won't leave me alone here?"

"No," says Conor. His face lightens. "Hey, Saph. Listen."

"What?"

"Maybe you should cut off your hair."

"*Cut off my hair?*"

"Because when it's so long and you're in the water, your

hair spreads out all around you. It makes you look like a – you know, like one of them."

"You mean, like a *mermaid*," I say icily. How can Conor possibly suggest that I cut off my hair? He knows I've been growing it since I was six. I've got the longest hair in our whole school. I wouldn't be me without it.

"Yes," says Conor, quite seriously. "They might see your hair floating in the water when you go swimming, and get the idea that you're one of them. That you ought to stay with them."

"So let me know when I start to grow a tail."

But Conor shrugs my comment away, as if I'm just the little sis trying to be smart. I'm about to snap back, when a strange feeling seizes me and I forget him.

How dark it is inside the cottage, with the doors and windows closed. You know that feeling when you come home after a holiday, and everything feels so familiar and comfortable, because it belongs to you and you belong to it? That's the feeling I usually have when I come home to our cottage.

But not now. The walls seem to be pressing in around me. I've never realised before that the cottage is so small. There's so little space that I can hardly move. I want to stretch. I want to get out. I want to leap and plunge and dive and be free, and I want the cool of the water rushing past my skin instead of this dry, scratchy air. Our cottage isn't a home at all. It's a prison.

Conor is watching me. "Saph, no!" he says warningly, as if he can read my thoughts.

"I'm not doing anything."

"I won't let you, Saph. You're not swimming off down any streams without me. I told Granny Carne I'd look after you."

I hold on to the strength of Conor's voice.

"Conor, listen. What else did Elvira say to you?"

"Everything I wanted to hear," says Conor. "But I can't describe it. You have to hear her voice."

I think of Faro, and all the power of Ingo.

"I know," I say.

"But I'm not going to Ingo again. If Elvira calls to me, I'll put my headphones on and turn my music up loud so I can't hear her. It's the only way."

Suddenly a thought cuts through me like a knife. "Conor! What about Mum?"

"What about her?"

"Mum might hear it too. You know. The singing. It might start to pull her. And then what'll we do?"

"She won't," says Conor confidently. "Mum hates the sea. Can you imagine her in Ingo?"

"No – maybe not—"

"Mum wouldn't even believe Ingo exists. And that'll make her safe."

In the cottage, with Conor there and Conor's music playing loud, doors and windows shut, curtains drawn, lights on and a bolognese sauce bubbling on the stove, Ingo seems far away.

But even the loudest music has pauses in it, and into those pauses the noise of the sea can break through, drop by drop, then faster, a trickle, a stream, and now a flood-tide—

No. I won't let it happen this time.

I make a huge effort. I close my eyes, my ears, my mind. Our cottage is warm and safe and friendly. It's our home, where we belong. In a minute it'll be time to drop the spaghetti into boiling water.

Ingo does not exist. Ingo is just a story, far away.

Yes, says a small, mocking voice inside my head. *Ingo doesn't exist. How true is a lie, how dry is the ocean, how cold is the sun?* And I think the voice sounds like Faro's.

CHAPTER THIRTEEN

um straightens up and turns from the oven to the kitchen table where we're all sitting. She places a pan of roast potatoes carefully on the heat-proof mat, next to the roast chicken which has been resting for ten minutes.

"The chicken's having a good rest before we eat it," Dad used to explain to us when we were little. "It's hard work to be eaten."

"Don't fill the children's heads with rubbish, Mathew. It rests so as to make the meat easier to carve, Sapphire," Mum would say.

Dad's not here, but we're still eating roast chicken. Isn't it strange that a meal can last longer in your life than a person? Sunday dinner, the same as ever. I stare at the golden skin of the chicken and the crunchy golden-brown roast potatoes. Mum always sprinkles salt on the potatoes before she puts them in hot oil to roast.

"I'll just have potatoes and broccoli, Mum," I say, when

it comes to my turn. Mum has already heaped Roger's plate with chicken breast and a leg as well, and he's staring at it carnivorously.

"You're not turning vegetarian again, are you, Sapphire?" asks Mum warily.

"I'm not turning *vegetarian*, it's just that I don't want any chicken."

"Great-looking chicken," Roger observes.

"It was better looking when it was running around, in my opinion," I answer. I'm on safe ground here, because I know this is one of the Nances' chickens, so I have definitely seen it running around many times. In fact I've probably even thrown grain for it, which makes the sight of it on the plate a little difficult.

"Is it better for a chicken to run around and have a good life and then die and be eaten, or for a chicken to be shut up in a box and never run around, and then die of natural causes?" asks Conor. Mum pours gravy on to Roger's plate in a long stream. Her lips are pressed tightly together with annoyance. Her face is flushed from the heat of the oven on a hot day, and suddenly I wish I hadn't said anything about the chicken running around.

"Lord, bless this food and all of us who gather here to eat it," says Roger. We all stare at him. His face is calm and bland. He nods at me, picks up his knife and fork, and starts to eat.

"No disrespect to your workplace, Jennie, but this roast beats anything I've eaten in a restaurant," he says, after swallowing the first few mouthfuls. I listen to his voice instead of the words and I hear something unexpected there. Mum never told us Roger was Australian. But his accent is not that strong. Maybe he went to Australia for a while, that was all. Diving on the Great Barrier Reef.

"I got gravy on my chin?" Roger asks, smiling. I must have been staring at him.

"No," I blurt out. "I was wondering if you were Australian."

Roger looks pleased. "Yeah, that's right. I was born out there, in a little place in the Blue Mountains near Sydney. My parents emigrated there after they were married. But things didn't work out for the family, so my mum came back here when I was ten years old. You can still hear the accent if you know what to listen for, I reckon."

"I never knew that," says Mum.

"Your daughter has a quick ear," says Roger, and I can't help feeling a bit flattered. I look down quickly to hide my smile. I don't want Mum thinking I'm starting to like Roger.

"Eat your broccoli, Sapphire," says Mum automatically, although I've already eaten it.

"She's looking better, isn't she?" Mum goes on. It's not really a question to anyone, and no one answers.

"You're feeling better, aren't you, Sapphy?"

"Um, yes—" I begin, when I realise that I'm not feeling better at all. In fact I'm feeling very strange indeed, as if the Sunday table is rushing away from me. Conor's looking at me worriedly. The room feels as if all the air has been sucked out of it, even though the kitchen door is open. The smell of food chokes my nostrils. Why are we all sitting inside when the sun is bright on the grass outside and the tide's moving, tugging...

"The tide's on the turn," I say, before I know I'm going to say it. Roger glances at his watch.

"You're dead right there," he says, surprised. "Right to the minute. You keep your eye on the tides, then?"

"So do you."

"I have to, I'm a diver. It's second nature."

"It's first nature for Saph," says Conor. I can't believe he's said that. Is he trying to give away our secrets?

"Is it?" asks Roger. He gives me a long, considering look. It occurs to me that divers probably have to be quite observant. "I've known people who get so that they can feel the tides, without ever needing to look at a watch or a tide-table. Lifetime of experience, I guess. But you're a tad young for that."

"The children have lived within the sound of the sea all their lives," says Mum. "Children more or less grow up in the sea around here. Or at least, mine have done."

"Can't think of a better way to grow up," says Roger. "Tell me, Sapphire. Does the sea sound different, when the tide turns?" He sounds as if he really wants to know, but I don't answer. I'm struggling to listen. The noise of the sea is loud, filling my ears. Conor diverts Roger's attention.

"I'd like to learn to dive," he says, looking directly at Roger.

"No, you wouldn't, Conor!" I burst out.

"You don't know everything I want, Saph."

"You'd need proper training," says Roger. "How old are you now?"

"Thirteen."

"If you're serious, I'll see what I can fix up. A week's beginner course is what I'd suggest for a start."

"I am serious," says Conor. "I'd like to learn."

"But it's dangerous," says Mum. "Isn't it, Roger?"

"No more than anything else, if you're careful. If you follow the rules, use your common sense and don't take risks, you'll be OK."

Follow the rules. Use your common sense. Don't take risks. Without my realising it, the roar of the sea has faded.

"But how can you discover anything, if you don't take risks?" I ask.

Roger considers again. "Maybe there's some truth in that. But you don't start off by taking risks. You start off by doing all you can to minimise them. You have to know what you're doing, go step by step, respect the force of the sea. Remember, you're in a different world down there. An alien world. You'll see what I mean when you make your first dive, Conor."

"It must be beautiful," I say innocently.

"Oh, it's beautiful all right," says Roger. " It's a world of its own, what you see down there. It has its own light, not like ours. When a dustbin-lid jellyfish goes by, or even a shark – well, you see some amazing sights, I can tell you that. You have basking shark in these waters, did you know that?"

"Yes."

"And there are weeds that grow as big as trees. It's a another world. You have to respect the sea. We don't belong down there. If you forget that, you're in big trouble."

But what you're really doing is spying on Ingo, I say inside my head. *The Mer don't want you there. What's so respectful about forcing your way in where you're not wanted?*

But I'm not going to say any of this aloud. Instead I nod and say, "Mm, maybe."

"Roger's going to take a boat out from the cove. He's going to dive round here," says Mum. Even though Mum hates the sea, she doesn't seem to worry about Roger going out on it.

But she was afraid when Dad went out. Always afraid, even though she tried to hide it from us. When he was home in the cottage, with the doors shut and the fire burning, when there was a storm and nobody could think of taking a boat out, then Mum was happy and relaxed.

"It's just an exploratory dive," says Roger quickly. But I'm not sure that I believe him. I can sense danger. He thinks there is something worth diving for: a wreck, treasure, something to be dragged up out of Ingo into the Air. Something to be taken away from the Mer. Something valuable that Roger is going to discover, and no one else.

"What are you looking for?" Conor asks.

"I won't know what's there until I've searched around a little," says Roger evasively. He glances round the table. "So I'd appreciate it if you kept all this quiet for the time being. I don't want other divers muscling in on the site."

"You mean, not tell our school friends and our friends who live around here?" I ask.

"That's right. Not for the time being, anyway."

"I won't tell them, then, I promise," I say, and I smile at Roger for the first time. A big, wide, warm smile that will put him off his guard. Mum looks at me gratefully. I can tell exactly what she's thinking. *What a relief, maybe Sapphy's going to like Roger after all.*

"Do you want this other leg, Roger?" asks Mum.

"You're not to tell them about the dive," hisses Conor as we wash up together.

I open my eyes wide. "I said I wouldn't, didn't I?"

"You know what I mean. I heard exactly what you said. You only promised that you wouldn't tell people from school, people round here."

"That's all Roger asked."

"Only because he didn't know who else you might tell."

"No, because he doesn't know anything, does he? He doesn't know or care about any of them. What's going to happen to Faro if Roger finds what he's looking for? It's probably gold or treasure or something. Other divers will find out too. They'll be swarming around here. And tourists as well. There'll be people everywhere, all over the sea just like they're all over the land. They'll drive the Mer away."

Very slowly, Conor wipes a plate dry. "Yes, I know. I've thought of that too."

"If you've thought of it, then why are you encouraging Roger? Why did you tell him you wanted to learn to dive?"

"Because I do want to."

"But you can, anyway! You can dive. You don't need Roger. You don't need air on your back and a black suit to go into Ingo."

"Give Roger a chance, Saph. He's all right. He's not the type that would want crowds of people diving for treasure round here."

I feel as if Conor's slapped me. I take a deep breath, and hit back. "*That* didn't take long, did it?"

"What didn't take long?"

"You're on his side already."

"Give that glass here, you're going to break it. Listen, Saph. It's not about taking sides. Look at Mum. Don't you think she looks better? Do you want her to go back to what she was like just after Dad went?"

Mum and Roger are in the living room. They're playing cards, and it sounds as if Mum's winning. As Conor and I stand listening, we hear Mum laugh. A warm, soft, chuckling laugh. She sounds relaxed and happy.

"She's a lot better," says Conor. "A lot. You want Mum to be better, don't you, Saph?"

"You don't care about Dad any more."

Slowly, Conor's face flushes under his brown skin. Slowly, spacing out his words, he says, "Don't ever say that again."

"I won't, I won't, Conor, I'm sorry—"

But Conor's gone. He turns his back on me and walks out quietly. He doesn't slam the door, but the way he shuts it is worse than a slam. I hear his tread on the stairs, going up to my room, and up the ladder into his loft. He pulls up his ladder and shuts the trapdoor, shutting me out.

Conor has turned his back on me. Conor doesn't want to be with me. He's angry and I know that Conor's worst anger is very quiet and it goes on for a long time.

It's all my fault. Why was I so stupid? I'll go after him. I'll tell him I'm sorry. I'll make him believe I'm really sorry for what I said.

"Conor?" I call from beneath the trapdoor, softly in case Mum hears and asks what's going on. "Conor? Con, I'm sorry. I didn't mean it. It wasn't true, what I said."

But there's no answer from Conor. I feel crushed inside from fear and loneliness. There's Mum again, laughing, and now she's saying something, but I can't hear what it is. Conor's right. Mum *does* sound happy. And there's Roger, laughing too, joining in.

I have the strangest feeling that, already, Roger belongs here more than I do. In a while, when he knows I'm not standing here waiting any more, Conor will come down the ladder. He'll play cards with Mum, and Roger will talk to them about diving. I can see the three of them together, belonging to one another, and the pain inside me grows stronger.

Why was I so stupid? Why ever did I say that Conor didn't care about Dad? I wish I could bring the words back. If only I knew how to make time run backwards. If I did, all the mistakes I've made could be undone.

Mum and Roger are laughing again. Mum is happy. Is

she happier because I'm not there? Maybe Mum doesn't want me here, reminding her of Dad every time I open my mouth. I look like Dad. Everyone has always said so.

If only Dad was here.

But just as I think that, for the first time a small, bleak voice inside me whispers, "Maybe they're right, and you're wrong. Maybe he's never coming back."

All the loneliest thoughts I've ever had crowd into my head. I feel cold and tired, and I don't know what to do. If only there was someone to help me. But there's only emptiness, swirling inside my mind.

Until I feel something. A pull, a tug, faint at first and then stronger, stronger. I know what it is. The tide is falling fast.

It's already an hour past the turn. I know it without knowing why I know it. I can feel the tide inside me, as if my blood has turned to salt water. There's the pull of it again, stronger, almost lifting me off my feet. *Now.* I've got to go *now*.

Hurry. Hurry. Hurry. You'll miss the tide.

CHAPTER FOURTEEN

"Where are we now, Faro?" I ask. We're swimming lazily side by side, our bodies wrapped in the warmth of a slow current that's taking us northwards. I'm back in Ingo. Safe. It doesn't seem strange any more, or dangerous. Everything has a familiar feeling about it, as if part of me has always lived here.

"We won't go too far this time. We might dap off the current westward," Faro says. "There's land there, another country of Air People, and then beyond there's the Great Ocean."

I can see it in my mind as if I'm reading a map. The ocean off our part of Cornwall is the Atlantic, then north-westward there's Ireland. West of Ireland the Atlantic spreads out again for thousands of miles, until you reach America.

Dad taught me about the oceans long before I studied geography at school. He drew a map of the oceans for me on the firm white sand of the cove, with a pointed stick. He said we'd sail them all one day. The Pacific, the Atlantic, the Indian Ocean, the Arctic and the Antarctic Ocean. The five oceans of the world, Dad said.

I loved the sound of their names. I believed Dad when he said we would sail them all one day. Dad said Conor and I could come out of school for a year, and we'd all go travelling.

Mum said, "Don't put that stuff into her head, Mathew. Where's the money coming from for us to sail the five oceans? We can barely pay the phone bill." But I knew Mum was wrong. She was always worrying about bills, but they got paid in the end. If we wanted to sail the world, the money would come from somewhere.

"Are you talking about the Atlantic when you say the Great Ocean, Faro?" I ask now. "Is the first land Ireland, and then there's the Atlantic again, and then America?"

Faro shrugs and his eyes sparkle wickedly.

"The Atlantic? Sorry, Sapphire. Never heard of it."

"You're *swimming* in it right now this minute, Faro!"

Faro spreads his fingers and lets the water spill through them.

"I can't seem to see the word *Atlantic* here anywhere," he murmurs, pretending to search. He flips on to his back and stares upwards. His tail flicks lazily, glistening in the deep green underwater light. "No, nothing's written on the surface either. Maybe the words washed off?"

"Don't be dumb, Faro, things like sea and sky don't have words printed right through them, like sticks of rock."

"Then how do you know this is the Atlantic?"

"Well, it just is."

"Not to me, it isn't."

"It's called the Atlantic on every map I've ever seen," I say firmly. Why can't Faro ever admit that he's wrong?

"Only people who don't know where they are need maps," answers Faro smugly.

"You'd get lost quick enough on land."

"Maybe. But who wants to go on land?"

"*You* did. That's where I first met you, on that rock."

"Ah, but then I had a reason."

"What?"

"I'll tell you one day. When you can speak full Mer."

I never argue when people say things like that. It only makes them more annoying. Changing the subject works much better.

"I suppose it doesn't have to be called the Atlantic," I say. "It's what we call it, that's all. It's got to have a name. *The Great Ocean* doesn't mean much. All the oceans are great, so you wouldn't be able to tell which one you were talking about. Is that really what you call it?"

"It's a name, that's all," shrugs Faro. "We don't carry maps around with *writing* on them, and everything with a name label on it. What do you think happens when the Atlantic meets the Pacific, Sapphire? Is there a thick black line on the sea?"

"You *do* know their names! I knew you did."

"I know all about your *maps* and your *writing*. You think I'm ignorant as a fish, don't you? Living in the sea, playing all day long, never thinking about anything, no car, no credit card—"

"Hey, do you really know about cars and credit cards? *How* do you know?"

"I listen," says Faro modestly. "It's surprising what you can hear when people are swimming or sunbathing or out in their boats. They talk a lot about their credit cards. Anyway, to go back to the subject, fish aren't ignorant. I've told you before that they share their memories. The memory doesn't die when a fish dies. It stays in the shoal. And because the memories are shared they get stronger."

"Do you do that, Faro?"

"What? Die?"

"No. Share your memories like that."

Faro sculls gently with his hands against the draw of the current. A frill of tiny bubbles bursts around his fingers.

"In a way. We share what we know," he says at last. "We don't keep our knowledge to ourselves, as if it's money we want to keep safe in a purse." His smile flashes at me triumphantly. *You see! I know all about 'money' and 'purses'.* The smile vanishes and he's serious again. "We have separate memories but sometimes they run in and out of us. I can touch Elvira's memory sometimes."

"Can you touch mine?" I ask suddenly, surprising myself.

Faro rolls towards me. We are face to face, with the same current holding us both. The inside of the current is so calm and still that it's only when I look sideways and see the fish flashing by that I know how fast we're travelling.

"I don't know," he says." Let's try."

"What do I have to do?"

"I'm not sure. I don't know how it happens with Elvira and me. It just happens."

I wait, tense and hopeful, while Faro stares into my face.

"No, it's not working. You're stopping me."

"I can't be stopping you. I'm not doing anything."

"You are. You're like a sea anemone when it feels a shadow on it. You've shut up tight. I can't feel your mind at all."

Part of me is a bit pleased at this. I'm stronger than Faro. He can't break into my mind like a burglar. But another part feels sad. I will never belong with the Mer if I can't share what they share. And it must be good to share memories – not be alone with them, hurt or frightened or not knowing what to do.

I think of what sea anemones look like in rock pools, with their soft open fronds waving through the warm water, exploring it. Soft, delicate fronds, purple and brown and red. Conor and I used to sit for hours by the pools, not letting our shadow fall over them, waiting until the crabs and baby dogfish grew confident and scuttled out from the weeds, and the sea anemones slowly unfurled like dark red flowers in a sea garden...

"You're with your brother," says Faro. "You're watching the flowers. You're very happy..."

"Faro, you did it! You saw what I was remembering!"

"We did it," says Faro. "I didn't know Air People and Mer could touch each other's memories."

"But we did," I say triumphantly.

"Maybe there's more Mer in you than I knew," Faro goes

on thoughtfully. "Elvira and I used to watch those hollows in the rocks for hours, just like you. When I touched what you were thinking, it was like touching my own memory. We learned how hermit crabs find their shells, how a male sea horse cares for his babies, where to find sugar kelp and strawberry anemones."

"Only *you* were underwater, and *we* were on the shore. But we were doing it at the very same time, maybe."

"Maybe. But you know, Sapphire, you're not the first Air Person I've met. Or even the first I've talked to. I know more than you think. I know all about *books* as well. Why are you smiling like that?"

"It's nothing." I can't tell Faro how funny he looked, so proud of himself for knowing this perfectly ordinary word.

"You're laughing at me." Faro narrows his eyes.

"I'm not. It was just the way you said 'books'. Like they were something out of a fairy story. Don't the Mer have any books?"

"Why should we? I told you, we don't need writing. If something is worth keeping, you can keep it in your mind. We don't copy Air things. We have our own life."

"It's strange, Faro, that's exactly the opposite of what humans do. They copy everything. I mean, we copy everything. That's how we get our ideas. I mean, that's how aeroplanes got invented, because people looked at birds and wanted to fly like them, and tried to work out how they did it. They were trying to copy birds for hundreds of years before they worked it out. And I suppose we copied fish when we built submarines—"

"But *why* did you want to fly?" interrupts Faro, with real curiosity. "You don't need to. Flying's for birds. What good is flying if you've got legs to walk?"

"Yes, but – if you see someone doing something, don't you want to do it too?"

"No," says Faro. "But *you* do, because you're human. That's what makes humans so dangerous. They want everything. They aren't satisfied with what they are. They want to be everything else as well."

"But how do you know what you are, until you've tried to be lots of other things?"

"I know what I am," says Faro. He closes his eyes, resting on his back and letting the current do the work. "I don't need to try to be anything else."

My legs look strange beside the strong, dark, glistening curve of Faro's tail. They look thin and feeble and forked. Almost ugly. I remember how Faro called me 'cleft'. I've never ever thought my legs were ugly before, but here under the sea they don't look nearly as good as a tail. One flick of Faro's tail can take him farther and faster than any swimming I can do.

"Look how well you're doing now, Sapphire," says Faro, opening his eyes. "I don't have to hold your wrist at all."

It's true. I think back to that first journey into Faro's country, and how afraid I was. How much it hurt to go into Ingo then. I thought I would die if Faro moved a metre away from me. It felt as if the salt water would rush into my throat and smother me. But now I don't even think about breathing. Faro doesn't have to tell me I'm safe, because I know it all through my body. Every cell of me knows that the sea is full of oxygen and it's streaming into my blood without my needing to breathe air. I am safe, in Ingo.

I squint down at my legs and wonder what it would be like if they joined together and the join fused and the skin grew strong and thick and dark, like seal skin. I wouldn't be able to walk any longer, up in the Air. Walking would hurt, and I'd have to drag myself over the stones. But I would be completely at home here in Ingo. How would a tail look on me? How would it feel? For a second the pressure of the current seems to grow stronger, grasping my legs and pushing them together, as if they were truly joined.

Like this, I think. *If my legs fused into a tail it would feel a bit like this. And then I'd be—*

Faro is humming a song and I know every word:

I wish I was away in Ingo
Far across the briny sea,
Sailing over deepest water…

"Faro, how do you know that song?" I ask cautiously. I don't want Faro to guess how important the song is to me.

"I must have heard it somewhere," says Faro lightly. But I can tell from his face that he's hiding something. There's a glint in his eye, teasing, daring me to ask more.

"I think you do know where you heard it, Faro. Who sang it to you?"

"I can't remember."

"Try. Please."

Faro looks thoughtful, but after a while he repeats, "No, it's gone. I can't remember."

I abandon caution. "You can! You've got to tell me!"

"Have I?" He flips over and turns to face me. "Why should the Mer tell you anything, Sapphire? Do you know what Air People do to us Mer?"

His eyes glower, his expression is fierce. The Faro I thought I knew has vanished from his face. I shrink back.

"I'll tell you what you do. You send ships with nets that scrape every living thing from the ocean floor. You crush the coral and destroy the secret places where life begins. Our gardens that we lay and watch are ruined. You rip up the life of Ingo and you don't even want it once you've wrecked it. You throw most of it away. You trap dolphins in your nets until they drown. You hunt for whales. You slash the fin off a shark and leave it to flounder in its own blood. You pour dirt into Ingo from pipes. You choke us with oil and cover the seabirds' feathers with filth until they can't swim or fly.

"You teach gulls to feast on rubbish instead of fish, until they're full of disease. And anyway you've taken the fish for yourselves. You steal our shore places and fill them with buildings so that Ingo can't breathe. You would build on the sea if you could, wouldn't you? You'd catch the Mer and take us away and put us in glass tanks in circuses. Don't ask me how I know, Sapphire. I understand what the gulls say, remember? Gulls go everywhere. They see everything. They tell us what they see.

You humans want everything to belong to Air, not to Ingo. But Ingo is strong. Stronger than you know."

"But Faro, I don't! I didn't! I didn't do any of that! I've never—"

His face relaxes, just a little. He seems to see me again. Me, Sapphire, instead of an enemy he hates.

"I've never tried to hurt you," I say. It sounds pathetic, even to me. The things Faro says strike heavy in my heart, and I know that they are true. I've heard of dolphins drowning in tuna nets, and tankers releasing thousands of tonnes of oil into the sea. I've seen seabirds on TV, coated with oil and struggling in the water until they die. And layers of dead, gaping fish on the tide line. What would it be like if oil swilled out of a tanker now, and coated our lips and our tongues and burned our eyes? Would it kill us too? Yes, it would cover us and we would choke to death.

"You think you haven't done anything to us," says Faro, more quietly. "But you're still part of Air, Sapphire."

"No, I'm not! I'm—" I break off because Faro is watching me so intently. Why? What is he waiting for? There's a pressure in my mind, as if someone else's thoughts are beating against mine.

"Faro, don't!"

"Don't what? I'm not doing anything." He looks surprised.

"Aren't you trying – you know, to see my memories?"

"No. Why do you say that?"

"It's as if there's something else inside my mind. It's pressing on me. It wants to come out. I can feel it but I can't quite tell what it is."

"Ah," says Faro. His breath comes out in a long sigh. "I know that feeling. Haven't you had it before? Don't you really know what it is?"

"No."

"It's you. It's yourself. But it's another part of you, a hidden part that you don't know about."

"That sounds crazy."

"No, it's not crazy. But it's... difficult. Don't think about it now, Sapphire. Think about something else."

"Faro," I try to speak calmly and quietly. "That song you sang. Have you ever heard of my father?"

"Yes," says Faro immediately. He's still watching me closely. "You mean Mathew Trewhella."

He knows my father's name. Or did I tell him? I can't remember.

"How do you know his name?"

"I told you. We hear things. We know a lot about humans when they live close to us. He was always out in his boat."

"Have you ever seen him?"

There's a pause, and then Faro says, "Yes."

"When?"

"I can't remember. Not long ago."

But time for Faro isn't the same as human time. *Not long ago* could be months – or years —

"Where was it?"

But Faro shakes his head. "No. It's gone."

"But it's important, Faro! You must try to remember."

"I can't. It's gone."

"Is there anyone, anyone at all who you think would know what happened to him? Anyone here in Ingo, I mean?"

Faro shakes his head. A ripple of movement runs through his body and down into his tail. Faro says no with his whole body, not just his voice. His hair sways like fronds of seaweed.

"Leave it, Sapphire," he says. "I've nothing to tell you. I saw him in his boat once, that's all. Let's get out of this current and go back south. I want to feel the sun."

Even though questions burn in my mind, I have to let them go. But I won't forget them. If Faro can't give me the answers, I'll search until I find someone who can.

We slip out of the current like eels. Outside it, the sea is cold. How far are we from home?

"Not very far," says Faro. "That was a slow current. We'll catch a faster one back."

We swim through the cold dark sea. We're in mid-water, Faro says, which means we are between the sea bed and the surface. The water is so deep I can't see the bottom.

"If we were up on the surface, we wouldn't be able to see land," says Faro. "Keep your eyes open. Now, Sapphire, see that current there? That's the one we want."

It's a cold current this time, and it settles itself around us like an icy, prickling glove. But when I'm in Ingo, I feel the cold but it doesn't hurt me. My blood is changing, Faro says. It's slowing down and becoming like his.

"Hold on!" shouts Faro suddenly. "This current is *wild*."

He's right. It's like the roughest rollercoaster in the world. I make a grab for Faro even though I know I don't need him any more. But the current's too strong and it tears our hands apart and sends me swooping and tumbling over and over as it rushes me south.

I hate it and I love it. If it goes on for one more minute I'll die, but at the same time I want it never to end.

"Pull OUT, Sapphire!" Faro's yelling. "Now!"

We burst out into warm, still water. The icy current is gone, racing south without us.

"Time to feel the sun," says Faro.

Feeling the sun doesn't mean going up into the Air. It means sunbathing a couple of metres below the surface, in the brightest water. Faro takes my wrist. We rise together, towards the shining surface. Faro knows something about Dad, I think. I'll find out. I won't let Faro know that I'm still searching. I'll keep it secret.

"Let's have a sleep," says Faro.

We close our eyes. I'm tired from the current pummelling me all over. Water rushes gently in my ears. Faro's right, it's good to feel the sun. All my worries are slipping away from me. I stretch out my arms and legs to the delicious warmth, and let myself rock and drift on the swell of the water. I will find Dad. But now I'm away in Ingo... far, far away, in a garden of seaweed and sea anemones.

Memories flood into my head. A boy and a girl, side by

side, peering into the depths where blue and silver fish flick from rock to rock like electric darts. The boy has dark hair, like Conor. I can't see his face. But where his legs should be there is thick, glistening sealskin. I try to move my legs and feel the powerful flick of my own strong tail and I shoot upwards through the water laughing as my brother chases me—

It's the cold shadow passing over me that wakes me. I open my eyes at once with a feeling of panic, and stare up through the water. The surface is black. Something is directly above me, blocking out the light. A shark. Fear whips though me. No. It's not alive. The dark shape is solid and dead-looking. Man-made. Not something of Ingo, but something of Air. *How do I know that?*

A boat, I think. It's a boat, but I'm seeing it from upside down and it looks quite different. That's why I didn't know what it was. I'm looking straight up through the water at its hull. The boat is about the size of a fishing boat. I can see the rudder and the propeller. A small boat that wouldn't hurt me even if it passed right over me. But the engine isn't running. The boat is drifting silently.

And then it happens. A face looms over the side of the boat. A face and shoulders, part of a body in a blue shirt. Someone looks down, staring deep into the sea where I am. The face is distorted by Air. It wobbles. But upside down and distorted as it is, I can see it. It's a man's face. And if I can see him…

That's when it happens. The eyes look down and catch

sight of me. The face goes still with shock. The man stares and stares as if he can't believe that what he sees can possibly be real.

With a shock, I know what he sees, and why he can't believe it. He sees a girl, deep under the water, looking back at him. We meet each other's eyes. He sees me and I see him. It's a long moment and even through Air and water I recognise the frozen disbelief in his face. It can't be real. A girl sunbathing way below the surface. A girl with her eyes open, who doesn't need to breathe like Air People. Not a drowned girl but one who is alive, and looking back at him. *A mermaid.* I think I see the word form on his lips. And as his mouth opens to cry out and tell someone else on the boat to get a net and catch me and take me away and put me in a glass tank in a freak circus —

I dive.

I dive with hot terror pulsing through me. Down, down, down, into the deepest water, where the Mer can live but Air People can't follow them. And in that moment for the first time I understand why Faro hates and fears divers. They are Air People who can put air on their backs and come where only the Mer should be. That man in the blue shirt can't follow me. But a diver in a wetsuit with air on his back could have swum down after me and caught me. Faro's right. Divers are dangerous.

I see that face again, staring down into mine. Shocked and disbelieving but something else too. *Recognising.* I know that I know the face, but whose is it? My memory is full of Ingo. Too much else is crowded out. I struggle to remember who that man could be... where I've seen him before...

No, don't struggle, Sapphire, I tell myself. You're safe in Ingo. The deep water rocks me gently. Yes, Faro's right, my blood is becoming like his. I put my finger on my wrist and feel how slow the pulse beats there. Faro says—

But where's Faro gone? Why am I alone?

CHAPTER FIFTEEN

"I'm here," says Faro's voice, soft and close.

"But where were you? I was so scared, Faro! I woke up and there was a boat up above, with a man looking down at me."

"I know. I saw him too."

Suddenly, when I'm not even trying, the name behind that man's face swims into my mind. Of course. It was Mum's friend. *Roger.* Roger, out in his boat, exploring. Not diving yet, just mapping out the area so he can come back and dive.

But I left Roger back at home with Mum, playing cards. I must have been asleep in the sunwater for a long time. Or maybe I wasn't asleep. Maybe it's only the difference between human time and time in Ingo again. *Why* is time in Ingo so different from Air time anyway?

I think of time folding and unfolding like one of those fans you make out of a piece of paper. Time folds up tight like a closed fan, then it spreads open wide. There's the same amount of paper in the fan whether it's open or closed. Maybe time is the same substance, whether in Ingo or up in Air. But it's folded differently, and so it doesn't look or feel the same. When I'm in Ingo, Ingo time seems natural. When I'm in the Air – at home, I mean – then that's natural too. But I can't belong in both times, can I?

I've got to stop thinking like this. My thoughts are making my head hurt. If you try to have Air thoughts when you're in Ingo, they don't work.

"He's a diver," says Faro. His voice is cold and hard. Faro hates divers.

"How do you know?"

"We've seen his boat before."

"I know him," I say.

Suddenly I want to punish Roger for laughing like that with Mum, both of them so happy and relaxed as if there wasn't a thing wrong in the world. As if Dad had never existed. Roger thinks he can go wherever he likes. He makes himself at home in our cottage, and he wants to dive into Ingo and make it his own, and take its treasures. But I'm not going to let him. None of what Roger wants is going to happen.

"He explores for wreck sites," I go on, headlong. "He's bringing a team of divers."

"He shouldn't be here at all," says Faro, like an echo of my own thoughts. "He should stay in his own place."

"It's *our* cove, not his."

"Air People are like that. They want to change everything."

I like the way Faro agrees with me about Roger. It's comforting. It silences the little voice that says I shouldn't have told him what Roger was doing. After all, I did promise...

No, you didn't. You only promised not to tell your friends at home and at school, I tell myself firmly, but I still feel uneasy. It's Roger's fault. If he would just disappear back to where he came from, everything would be all right again. Mum wouldn't really mind. She hasn't known him long, so she couldn't miss him that much.

"I heard him talking to Mum about diving near the Bawns," I say.

"What are the Bawns?"

"You know them. Those rocks about a mile off our cove. There's a big reef below water."

Faro's face goes still as a mask. "You call those rocks the Bawns?"

"Yes. What do you call them?"

"It doesn't matter. He can't go there."

"But he's going to, Faro."

"He doesn't understand. That place is ours. It is where we—"

"You what?"

"No, Sapphire. I can't tell you. But I can tell you this: your Roger will never go there. All of Ingo will defend it."

Faro's perfect teeth are bared. Ingo looks at me out of his eyes, and Faro's a stranger to me, full of cold, furious determination. And then the tide ebbs, and he's Faro again. My friend and my guide in Ingo. "Take my wrist, Sapphire," he says. "We're going back. If you reach home before he does, he will never believe that he really saw you in the sunwater. He'll think it was all a dream."

I remember Roger's shocked face. I'm not convinced it'll be that easy to make him forget, or think that it was all a dream. Roger doesn't seem the kind of person you could fool easily. But how can he possibly tell Mum he saw me lying under the water, not breathing? She'll think he's crazy. She certainly won't want him to come and have Sunday dinners and games of cards with her any more.

I put my hand around Faro's wrist, like a bracelet.

"Where are we now, Faro? Are we far from shore?"

"Not far. It depends how we travel," says Faro mysteriously. "There are ways that are even faster than riding the currents. You'll see. Wait."

We tread water, side by side. I can't see what Faro's looking for, and I can't hear what he's listening for. His face is tight with concentration. He looks like a surfer, poised, waiting for a wave.

Suddenly he turns to me, his face blazing with excitement. "They're coming. They're close enough now. Watch."

His mouth opens and a stream of fluting sound pours out, mixed with clicks. It sounds like sea music, something that belongs in the heart of one of those huge curved shells that you hold up to your ear so that you can hear the sea in them. Faro pauses, looking into the depths of distant water and listening for an answer. But if there is an answer, I can't hear it. I wish I knew that language. I wish I were less human, and more Mer.

"They're coming!"

"Who are coming?"

"Wait. You'll see."

And then I hear it too. The water's filling with sound. It's like Faro's music, but richer and more strange. It comes from all sides, clicking, whistling, echoing, fluting. And now they rise out of the deep water, sleek and shining and twice as long as I am. They come so fast that I flinch, thinking they'll hurtle into us. But they stop dead, and the water churns from their suddenness. They are smiling at us.

"Dolphins!"

"They'll let us ride them."

The dolphins swish into place alongside us. They watch me with their small, clever eyes, and they click and whistle, waiting for me to answer.

"Tell them I can't, Faro. I haven't learned their language yet. Tell them I'm sorry."

"They want you to climb on. Lay your body against her back, Sapphire. No, not like that. You're too stiff, she won't be able to hold you. Watch."

I watch Faro. The dolphin dips to let him climb astride and then he lies on its back. Faro's whole body seems to melt as he relaxes against the glistening dark skin of the dolphin. I can't even see where Faro's tail ends and the dolphin's body begins. I touch the shoulder of the dolphin who is butting gently against my legs, and she dips down, ready to carry me.

"But Faro! Dolphins don't swim underwater all the time, do they? They show their backs above the water. They'll take you into the Air. It'll hurt you."

"As long as I'm with her, riding on her back, I'm still in Ingo," says Faro, not lifting his face from the dolphin's skin. "Dolphins are always part of Ingo. Come on, Sapphire. Hurry. We have to go as fast as we can."

I lean gently forward on to the dolphin's back, and as my skin touches hers I'm held firm, as if some suction is gripping me. The clicks and whistles of the dolphins seem to be pouring through my body, turning into a language I nearly understand. I almost know what the two dolphins are saying to each other.

The dolphins move apart. They balance themselves in the water and then spring forward with a rush that plasters my hair over my face. I can't see anything. I don't know where I'm going or even where Faro is. But I have never felt so safe. My dolphin speaks to me and I wish I could answer, but I think she can tell through her skin that I trust her. I'm sure I can hear her heartbeat. The closeness of her is like a cradle.

"I know you're my friend," I say, and I don't know what language I'm speaking or if it's only thoughts in my head. I peep at my arms and they're wearing a coat of bubbles from the dolphin's speed. The water round us churns white but our rush is effortless. All at once we are going up and before I know what's happening we've flashed through the skin of the sea and we're out in a shock of dazzling sunlight. We crash back into the dark water and I can feel my dolphin laughing. Again and again and again we rise and dive, going faster and faster, the dolphin jumping higher each time. Faro's dolphin jumps at our side and I know the two dolphins are racing, urging each other on, laughing with us and with each other.

"Faro!" I shout, not because I want him to answer but because nothing as wonderful as this has ever happened to me before. Our speed is like time unzipping and running backwards. Hope surges in me that where the dolphin's journey ends I'll find everything that time has destroyed. Dad'll be home again. Dad'll come down to the shore to meet me, saying, "Well now, Sapphire, have you been a good girl while I've been away? Should we give school a miss tomorrow and go fishing instead?" There won't be any Roger, or games of cards, or Mum looking new and different with another man sitting at our kitchen table instead of Dad. The dolphins have the magic to take away everything that's gone wrong, and bring back everything I love.

"Faro!" I shout again, wanting to tell him how great it's all going to be. And he yells back something I can't hear before we plunge back into the sea and down, down, skimming along a fast rope of current. And then the white sand zooms up to meet us and I know we're coming to the borders of Ingo, where the earth and water meet.

Our dolphins slow down. I feel my body peeling away from the dolphin's back. She is letting go of me, and I have to let go of her. But I want to stay with her, so much.

"Can I see you again? Please?" I ask her, but she pushes against me, shoving me gently towards the shore as if she's telling me that that is where I belong. I must leave Ingo. I'm human, not Mer.

"But I belong in Ingo too," I whisper, and she looks at me with her small, thoughtful eyes, as if she's considering the question.

"Don't go," I plead, but I already know she's leaving, and taking her magic with her. She turns to her companion and they point their blunt noses to the deep water, and spring away from us. The clicks and whistles fade. The dolphins are gone.

"I wanted to thank them," I say, but Faro takes no notice.

"You can swim in from here. Hurry," he says.

He won't come any farther inshore, because the water's too shallow. But I'm not going to leave without asking Faro something that's been troubling me more and more. "Faro, why is it that I only ever see you? Where are all the other Mer? I don't even see Elvira."

"You saw the dolphins just now."

"Yes, but I mean people. Mer People."

Faro throws back his head angrily. "That is so typical of Air, Sapphire! People, people, people, as if people are all that matter."

"I didn't mean that, I liked the dolphins…" I argue, but even to me it sounds pathetic.

"You think you can have everything, don't you, Sapphire?" demands Faro. He sounds nearly as angry now as he was when he was talking about oil-spills and dead seabirds. "Do you think you can have a tour of Ingo, stare at us all as if we're creatures in a zoo – yes, believe me, I know all about your zoos! – find out all our secrets and then go home? *Ingo is not like that.* As long as you belong to

Air, you'll only see this much of Ingo," and he dives to the sea floor, takes up a handful of sand and pours it through his fingers until there's one grain left. He holds out the single grain to me. "*This* much."

"I've got some Mer in me," I say sulkily. "You told me so yourself."

"I know." Faro looks at me, his eyes serious, not so angry now. "Listen, Sapphire, that's why we can meet. You and me. It's because you've got some Mer in you. But I still don't know how much, or how strong it is. You don't either, do you?"

"Sometimes, when I talk to you, Faro, I feel as if I don't know anything any more. I'm so confused."

Faro lets go of the grain of sand and it spins down through the water to join its brothers and sisters on the sea bed. "We can't talk about it now. You must hurry. But you *have* got Mer in you, Sapphire. And I—" he hesitates, and looks at me intently, as if he's deciding whether or not to trust me. "I've got—"

But at that moment noise hits the water like a bomb. My ears sting with pain. The sea throbs as if it's got thunder in it.

"Quick, Sapphire, swim for the shore! It's the boat coming!"

As soon as Faro says it I recognise the sound of an engine. Faro grabs my wrist, grips tight for a second and then launches me towards the shore. I ride on the wave he's made for me, and it hurls me up, swooshes me in, and throws me flat on the sand. I struggle to my feet, coughing and choking, my eyes blind with salt. My ears are full of sand. I can't see and I can't hear. I'm back in the Air, where I belong.

Faro has disappeared. The boat is chugging round the other side of the rocks, towards its mooring. The noise of its engine thuds around the cove like a warning of danger.

"lease don't go off like that again, without telling me where you're going, Sapphire," says Mum. "If Conor hadn't said you were taking Sadie for a walk, I'd have been worried."

"Sorry, Mum. It was so hot that I took Sadie to play in the stream."

"I can see that. You're soaked through. You've been gone hours."

Only *hours*, I think. So Mer time and human time haven't been so different from each other this time. If time is a fan, then for once it hasn't opened wide enough to separate Mum's time from mine. Clever Conor, to think of saying that I'd taken Sadie out. Mum wouldn't doubt what he said, because Conor doesn't lie.

But Conor's just told a lie for my sake. Or maybe it was for Mum's sake? Conor wouldn't want Mum to be frightened.

I don't always tell the truth, I must admit. When I was little I used to scream and yell if people didn't believe what I told them about fairies living in a cave I'd made for them under the rosemary bush. And I had an imaginary kitten which had to have milk every morning and only ate Whiskas, just like the cats I'd seen on TV. Dad bought a can of Whiskas for the kitten, but Mum got really annoyed and wouldn't let me open it.

"Sapphy has a vivid imagination," Dad said.

"Stop humouring her, Mathew. She's got to learn the difference between what's real and what's not," said Mum.

But sometimes real and not-real are hard to tell apart, and life is easier if you bend the truth, just a little...

"Where's Conor now, Mum?" I ask casually.

"He's gone out in Roger's boat. They were planning to take it right out, to test the new engine, and then Roger's going to come in to take soundings by the Bawns. You know, he needs to prepare for diving there. Now, Sapphy, why don't you go up and change, and tidy your room while I finish this ironing. And then maybe you'd sort the washing for me. I need to put another load in the machine before the boys get back. The trouble with Sundays is that there's always so much to do."

The boys, I think angrily. As if Roger is part of our family. I go slowly upstairs, thinking hard. I know what *soundings* are. Roger's trying to find out how deep the water is in different places, and how difficult it will be to dive there. The Bawns are part of a reef about a mile offshore. Most of the reef is underwater, but the Bawn Rocks show above the surface. The part of the rocks that you can see is black and jagged, but what you can't see is the line of the Bawns that runs beneath the surface, like teeth. These hidden rocks are the most dangerous. In the old days, when shipping routes ran closer inshore than they do now, ships would lose their way in storms. The wind and tide would drive them on to the rocks. Sometimes, at night or in fog, a ship would break her back on the Bawns.

When the weather's bad the Bawns are lost in a white thunder of waves. Spray breaks and tosses high, as if the rocks themselves are spouting water, like whales. It makes me shiver to think of having to swim in those seas. Dad told me that a boy was found in our cove one morning after a wreck. He was thrown up on to the sand, still clinging to a piece of slimy wood. The people who climbed down to rescue him couldn't get the wood out of his grasp at first.

The miracle was that the boy was still alive. They wrapped him in blankets and carried him up the cliff path, and put him in front of a fire and poured brandy down him. He couldn't speak a word that anybody understood. They never found where he came from, or what language he was speaking. They named him Paul, because St Paul in the Bible was rescued after a shipwreck too. The Treveals took the boy in, and he grew up with their children. His grave is in the churchyard.

Shipwrecked Paul was my age. He was the only person who survived that wreck. No one ever knew where his ship came from, or what cargo it was carrying. Even when he learned to speak English, he never talked about the wreck, or what his life was like before he was found in the cove. On his gravestone it says that he died in 1852. He married Miriam Treveal and they had eight children. And then maybe all of those eight children had eight children, and then *those* eight children had eight children, Dad said. So no doubt all of us around here have got a drop of that shipwrecked boy's blood in us somewhere.

Dad won't go near the Bawns, even on a calm day.

And don't you ever go there, Sapphire, when you're old enough to take the boat out by yourself. Those rocks are a powerful place, and they've got a bad appetite for boats and human flesh. To sail near them is like putting your head into a wolf's jaws. After Dad said that, I could always see the shape of a wolf's head in the farthest of the Bawns. We never went in close, not even for fishing. But now Roger has taken Conor there. Conor must have agreed, even though he knows how bad the Bawns are.

I rush downstairs. "Mum! Did you tell Roger not to take Conor close to the Bawns?"

"Roger's a very experienced diver, Sapphy. He knows all about risk assessment."

"Oh, Mum! He doesn't know this coast like we do. It's dangerous by the Bawns."

A shadow of fear crosses Mum's face, but she makes a big effort and answers cheerfully. "Conor's safe with Roger. And look how calm it is today. Now, have you sorted the washing? I want the whites first."

"Mum, it's the Bawns, they shouldn't go there—" but Mum's closed her ears. I can't believe that this is Mum, who hates the sea and fears for everyone that goes on it. And now, the one time she should be frightened, she isn't. Mum, who used to issue storm warnings every time Dad took me out. I can remember when I was little the way Mum used to pick me up and hug me tight after I'd come back from fishing or taking photos with Dad. She would squeeze the breath out of me with relief.

Mum even chose the back bedroom for herself and Dad, because it faced inland.

Now she lets Conor go off in Roger's boat, even though he's almost a stranger, and he doesn't know a zillionth of what Dad knew about the coast and the currents here. Dad knew the sea almost as well as the Mer.

I mustn't think about it now. I mustn't let Mum guess about the Mer, or Ingo, or any of it. She wouldn't understand and it would only make her more afraid of the sea than ever.

"How long have they been gone, Mum?"

"For heaven's sake, Sapphy, stop fussing! Conor will be fine with Roger. Roger's got full safety equipment, and his mobile."

"There's no reception out there."

"All they're doing is testing the engine, taking the boat near the Bawns, doing some soundings and coming back. And then we'll all have tea."

I can't believe it. Mum's making it sound like an Enid Blyton story: have a nice adventure, and then home for tea. But Ingo isn't like that. *They weren't anywhere near the Bawns when I saw Roger*, I want to say. *They were much farther out than that. Testing the engine, eh?* But never in a million years can I tell Mum about lying in the sunwater, far out to sea, and feeling the shadow of Roger's boat come over me.

"There they are now!" says Mum, going to the door. She can't stop herself from sounding relieved. She heard the sound of footsteps and voices before I did. Roger's deep voice says something muffled, and Conor answers. Mum flushes slightly. A little smile grows at the corners of her mouth, and I know she's happy because Roger and Conor are getting on well. But that's what Conor is like. He's the easy one, who makes friends everywhere he goes.

Conor and Roger take off their shoes outside the door. I stay inside.

"Is Saph back yet?" calls Conor. I can hear the anxiety in his voice and I wonder if Mum can.

"Yes, she's in the kitchen," says Mum casually, going out to meet them.

"When did she get back?"

"Oh, just a little while ago. You were right, she was out walking Sadie. You two sound as if you've had a good time."

"We have," says Roger heartily. "Or at least, I have. It was a pleasure to have you along, Conor."

What a creep. But then I hear Conor. "Yes, it was good. Can we go out again next time you're down?"

"No problem," agrees Roger. "I'm grateful for the local knowledge. I'd have scraped when we came off the mooring, Jennie, but for Conor."

Conor protests that Roger would have done fine without him, and they all laugh. And now they come in through the dark doorway, blinking as people do when they've been out on the bright sea for hours. My eyes are already used to the indoors, and so I see Roger's face clearly. He startles when he sees me, just a little. He wants to hide it, but he can't. He comes farther into the room, trying to look as if he isn't staring at me. But he is. He's measuring my face against something in his mind. He's trying to tell himself that what he thinks he's seen out on the deep water can't possibly be true.

"Hi, Roger," I say cheerfully. Mum gives me a pleased look, because I'm being friendly at last, and forgetting all that nonsense about not liking Roger.

"Let's all have some tea," she says. "I've made a coffee and walnut cake."

"Wow, coffee and walnut, my favourite," says Roger enthusiastically. But he is still staring at me, and a frown knits on his forehead. Maybe he isn't going to enjoy the coffee and walnut cake quite as much as Mum hopes.

Roger's not the only one who is watching me. Conor sends me a meaning look. "*Upstairs*," he mouths silently. Aloud, he says, "Be down in just a minute, Mum. Got to change my jeans – there was water in the bottom of the boat."

But Conor's jeans are dry. Another lie for Conor. I follow him upstairs. If he keeps on lying like this, how long will it be before people stop always believing him?

"*What are you playing at*?!" whispers Conor angrily as soon as we get to the top of stairs. He grabs my arms so I have to turn and face him.

"What d'you mean? Shut up, Conor, they'll hear! You're hurting my arms."

"No, I'm not," says Conor. "I never hurt you. Saph, you must be crazy. First of all you go to Ingo again, and on your own. How many times do I have to warn you?"

"It was all right, Con. Their time was nearly the same as ours today."

"Today, maybe," says Conor grimly. "You were lucky. I had a feeling it would be OK though, I don't know why. I wasn't as frightened as I was the time before. So I made up some stuff for Mum about Jack calling to ask if you'd walk Sadie because he was going surfing."

"Conor, you're such a bad liar. The sea's flat."

"Yes, but Mum didn't think of that. You got away with it this time. Or at least you nearly did. *Roger saw you*. Now he's trying to convince himself it was some weird refraction of your image. You know, like a mirror image of you got beamed up into the air and reflected underwater, because of freak weather conditions."

"He can't believe that. It's impossible."

"Not as impossible as looking over the side of the boat and seeing you relaxing underwater with a big smile on your face. And seeing that you didn't need to breathe. And you were miles out as well."

"Did you see me too?"

"No. He didn't say anything straight away. I guessed something was wrong because of the way he went all still and tense, but I don't know him well enough to ask. Then after a while he turned round and said he'd seen something that couldn't possibly be there. A girl underwater. Not a drowned girl, but a real girl looking up at him. And then he said: *You're not going to believe this, Conor, but she looked exactly like your sister. She could have been her twin*. And then he started saying all that stuff about light rays bending and images refracting. But I knew he didn't really believe it, he was just trying to convince himself. So I said that there have always been mermaids around here, and maybe you had a mermaid double. That made him laugh."

"He laughed at the Mer?"

"Sapphire, *please*. I was *trying* to make him laugh. I wanted him to think it was all crazy and impossible and so he couldn't have seen anything. He said, *Well, one thing I know for sure is that your sister isn't a mermaid. I've seen her walking and she definitely has two feet.*

I can't stop myself. I glance down at my legs to make sure, and yes, there are my feet, safely inside my trainers. Relax, Sapphire, relax. Conor is on your side. He's only trying to cover up for you, and make Roger believe that he can't have seen you down there in the sunwater.

"I'm sorry, Con," I say. "I know you still do."

"Still do what?" asks Conor blankly.

"Still care about Dad. Still want him to come back."

"Of course I do," says Conor impatiently, as if he's forgotten all about our argument. "But Saph, listen—"

"What?"

"You don't need to be so against Roger. He's all right."

"He is not all right! He's a diver. He's the enemy of the Mer."

Conor doesn't answer for a little while. He watches my face very carefully, and then he says, in a cautious voice,

"But Sapphire, *you're* not Mer, are you? You belong to the Air. You're human. Like me and Mum and Roger."

"I'm *not* like Roger!" I spit out, before I know what I'm going to say.

"But you are like me, aren't you?" Conor goes on, still in that careful voice, as if he's not quite sure what I might do or say next. "We're brother and sister. Same genes. *Human* genes, Saph."

"Yes," I say uncertainly. Of course I belong with Conor, my brother. But I'm remembering what I said to the dolphins. *I belong in Ingo too*. Even though Faro is right, and what I know about Ingo is as small as a grain of sand, I don't feel like a stranger there. I feel different when I'm in Ingo. More alive. More... more *myself*.

"Conor. Tell me truthfully. Do you truly believe that we're all Air, and not Mer at all? You and me, I mean?"

"But Saph, what else could we be but human? We've got a human mother and a human father. That makes us a hundred per cent human. Why do you want to believe anything different?"

"I don't know." Suddenly I feel tired all over. Conor is standing right next to me, but he's far away. "I don't know why I believe it, but I can't help it. I *feel* it, Conor. When I'm in Ingo I'm free. I can go anywhere, wherever I want."

"Only if you're holding on to Faro's wrist," says Conor sarcastically. "I don't see what's so free about that."

"But I don't need to do that any more."

"What? *You don't need to do that any more*?" repeats Conor slowly. "No. Of course, you're right. It's true. You can't have been with Faro when Roger saw you, otherwise Roger would have seen *him* too. You mean you can breathe and move and do everything on your own, all the time you're down there?"

"Yes. If I want to go really fast though, I hold on to Faro or we get the dolphins—"

"You should never have gone back there, Saph. It's dangerous. It's changing you. Each time you go, it draws you deeper in. I keep trying to make you understand. Why won't you listen?"

"No, Conor, why won't *you* listen for once? You should have been with us today. You don't understand what it's like. We rode on the dolphins and I nearly understood what they were saying. It doesn't hurt at all to go into Ingo now, not like it did the first time. And Faro and I—" I stop. I'd been about to blurt out that Faro could hear my thoughts.

"Faro and you what?"

"Oh, nothing."

"Faro and you what?"

"Conor, it's nothing. Don't look at me like that. It's just that he can – I mean, *we* can – we can see into each other's minds. Just a bit. I can see his thoughts and he can see mine, the way fish do in shoals. They share their memories, did you know that?"

"I do not *believe* I'm hearing this. Sapphire. You – are – not – a – fish. You are not even *partly* a fish. Get over it. You are my sister and you live in Senara Churchtown, West Penwith, Cornwall, the Earth, the Universe. Not in ***!!!!*** Ingo!"

"I wish Mum could hear you swearing like that."

"Why don't you swim off and tell her? Assuming you can still remember enough human words? Mum can't share your thoughts like *Faro*, remember. She's only human."

"Conor, we mustn't!"

"Mustn't what?"

"Argue."

"I'm not arguing."

"Nor am I."

Face to face, not arguing, we can't think of anything else to say. But without saying anything, I know that something has shifted. Conor is my friend again. Maybe that sounds a strange thing to say, because how can your brother not be your friend?

"All the same, Saph," says Conor after a while, "I *am* going out with Roger again. I do want to learn to dive. Roger's going to fix up a course for me. He's got a mate who'll give me the course for nothing, in exchange for a favour Roger did him. It's really interesting, what Roger does. It's the kind of thing I'd like to do one day."

"It's dangerous," I say, and then I realise I'm echoing what Conor's just said to me. "The Mer don't like it, Conor. And in their own world – in Ingo – they're powerful. We aren't."

"I know, I know. Can you please stop being the Mer Broadcasting Company for two seconds? Listen. Roger's not trying to do harm. He's not working for an oil company or anything like that. He knows loads about marine ecology, Sapphire. He cares about it. That's what he's interested in. You ought to talk to him."

"Don't go out with him, Conor."

"But why not? You've been out in Dad's boat hundreds of times and nothing's ever happened. Well, not much, anyway. So have I. What's so different about Roger?"

"I don't know. I can't say. It's feels like – I don't know. Like bad weather coming, when the sun's still shining. But you can see the storm moving in from the sea. And you feel the pressure inside your head."

"OK, I promise, if it's bad weather, or if it even looks like bad weather, I won't go," says Conor. But it wasn't bad weather I was talking about. It was a different kind of storm. If I could put what I'm afraid of into the right words, then surely Conor would understand.

"And Roger won't go out if there's a bad forecast. He's very careful. Divers have to be. Come on, Saph, we'd better go downstairs."

I'm not finding the right words. But at least Conor won't be going out again with Roger for a while, so I'll have time to persuade him.

"Hurry up, Saph, Mum'll be waiting."

"She won't. She's happy talking to Roger. Anyway, you'd better change your jeans first, hadn't you?"

"Why?"

"Because you told Mum they were wet. And it's a good idea for Mum to keep on thinking that at least one of us tells the truth."

CHAPTER SEVENTEEN

ll through tea I'm on edge in case Roger says something about seeing me underwater. I can't eat more than half my slice of cake, even though it's one of Mum's best, and Mum is trying to feed me up. After Roger's eaten two fat slices, Mum asks if he'd like a fresh pot of tea.

"You sit down," he says, "I'll make it, Jennie. You deserve a rest." Then he turns to me and Conor. " Your mother is an amazing woman," he announces, sounding like a character in a TV sitcom. "The best waitress in town, best cook I know – finest coffee and walnut I've ever tasted, Jennie."

"Is that all I'm good for? Baking cakes and running around the restaurant?" asks Mum, but she doesn't sound cross at all. Her voice is full of teasing laughter.

"I think you know that's not the case," says Roger, and they laugh together.

For several reasons this conversation makes me prickle. We *know* that Mum is a good cook. We *know* how hard she works. Isn't that why we try all we can to help her? We don't need Roger to tell us. It's our life, not his – none of it is Roger's business at all – and yet the way he laughs with Mum makes me feel as if I'm the one who is left out. I try to catch Conor's eye to see what he thinks, but he's on his way out already.

"Got to fetch the milk, Mum. See you in a bit."

"I'll make that tea," says Roger, dragging his eyes away from Mum.

"Sapphire'll help you, won't you, Sapphy," says Mum, settling herself luxuriously in her chair and closing her eyes. "Now this is heaven. All the meals cooked, nothing to do for the rest of the evening... Sapphy, love, show Roger where things are in the kitchen."

Roger and I traipse into the kitchen. As soon as I'm alone with him, I suddenly realise how big he is. Not heavy, but broad and strong and tall. He has to duck his head to go through the kitchen doorway.

I don't like being alone with him. I'm scared of what he might ask, so I start to gabble to fill up the silence." We keep the tea bags in this tin up here, and the kettle's over here. It doesn't switch itself off, because the switch is broken. Mum's going to buy another kettle when she's been paid. If you fill it up to five there'll be enough for a pot."

"I have seen a kettle before," says Roger mildly. He is watching me. He's going to say something – ask me something. I must get away—

But I only get as far as the fridge before he asks casually, "Sapphire, how far can you swim?"

"I don't know, quite a long way, I mean, not all that far, depends how flat the sea is—"

"Your mother tells me that you and Conor aren't allowed to swim outside the cove."

"No, because of the rip. Only if we're out in a boat with... with someone. Sometimes we swim off the boat."

"Have you been out in a boat with... *someone*... lately? In the last day or two?"

"No," I say firmly, and I look Roger in the face because I can prove this isn't a lie. "I haven't been out in a boat since... since..." But I can't say it. Not to Roger.

"Since what?" he insists. Anger springs up in me. Roger's trying to act like my father, as if he has a right to question me.

"Since Dad took me out in *Peggy Gordon*," I say. I feel my face burning, but I'm not going to cry. I'm not going to let Roger see me crying.

"Oh. I see." Roger is quiet for a while, then he says, quite formally as if I'm an adult like him. "I'm sorry, Sapphire. I didn't mean to distress you."

His face is troubled. For a moment I can't help believing that he really is sorry. But I don't want to believe it, or I might start having to – well, to tolerate Roger.

"S'OK," I say grudgingly.

"No, it's not OK," says Roger slowly. "None of this is OK, I know that. Your dad dies, a year later I come along... It's not easy for anyone. Have you thought about how hard it is for your mother?"

"Dad is not dead," I flash out furiously. Roger stares at me.

"He is not dead," I repeat, more quietly, but with all the force I can find. If only Roger would believe me, how much trouble it would save.

"You're a complicated young lady," he says slowly. "And I wish – I wish I could see inside that head of yours."

"Well, you can't. We're human. We don't share our thoughts. The kettle's boiling. I'll wash the mugs while you make the tea."

I'm not sure if I'll get away with this, but I do. Roger and I finish making the tea in silence. But just before we take it in to Mum, Roger asks, "Sadie. The dog you were walking. She's one of the neighbour's dogs, right?"

"Yes."

"What breed is she?"

"Golden Labrador."

"Nice breed."

"Yes, she's—" Suddenly Sadie is so clear in my mind that I can almost feel her warm golden body, her soft tongue licking my hand, her quivering excitement when she knows she's going for a walk.

"You like her. You ever had a dog of your own, Sapphire?"

"No. Mum says it's too much work."

"Well, that's true, a dog is a lot of work. I had one as a boy myself, and I found out the hard way that my dad meant what he said when he told me: *If you get a dog, then it's you that's got that dog as long as it lives.* But Rufie was the best thing in my life, after we came back from Australia and I found myself stuck in Dagenham. You and Conor could take care of a dog between you, I reckon."

"Except when we're at school."

"There's no one in the neighbourhood who'd keep an eye?"

I have never thought of this. Never thought beyond pushing against Mum's prohibition by telling her over and over again that me and Conor will do everything.

"I don't know…"

"Worth thinking about, it seems to me," says Roger. "Your mother would feel easier that way."

"What kind of dog was Rufie?"

"Black Labrador. Beautiful breed. They get problems with their hips as they grow older, that's the only thing."

I nod. I already know that, and that Labradors don't live as long as some other dogs.

"But for good temper and loyalty there isn't a breed to touch them. Beautiful breed," says Roger thoughtfully, and he opens the door for us to carry in the tea.

It's late at night now. I'm in bed, and everyone else is asleep. Roger's gone back to St Pirans, and Mum went to bed early because she's doing the breakfast shift at the restaurant tomorrow. There's no sound from Conor's loft. I heard his light click out a long time ago.

I feel like the last person left awake in the world. If I had my own house, I'd let my dog sleep in my bedroom. Dogs wake up the instant you stir. If Sadie was here she'd know I was awake and I could talk to her.

I'm not going to think about Roger any more. It's all been going over and over in my head for hours. Mum, Roger, Dad. Sometimes I wish I wasn't a child, and then I could be like them and make my own decisions and my family would just have to live with them.

I'm going to think about Ingo. Dolphin language and sunwater, basking sharks and grey seals, sea anemones, shrimps and cowries and shoals of jellyfish, wrecks and reefs and the Great Currents taking you halfway around the world. Ingo. *Ingo*. Once you're through the skin of the water, it doesn't hurt any more. You dive down and there's a whole world waiting for you. Blue whales and Right whales and Minke whales, schools of porpoises leaping in perfect formation as if each one knows what the others are thinking. Maybe they do.

Thong weed and cut weed and sugar kelp, all the names Dad taught me and all the creatures we've ever seen. By-the-wind sailors, shore crabs and hermit crabs, bass and wrasse and dogfish and squat lobsters, rips and currents and tides. *I wish I was away in Ingo, I wish I was away in Ingo…* and as I'm saying these words, I fall into sleep.

I wake with a start out of deep dreams. Something's woken me. I push the duvet off me and sit up, listening, but now everything's quiet. I'm certain I heard something. My skin prickles with fear as I climb out of bed, cross to the window, pull back my curtain and see the moon, strong and riding high.

"Sssssssapphire!"

I open the window to hear better. The voice is as soft as a breath, as if it's travelled a long way to get to me. As soon as I hear it, I know it's the voice that woke me. It's not Conor's voice, or Mum's. It's eerie and full of mystery. My skin prickles again and I shiver all over. *I don't think it's a human voice at all.* It's like the voice the sea would have, if the sea could talk.

How I wish I could speak full Mer. Can the sea really talk? Can it tell you all its secrets? I'm sure the sea is trying to tell me something now.

No sound comes from Mum's room, or from upstairs where Conor's sleeping. Nobody else has woken.

"Ssssapphire!" The voice is urgent now. It wants to get close to me but it can't. The sea can't reach you on land. It can only come as far as the high-water mark. Granny Carne said that Ingo is strong, but I'm sure it isn't strong enough for the sea to come to me, washing up the cliff and across the fields and flooding our garden so that waves break below my window.

"SSSapphire… SSSSapphire…"

It sounds like waves breaking. All at once I'm completely sure that I'm hearing the sea's own voice. I can hear salt in it, and surging water, and the roll of the tide. It's sea magic, talking to me.

Granny Carne stopped me going to Ingo, but that was in daytime. Sea magic might be stronger than earth magic, when the time's ripe. I stand still, bracing my feet on the floorboards. What's the time in Ingo? My watch shines on my wrist. The hands point to five past seven, the time I first walked into the water.

From the other side of the room my dressing-table mirror gleams back at me. Moonlight picks out the pattern of a starfish in the mirror's shattered glass. Even though the mirror is broken I can still see my reflection. It looks like me, and yet not like me. My hair is tangled like weed, my face shines like water.

"*Sssssssapphire!*"

I can't keep silent. I have got to answer. But just as I turn back to the window and open my mouth to speak, two things happen.

An owl swoops past my window. Its wings are spread wide, and as it passes the owl turns and stares straight into my room. Its fierce amber gaze burns into my mind, and then is gone. At the same moment a volley of barks bursts across the night. It's Sadie! I know it's her. I'd recognise her voice anywhere. It's Sadie, barking wildly, as if she's heard an intruder and is desperate to wake the whole house. Oh Sadie, I wish you weren't so far away! I wish I was where you are, then I'd know what's wrong.

Sadie barks even more wildly, as if she's answering me. I have the strangest feeling that Sadie is barking because of me. She wants me to hear her. She wants to warn me–protect me...

"It's all right, Sadie girl," I say, even though my voice can't possibly reach her. "It's all right, there's nothing wrong, nobody's hurting me."

But Sadie just carries on barking, telling the whole night to watch out. I bet Jack's dad has already stumbled downstairs in his pyjamas to see if there's a burglar, or a fox after the chickens. Sadie keeps on barking out her message, and I find myself smiling. It's almost as if she were in my room, thumping her tail on the floor, telling me she's here, it's all right, she's not going to let anything hurt me.

Suddenly I'm very tired. What's my window doing open? I close it, fasten the catch, and tumble into bed.

"Goodnight, Sadie," I say. "It's all right now, I'm safe in bed, you can stop barking. But thank you anyway..." As if Sadie really can hear me, the barking dies away. I snuggle deep under the duvet, and fall into a dreamless sleep.

CHAPTER EIGHTEEN

"*Wake up, Sapphire. Wake up. It's important. You've got to remember.*

Who said that?

White wall, bedroom wall. I'm awake, or I think I am. It's early. Mum hasn't gone to work yet, I can hear her downstairs.

Inside my head everything slides into place. Yes, something happened last night. The sea was talking to me but then Sadie started barking and the sea's voice went away. And an owl flew past too. It came so close that if I'd leaned out of the window I could have touched its feathers. And it turned and looked at me. Its eyes reminded me of something... but I can't remember what, now.

I'm sitting rigid, upright in bed. It wasn't a dream, it was real and it was important, even though I don't understand what it meant. I've got to tell Conor.

It's hard work waking Conor. He keeps fighting his way back under the duvet.

"Go WAY, Saph. Nogonnagerrup—"

But I'm brutal. I drag the duvet right off him and when he rolls over to the wall I haul him back.

"WhassMAAERSaph?"

"Conor, something really important's happened. You've got to wake up."

At last words penetrate the fog of Conor's sleep. He says clearly, "Go away. I'm asleep."

"How can you be asleep when you're talking to me?"

Conor groans. "Go AWAY, Saph. Just cause *you* want to get up at dawn—"

"The sea was calling to me last night. It was saying my name. The sea's got a voice, Conor! I think it was saying my name in Mer, and guess what, I understood!"

Conor's eyes fly open. "What?"

"Moryow were calling me."

"What? What did you say? Who are Moryow?"

"Did I say that?"

"Don't you even know what you said?"

Suddenly the meaning of the word opens up in my mind.

"Moryow are the seas of the world," I tell Conor.

"You're making this up, aren't you?"

"No, I'm not, I swear and promise. Moryow came close last night, as close as they can. But Sadie wouldn't let me hear the voice any more... and I think the owl stopped it too."

Conor props himself up on his elbows. He looks rumpled and worried.

"It was a dream, Saph. It must have been."

"It wasn't. I definitely heard a voice. It was as clear as yours, and it was calling me."

"I don't know. Maybe it was some weirdo." He shivers. "Thank God you didn't go."

"But I would have done. It was only Sadie barking that stopped me."

"Jack's house is more than two miles away. How would Sadie barking from there have stopped anything?"

"I know, but the barking was close, as if Sadie was in my room. I could hear the lev of the Moryow, then the lev of Sadie hid it."

Conor flops back on his bed. "This is all so crazy. *Moryow – lev* – I don't know what you're talking about."

"It's not crazy, Con. Listen. I think it only sounds crazy when you try to understand it all in a – well, in a human way."

"Which other way can I look at it? I'm human. And so are you."

"But imagine if I could speak full Mer, and talk to everything in Ingo. Maybe I'm beginning to learn the language."

Conor suddenly stops being angry with me.

"I'm not saying I don't believe you, Saph. It's just that it's really, really scary to have a sister who suddenly starts speaking a different language. It makes you seem like a stranger."

"How could I ever be a stranger to you, Conor! We're broder and hwoer."

Conor clasps his head in his hands. "Saph, *stop it*. And whatever happens, if you hear a voice like that again in the middle of the night, don't follow it. You mustn't do what it tells you to do. Swear and promise."

"I can't—"

"You must."

"But Conor, don't you understand? Promises made in this world only cover this world. I can't promise here for what I might do in Ingo."

Conor nods reluctantly. "All right, then. I suppose that'll have to do. Swear and promise?"

"Swear and promise," I say, and we each spit on our right hands and slap them together.

Conor believed me when I said that the seas of the world talked to me last night. Yesterday afternoon I felt as if I was on the outside of the family, on my own, while Conor was inside, close to Mum and Roger. But now Conor and I are back together.

"Hey, Saph, what's the matter? You're not crying, are you?"

"No, I'm just glad that…"

"That what?" asks Conor, wiping tears off me with the corner of his duvet. "You know Saph, you cry the biggest tears in Cornwall. We ought to bottle them and sell them to the tourists."

"That you don't think it was just a dream."

"No. I know when you're making up stuff. Those words sound real to me. But I wish I knew what to do."

"Let's talk to Granny Carne," I say, not because I've

thought about it, but because that's what people round here say when they have problems they can't work out.

But to my surprise Conor seizes on the idea. "You're right, Saph! That's what we'll do. I should have thought of it before."

"You mean we should go up there now?"

"Yeah, why not? Let's go up there as soon as Mum's gone off to work."

Mum's in her bedroom, brushing her hair and twisting it into a shiny knot for work. She smiles at my reflection in the mirror.

"There you are. You were sleeping so heavy this morning. I crept up and took a peep at you and you never even stirred. You look a lot better for the rest. Roger said he had a chat with you while you were making the tea yesterday."

"Yes."

"That's good. He thinks you're a bright girl. I said that he ought to see your school reports. It's the same every time. 'Bright, but can't be bothered'."

"You didn't tell him about my reports, Mum!"

"No, I didn't. I'm too kind, that's my trouble. But Mr Carthew's always saying that you don't do justice to your intelligence in your schoolwork. You could do really well, Sapphy, if you made an effort. You could get yourself to university, get a good job, get out of this place."

"I don't want to get out. I want to be here."

Mum sighs, and lays down her brush. "I know. You think

you want to spend the rest of your life swimming in the cove and running about with Conor. I don't blame you, I was the same at your age. I failed all my exams and I didn't care. But I don't want you to end up like me, Sapphy, counting up your tips at the end of the night and hoping you'll be able to pay the electricity bill."

"But Mum, I thought you liked it in the restaurant."

"It's all right. But I want more for you. Don't you see that? I want you to have a different life. Everyone wants more for their kids, it's human nature."

I wonder if it's Mer nature too, I think, and hope that the thought won't show on my face.

"Conor'll be all right," Mum goes on. "He works hard, and he knows what he wants. But you're such a mazeyhead, Sapphy, sometimes I want to spifflicate you to make you see sense."

Mum laughs, and I laugh too.

"Roger's a good man," goes on Mum abruptly. "I only want what's best for you and Con."

"Mum, you sound like you're going to marry him!"

A flush rises in Mum's face. She looks so like Conor. "Nobody said anything about marriage, did they?" she says. "We've only known each other five minutes. All I mean is, give Roger half a chance, Sapphy. He wants to be a friend to you, if you'll let him."

I can't think of anything to say about Roger. I don't even want to discuss him. "Why's your hair so much shinier than mine, Mum?"

"Because I brush it from time to time," says Mum.

"I keep asking you to do a henna wax for me, but you never have time."

"I will, Sapphire, I promise. Now stop fiddling with my hair and let me get on. I'm going to be late. Oh, these school holidays, they go on for ever and ever amen. I'll be glad when you're back in school and I can stop worrying about you all day long. Be good, Sapphy, and don't go off on your own. Stick with Conor."

"But Mum—"

"What?"

"Mum, do people ever hear voices – of things that aren't there?"

"What sort of voices?"

"Voices calling, but there's no one there. Maybe calling your name."

Mum puts one hand on each side of my face, framing it. Her fingers are soft and cool. "I think there are more things that happen than we know about," she says. "You remember I told you that I was working upcountry in Plymouth, when my Mum died?"

"Yes."

"No one was expecting her to die. She had a chest infection, but she was on antibiotics and people hardly ever die of chest infections. But she got an embolism in her lungs and she died at three o'clock in the morning. Dad rang me at four."

I don't know what an embolism is, but I'm not about to ask.

"So I never saw her again before she died," says Mum.

"But about two weeks later, after the funeral, when I was in the garden of our house – I hadn't gone back to work yet, I was helping Dad – I heard Mum's voice. She said, 'Jennie?' and I said, 'Yes.' And then she said, 'Don't worry about me, Jennie, I'm fine.'"

I stare at Mum. She's never told me anything like that before.

"Did she say anything else, Mum?"

"No. But I felt her come up close. I didn't see her, but she patted my cheek just like she used to when I was little. It was as real as that."

"Was she a ghost, then?"

"No. She was Mum, same as always. And then she wasn't there. Do you know, Sapphy, I've never told anyone about it until this minute."

I look at Mum. She's smiling, but her eyes are shiny. "Does it make you sad," I ask, "when you remember your mum?"

Mum shakes her head. "No, I like talking about her. Come here, Sapphy, give me a big hug."

I hug Mum tight, squeezing her until she gasps for breath. What if Mum died, and all I had was a ghost who walked up a path and then disappeared? Mum seems to be happy about her mum doing that, but I certainly wouldn't be.

"Promise me you won't," I whisper.

"Won't what?"

"You know. *Promise.* You won't ever just—"

"Ever just *what?*"

"Disappear."

Mum takes a deep breath. I can feel her ribs rise as her lungs fill with air.

"I promise, Sapphy," she says.

CHAPTER NINETEEN

A s soon as Mum's left for work, we're on our way to Granny Carne's. Her cottage is up on the Downs, tucked into the hillside, half hidden. The grey granite walls look like part of the hill until you get close. There's no track, only a narrow path, so even a Jeep can't get up here. The path is steep, and the sun beats on our backs so that we're sweaty and out of breath by the time we get up to the cottage.

We stand side by side in front of Granny Carne's door.

"Go on, knock."

Conor's knock is loud in the stillness. A few bees buzz and the wind riffles. The knock echoes, but nothing moves. He knocks again, more loudly.

"She's not there."

"Oh." We stare at each other in disappointment. All that climb for nothing.

"What shall we do?"

"I don't know."

"Go back?"

"No, let's wait. She might come back soon."

We sit on the rough grass. This is where people come when they have troubles. They talk to Granny Carne and she tells them things no one else knows. Things about the future, and the past too. People say she can look into the future, like a fortune-teller. Dad used to say that the doors that are closed to most of us are like windows to Granny Carne. She can see straight through them. I used to think he meant real doors, and imagined Granny Carne waving her wand to turn them into glass, like a witch in a storybook.

Conor's trying to make a beetle walk along a grass stalk. We both crouch down to see if it will. I squint, and my squint makes the stalk look as big as a log. This is what it must look like to the beetle. A big rough log, a climbing conundrum that he has to work out. Maybe there's a Beetle world, just as there's a Mer world. In Beetle world, shoes look like boulders, and flowers are as big as bike wheels. We're giants, and a puddle of water would be as deep as Ingo...

"I wish we'd brought a bottle of water, Conor," I say. "I'm really thirsty."

"There's a stone trough round the back of the cottage. It's spring water."

"How do you know?"

Conor hesitates. "I came here with Dad once."

"You never told me! When?"

"Last summer. Early last summer."

"Before he left."

"Yeah, that's right. Before he left."

"What happened?"

"Me and Dad were out walking. He was taking photos at the top of the Downs, and we came back this way. He said he would just call in on Granny Carne."

Conor stops. Like me, he can hear the echo of Dad's voice saying those exact same words. Dad's voice always made you want to hurry along where he was going.

"Dad went inside the cottage, but I didn't," Conor goes on. "I was thirsty and I heard water trickling, so I went round the back and found where the spring ran into the trough. There were some baby frogs."

"What do you think Dad asked her about?"

"I don't know. He was in there a long time, but I didn't bother, because I was watching the frogs."

Conor is good at watching. He'll watch the seals for hours until they lose their fear and come right up on the rocks, close.

"Then he called me," Conor says. "He and Granny Carne had finished talking. She stood in the doorway and watched us go, with her arms folded like this. I don't think they even said goodbye. I thought maybe they'd quarrelled."

"Did she look angry?"

"I'm not sure. Maybe not angry. But they both looked serious."

"Did Dad tell you anything?"

"No. He walked so fast I almost had to run to keep up with him. But he did say one thing."

"What?"

"He said, *That's the last time I ever go there.*"

"Then they must have quarrelled."

"Maybe Granny Carne told Dad something he didn't want to hear."

I try to think what that could be. It must be terrible to see into the future. To know what's coming, but not be able to change it. Like a curse.

But if Granny Carne has earth magic, then maybe she can use her power to change the future. Then the future wouldn't be like an accident rushing towards her – it would be a thousand possibilities. Not all of them have to come true.

The beetle has decided it's not going to bother walking down the grass stalk, however invitingly Conor waggles it. It scurries away, back into Beetle world, away from the two mysterious giants who do things it can't understand.

Suddenly, the bright sun on Conor's hand is covered in shadow. We look up at a tall figure dressed in white, with a white veil over its face, and white gloves. It takes me a moment to recognise that it's Granny Carne.

"I've been seeing to the bees," says Granny Carne. She takes off her bee keepers' hat and veil, and carefully peels off her gloves. She's wearing a white smock, with trousers tucked into her boots.

"Where are the bees?" I ask.

"Up on the moor," she says. "I'll take my things off in the shed and then we'll go in."

People say strange things about Granny Carne's home,

but they don't say them aloud and they don't say them in front of children. But we know it all anyway. Nobody says they believe in witches these days, but whether you say you believe or not, it doesn't alter what's there. It's probably dark and a bit creepy in the cottage. I'm glad Conor's here with me.

Granny Carne emerges from the shed in her usual shabby old clothes that make her look like part of the moor.

"I made a honey cake, seeing as you were coming," she goes on, taking us in. Inside, it's not at all as I'd imagined. The downstairs is all one room, clean and white and bare, like a cave. It is cool and calm, with all the things in it you need and none that you don't. A strong wooden table that looks as if you could dance on it without breaking it, wooden chairs with red cushions, a smooth dark floor.

"Sit down."

There's a sticky-topped honey cake on a blue plate. There are three mugs, ready for tea, and a blue pitcher of water with three glasses. One for her, one for Conor, one for me. Did she really make that honey cake because we were coming? Did she put out those three glasses before we arrived? She can't have known. We only just decided to come this morning. Maybe she saw us climbing up the hill, from a long way off? But no, if she was tending the bees, she couldn't have been here in the cottage at the same time, making cake and setting the table.

"My kettle takes a while to boil," says Granny Carne. "But

it's a hot day and you'll be thirsty from walking up. Drink some water."

Conor pours, and I lift my glass. The water smells pure. But it's earth water, sweet, not salt. It belongs to the earth. I lift it to my lips, then put it down. I want salt. I want the taste of the sea. The green and turquoise sea with its deep cool caverns underwater where you can dive and play. I want to plunge through the waves and roll over and jack-knife deep into the surging water that is full of bubbles and currents and tides. But Granny Carne's cottage is more than two miles from the sea. It's buried in the side of the hill, locked into the land.

I feel trapped. I want to get out. Mum and Dad took us to London once and we went in a lift in a tube station. I thought it was already packed as full as it could be, but people still kept shoving in and squashing up until my face was crushed against a fat man's suit and I could hardly breathe. I could smell the man's sweat. Everyone kept pushing until I was so squashed I couldn't see Mum or Dad or Conor. I felt as if the lift was closing in on me. I feel like that now. The cottage walls press in around me. My chest hurts. I can hardly breathe.

I want the space of the sea. I want to taste salt water and open my mouth and know that I can breathe without breathing. Down, down, down into Ingo...

I push back my chair and it clatters on the flagstone floor. Instantly, Granny Carne is beside me, tall and strong as an oak.

"Sapphire. Sapphire! Drink this."

She's holding the glass of water to my lips. I try to twist my head away but she insists. "Sapphire. I know you're thirsty. Drink your water."

The glass presses against my lips. Earth water, sweet, not what I want. I want salt. But I'm thirsty, so thirsty. I need to drink. I open my lips, just a little. The water touches them, then it rushes into my mouth. It covers my tongue and it tastes good. I swallow deeply, and then I drink more and more, gulping it down. The more I drink the more I know how thirsty I am. I feel like a plant that's almost died from lack of water. Granny Carne refills my glass from the jug and I drink again.

The cottage walls aren't pressing in on me now. They're just ordinary cottage walls again, white and clean. I don't know why I was so frightened.

"Good," says Granny Carne. "Remember, my girl, you mustn't ever drink salt water. Even if you crave it, you mustn't drink it. It makes a thirst that nothing can satisfy."

"What does crave mean?"

"When you crave for something you want it so much you'll stop at nothing to get it," says Granny Carne. "But salt water's poison to humans."

"Sapphire's been ill," says Conor.

"No wonder, if she goes drinking salt water," answers Granny Carne. "Now, tell me what you're here for."

"She's started speaking another language," Conor says.

"What's that then? French or German?" asks Granny Carne, watching us keenly.

"No, she knows it without learning it. Tell her, Saph. Tell her the words you spoke this morning."

"I can't speak to her in that language. She belongs to N—" I manage to stop myself, but Granny Carne has noticed.

"What do I belong to?"

"To Earth."

"Yes, but that wasn't what you were going to say. You were going to say that I belonged to Norvys, weren't you?"

I stare at her, astonished. "You can say it too! But you're not part of Ingo."

"Earth and Ingo share some words. But that's not the question, is it? The question is, how do *you* know about Norvys?"

I am silent for a long time, while Granny Carne's question presses in on me. Her eyes light on mine. They are amber, piercing—

"It was you," I say. "Wasn't it?"

Slowly, a smile fills her face. "Ah," she says, "you were wide awake in the middle of the night, weren't you? And why should you think that Norvys can't go into the Air, if you can go to Ingo?"

Conor looks from one to another of us, bewildered.

"Granny Carne was the owl who came to me last night," I explain.

"No," says Granny Carne. "It's not as simple as that. I'm not the owl, but the owl is maybe one of my... shadowings."

"But your eyes are exactly the same."

"Yes."

"We came because of what happened last night," Conor says. "Tell her, Saph. Tell her about the voice."

"It wanted me to come to it. It called me like this: *SSSapphire... SSSSapphire...*"

"But that's not your name!" interrupts Conor. "It doesn't sound anything like your name. They must have been calling someone else."

"But in another language, Conor," Granny Carne points out. "And who was calling? Do you know that?"

"I think it was the seas of all the world," I whisper, as if someone might overhear us.

"Moryow," says Granny Carne.

"Yes."

"But she didn't go," says Conor, as if that's the most important thing of all.

"Why not?"

"I don't know. I think it was because of Sadie barking. And the... the owl."

"Sadie," says Granny Carne thoughtfully. "Wasn't Sadie that dog who came to you when I met you in the track below your house?"

"Yes."

"Granny Carne," says Conor abruptly, "my dad came to see you here, not long before he left. I was with him that day. Did he say anything – did he tell you anything? Anything that we don't know? Did he know then he was going to leave us?"

"The things that people say here are between them and these walls," says Granny Carne.

"But he's disappeared. He might be in danger."

"He might," agrees Granny Carne.

"But if he is, we've got to help him!"

"We won't help him that way. We have to go gentle. But I will tell you this. When your father came to me he had a mark on his face that I see on your faces now. It was a mark you don't often see... in the Air," she adds, watching us carefully to see if we understand. We stare at her. My hand goes up, as if to cover my face. Granny Carne half smiles.

"You won't hide such a mark that way," she says. "Not from me. We talked about it before, you remember, the last time I met you. Ingo puts that mark on a face. You know it, Sapphire. You've been there, in Ingo. You feel it pulling you, sometimes soft, sometimes strong."

I don't say anything. I am frightened. How is it that Granny Carne knows so much?

"Conor's got the same inheritance," Granny Carne goes on, "but it's not so powerful in him. That's the way things come out. Even brother and sister don't inherit things from their parents equally."

Conor nods as if he understands, but I know he doesn't. He must feel as dazed as I do.

"But, Conor," goes on Granny Carne, leaning forward and looking seriously into his face. "You have your own power that belongs to you, never doubt that. The time will come to use it. Sapphire has more of Ingo, but you have more of Earth. Both have their equal power. It's when they become unequal that there's danger."

They look at each other. I think again how alike they are. Granny Carne could be Conor's ancestor. The same dark skin, the same shape of the eyes, the same shape around the lips when they smile.

"There's always been powerful Mer blood in the Trewhella family," Granny Carne goes on. "The Mer blood goes way back beyond the first Mathew Trewhella."

"But it couldn't have been passed down to us," says Conor. "Mathew Trewhella went off with that mermaid, didn't he? He didn't have human children. He was a young man and he wasn't married. It says so in the story."

"No, he wasn't married, but he had a girl," says Granny Carne. "He was in love with Annie, before the mermaid called to him. She was carrying Mathew's baby when he disappeared. Annie gave the baby Mathew's name, even though he'd left her and people were saying he'd betrayed her. It's that little baby Mathew who carried the Mer blood down and gave you the inheritance.

"Poor Annie, how she loved Mathew Trewhella," goes on Granny Carne, as if she can see it all before her, clear and real as the honey cake on the table in front of us." She would have fought the Zennor mermaid tooth and nail, and won Mathew back, if they'd met as equals. But she wasn't just fighting the Zennor mermaid. She was fighting the old Mer blood in Mathew, that wanted to be away in Ingo."

I stare at Granny Carne. The way she talks about all these long-ago people makes me shiver.

"So you're saying that the story's true? That Annie's baby is our ancestor?" asks Conor.

"Of course he is. How could it be otherwise?" asks Granny Carne harshly. "No more now. No more. I'm tired."

She *looks* tired. Not strong and tall any more, but empty and grey, as if the colour of life has poured out of her. She huddles back in her chair, shuts her eyes and takes a few deep breaths, then with her eyes still closed, she says in a low monotone that is almost like a chant: "But you've got a choice too. No inheritance can force you to accept it. You are the ones who choose. Salt water or sweet water."

"But we need to *know*—" I'm burning with impatience. Granny Carne has got to tell us more. *Away in Ingo* – why did she use those exact words?

"Granny Carne, you've got to tell us more—"

"Got to? *Got to*, my girl?" Granny Carne's eyes flash amber. She fixes me with a gaze so stern that I flush red and drop my eyes. Her eyes blaze amber, like an owl's eyes when it sees its prey. "Never throw a gift back to the giver, don't you know that? Cut the cake now. Conor, open the damper on my stove. That kettle's slow to boil."

And we know she won't say one more word about Mathew Trewhella or the mermaid or Ingo or any of it. I pick up the knife to cut the cake, and the scent of honey and ginger makes my mouth water.

Granny Carne won't talk, but she can't stop me thinking. The olden-days Mathew Trewhella, the one in the story, he never came home. Is that what he really wanted? Or did he decide in a split second to follow the mermaid, without realising that he could swim down that stream with her, but he'd never be able to swim back up it again? How did he feel when he knew there was no going back, ever?

How hard it must be to make such a choice. You'd be pulled from both sides, until you felt you were going to be torn apart. Choose Annie, or choose the Zennor mermaid. Choose home and family, or the love he wanted to follow. Maybe it was Annie who slashed the wooden belly of the carved mermaid. Maybe she hated her that much.

Have I got to choose too? The question beats in my head like the sound the waves make when they rush up on to the sand, and drain away. Swash and backwash, that's what it's called. Dad told me. He said, *Isn't it wonderful to think, Saph, that all the time we're alive those waves are beating on the shore, just as our hearts are beating in our bodies. It never stops. And when our hearts stop beating, the waves will still be coming in and out, the same as ever, until the world ends.*

"I think you've cut enough of that cake now," says Granny Carne. I look down in surprise at the slices lapping over the white plate, beautifully neat and even. I didn't realise I'd cut so many. The honey cake is sticky and golden, studded with pieces of crystallised ginger. Granny Carne makes tea, and we all sit round the table. Conor and I talk to Granny Carne about Sadie, and how Jack's mum had said we could have her a year ago, and Jack didn't mind because they already had Poppy and Jasper. But Mum thought it would make too much work, with her having to get a job in St Pirans.

"But it's you that really wants Sadie, Saph," Conor says, to my surprise.

"You do too."

"Not as much as you. I like her, but she'd be your dog, if she came."

"Would you mind?"

"No. It'd be good. I wouldn't have to worry about you when you were at home on your own."

"I wouldn't ever be on my own, if I had Sadie."

Granny Carne says nothing much, just fills cups and plates. Later she tells us about a bull terrier with one eye that she had once, years ago, and how she's never had a dog since he died, because she didn't want to replace him. *I wonder how many centuries ago that was?* I think.

"What's so funny, Saph?"

"Nothing. Granny Carne, can I have a bit more cake?"

Conor has three slices, and I have two. It's one of the best cakes I've ever tasted, moist and light and meltingly sweet. My stomach is warm and full and I feel drowsy. I could sit here for hours, chatting over tea. You could almost believe that Granny Carne is just like any other old lady who lives alone and remembers you when you were a baby, and knows everything about everyone in the village, and keeps a delicious cake ready in a tin, in case someone comes.

A bee knocks against the window, buzzing. Granny Carne goes to the window, opens it a crack and tells the bee to go away, she'll be up later. The bee flies off at once, up into the blue, as if it understands.

"They like to know what's going on," Granny Carne explains. "You always have to tell the bees. If there's a birth or a death, you tell them before you give the news to anyone else, and then they're satisfied."

Yes, you could *almost* believe that Granny Carne is just like any other old lady who lives alone. But not quite.

"Could I visit the bees?" asks Conor abruptly. I stare at him in surprise.

"You want to talk to my bees?" says Granny Carne.

"Yes. If that's OK."

Granny Carne gets up, and stands tall as a queen, considering Conor. She says nothing more, but after a long moment she turns and walks out of the cottage door.

"I think she's angry," I say nervously. "I wish you hadn't asked. They're *her* bees."

"She's not angry," says Conor calmly. "She'll be back in a minute."

He's right. Granny Carne comes back in with her beekeeping clothes over her arm.

"I keep them out in the shed," she says. "Bees don't like the smell of houses. Now then, Conor."

She hands him a pair of baggy white trousers and a beekeeper's smock. Conor pulls them on over his jeans and T-shirt.

"My boots will be too small for you, but you'll be all right with your trainers. Tuck the trousers in so the bees can't crawl on to your skin. They don't want to sting, since it's death to them, but if they find themselves trapped in your clothes they'll panic. Now the hat."

Conor puts on the beekeeper's hat and veil. Granny Carne adjusts it, and stands back to check he is completely protected.

"You'll do."

We walk in single file up a little path on to the highest part of the Downs. Granny Carne first, then Conor, then me. The sun blazes on us. The buttery, coconut scent of gorse fills the air, and sparrows flit out of the bushes as we go by. We tread heavily, to warn any snakes there may be. It's the kind of day an adder would come out to bask on a stone.

The ground dips, and there in a protected hollow ahead of us is a beehive. Even from this distance I can see a smoky blur of bees going in and out, and hear the low hum of their busyness.

"We won't go any closer, Sapphire," says Granny Carne, "and you keep nice and still now, and talk soft."

She steps forward a pace and stands there, listening. "Yes, you can visit them," she says to Conor after a while. "There's no trouble in the hive. They're happy."

"What do I do?"

"Walk forward slowly. Don't worry if some of them settle on you. They'll want to know what you're made of."

"Won't they think Conor is you, if he's wearing your clothes?"

"No. You can't fool the bees. Then when they're used to you, go right up to the hive and tell them what you want to tell them. Only go gentle. Bees don't like a flurry."

"What if it's a question? Is that all right?"

"There aren't many who can get an answer from the bees," says Granny Carne seriously.

"But *you* can," Conor says, and she nods.

"Me and the bees have lived together a long time. We're like family. You go on now, show respect and they won't harm you."

Conor steps forward slowly. It seems a long journey to the beehive. A small cloud of bees comes out to meet him, and circles his head. Conor doesn't seem worried. He just keeps going until he reaches the hive, and then he settles very gently on to his knees, so that his face is level with the hole where the bees are coming in and out.

I watch. Conor stays very still. I can't see his face, only his back. I can't hear anything but the buzz of the bees.

"Ask them now," murmurs Granny Carne, as if to herself. But Conor seems to hear her. I hear the sound of his voice, but not what he's saying. The steady hum of the bees dips into silence for a few moments. They're listening! They're really listening, just as Granny Carne said. And then the sound of the bees swells back again. Conor stays there a little while longer, then very slowly he rises and begins to move backwards, away from the hive.

"Go gentle," mutters Granny Carne, but she doesn't need to remind him. The bees don't seem bothered by Conor at all.

We walk back to the cottage. I'm longing to ask Conor what happened, but Granny Carne's silence forbids questions. He takes off all the bee-keeper's gear in the garden, so she can put it directly into her shed.

"You asked your question then," says Granny Carne as we're leaving.

"Yes."

"It's not for me to know if you had your answer. But I can tell the bees liked you."

Conor grins. "I liked them. I want to keep bees one day."

"You work on that then. Anything you want will happen if you work on it. Sapphire'll only get that dog if she makes it happen."

"Did she mean I *will* get Sadie?" I burst out as soon as we're far enough from the cottage. "Was it like a prophecy, when she sees into the future?"

"I don't think so. I think it was just a piece of advice."

"Oh. That's no good then." My curiosity gets the better of me. "Go on, Conor, tell me what you asked the bees."

"I asked them if Dad was still alive."

"What?"

"You heard. I asked them—"

"But why? How would they know?"

"You remember what I said about Dad coming up here last year? I thought that maybe Granny Carne had talked to the bees about Dad. Or even that Dad had talked to them. Maybe that's how it works. Maybe the bees help her to see into the future."

"You'd have noticed if Dad had gone up to the hive with her."

"I might not have done. I was round the back, remember,

watching the frogs. Anyway, when Granny Carne said that the bees have to be told about births and deaths, suddenly I thought that maybe they would know about Dad. And they would remember, because they keep their memories in the hive."

I stare at Conor in dread. What have the bees told him? But surely he couldn't look so normal if they'd said Dad was – not alive any more.

"So? What did they say?"

"Nothing," says Conor. "I was an eejit to think they would. But there was something all the same..."

"What?"

"I don't know. I can't describe it. A warm feeling. A good feeling. I think they did listen to me. They didn't mind me being there."

"Conor, do *you* still really think Dad's alive?" There. I've dared to say it at last. Sometimes I'm so scared that we're just pretending to ourselves, month after month after month...

"Yes," says Conor.

CHAPTER TWENTY

"**M**um, what are *you* doing home already? It's only two o'clock!"

"Are you all right, Mum?"

Mum blushes. "I thought you two were out for the day," is all she can think of saying. There on the table is a pile of chicken and tomato sandwiches. Mum's got the bread knife in her hand, ready to slice them. But what a huge pile: far more than Mum could ever eat. She must have made them for all of us.

I thought you two were out for the day.

No. Not for us, then. Thoughts whizz about in my head. The sandwiches are not the only food on the table. There's a pot of olives, a straw basket of cherry tomatoes, a bag of cherries, a packet of my favourite crisps, which we hardly ever buy because they cost so much, and a bottle of wine. The kind of expensive stuff that doesn't come into our house unless it's left over from the restaurant. But these don't look like leftovers.

Conor's hand snakes into the cherry bag. Mum slaps it away.

"Get off! Those aren't for you."

"Who are they for, then?" asks Conor, but both of us have already guessed the answer. *Roger*. Roger has come home with Mum, while we were up at Granny Carne's. Mum thought we were out of the way, so she said, *Dear, darling Roger, do come to my beautiful cottage. My horrible children won't be there.*

"Won't you lose your job if you just go home whenever you feel like it, Mum?" I ask her.

"Saph," says Conor in a quiet, watch-what-you're-saying voice, but I take no notice of him.

"So where's *Roger*, then?" I ask.

"Right," says Mum, dropping her knife with a clatter. "That's it. I've finally had enough. You don't want me to have any life at all, do you, Sapphire? As long as I'm working all the hours God sends and looking after you the rest of the time, you're happy. But if I try to go out – or have a friend – oh no, that's not allowed. Well, I've got news for you, my lady—"

Don't say it, Mum, I beg inside myself. *Don't tell me you're going to marry Roger.*

"—I've got news for you." Mum's finger stabs the air. "I have got a life, not much I grant you, and just for once I'm going to do something for myself. Yes, I know those are your favourite crisps but just for once you're not having them, and Conor's not having those cherries either. I'm going on a picnic and it is NONE OF YOUR BUSINESS," yells Mum, and now her finger is stabbing right in my face. I jump back. The pile of sandwiches wobbles and begins to collapse. Conor leaps forward, but he's too late. Chicken and tomato filling spatters over the floor.

I dive down to help but Mum shouts, "Leave them! I'm not giving anyone sandwiches that have been on this floor. Look at the state of it. I've asked you a dozen times to clean it, Sapphire."

An evil spirit jumps into my mouth. "If we had a dog, the sandwiches wouldn't be wasted," I say. Mum's hand slaps down on the table.

"Saph, *go out*. Just go outside," urges Conor. But I can't. I can't even find the door, I'm crying so much.

"Oh Sapphy." The next moment Mum's arms are around me and I can feel that she's starting to cry too. "Why do you do it? Why do you always make things so hard for everyone?"

"I don't, it's you that does—"

"It's both of you," says Conor flatly. "You're both just as bad as each other."

Mum pushes my tangly hair back and holds my face between her hands so that I've got to look at her.

"Listen to me. I wasn't planning to come back, that's why I didn't tell you. What happened is that Roger came in while we were setting up for lunches, and said he was going to do his first dive today," she says, in a voice which I know is meant to be soothing. "The weather's perfect for it, and the tide. Gray was there too – he's Roger's dive buddy for this trip. They're going to do an exploratory dive out by the Bawns. And Roger said he'd already asked Alissa at work if she'd swap shifts with me, and she was OK about it. So I'm going in to work tomorrow, on Alissa's shift, instead of having my day off then."

If Mum thinks I'm going to be distracted by details of her shifts, she's mistaken. "But you don't *ever* come down to the cove, Mum. You hate the sea."

I feel as if Mum's betraying everything. She's turning into a different person. Dad always wanted her to come down to the water, and she never would. We never went out in the boat together. But now, because of *Roger*, suddenly everything's changed and Mum's longing to go for a seaside picnic.

"You won't really go down to the cove, will you?" I ask disbelievingly.

"Oh yes, I will," says Mum. "It's all gone on long enough. It's time to open up my life a bit."

"You're never going out in the boat with Roger and Gray!"

"No," says Mum. "I can't push myself as far as that yet. But maybe one day I will. Roger'll help me."

"*Roger*," I say, trying to put everything I feel into the name.

"You shouldn't be so dead against him," says Mum.

"Why not?"

"Because you don't know what he's like. You don't even want to find out. He's a good man. He cares about both of you. He even—"

"Even what?"

"Never mind. I shouldn't have said anything."

"Mum! What shouldn't you have said anything about?"

Mum glances at Conor for help, but Conor's not saying anything.

"All right, then. Roger thinks – for some unknown reason – that I'm not being fair to you about the dog business. He reckons you're old enough and responsible enough to have a dog. But if he'd seen today's carry-on, he might change his mind."

"Mum!" My thoughts are not just whizzing around now, they are performing loops and swoops and dives and turning back on themselves. Roger – *Roger* – thinks Mum's not being fair about Sadie. And he's trying to get her to change her mind. Trying to persuade her that we can have a dog...

Pictures crowd into my head. Sadie, in our house, in her own basket. Sadie, padding upstairs to my room to wake me in the mornings – or maybe even sleeping in my room. Me taking Sadie for long walks whenever I want. Taking Sadie on the coast path, up on the Downs, checking her paws for thorns, brushing her coat, giving her a bath outside, taking her to the vet, whistling for her when she's roaming around outside...

Come on in, Sadie girl, Conor's gone up to Jack's so it's just you and me this evening, but we don't mind, do we? We've got each other.

"Don't look at me like that, Sapphy. It's not decided yet."

"Oh, Mum."

"I'm still thinking about it. Mary Thomas says she'd keep an eye on the dog during the day, when you were back at school."

"I can't believe it."

"Take it easy, Saph," says Conor.

"We won't say any more about it now," says Mum. "I must get on with this picnic. They'll be here soon."

"You're really going down there, then, Mum?" Conor asks. He sounds like an adult, not a boy. "Are you sure you'll be all right?"

"Maybe she'll take up diving," I say, before I can stop myself. Mum shudders.

"One day at a time," she says. She lets go of me, and I step back.

"*One day at a time, sweet Jesus*," I sing, then I continue, because Dad always did, "*One drink at a time, sweet Jesus.*"

"I'd be angry if I thought you knew what you were singing, Sapphire," says Mum severely. "Making mock like that."

"She's only singing what Dad used to sing," says Conor. Dad's name falls awkwardly, and conversation stops. Mum looks from one of us to the other.

"I'd better get on," she says at last. "Roger and Gray are bringing the boat around," and she begins to butter more bread.

Conor and I look at each other. For the first time, what's about to happen seems real. I'd rather keep on thinking about Sadie, but I can't. Roger and Gray are coming here. They're going to dive. *An exploratory dive by the Bawns*, Mum said.

Roger thinks it's an ordinary dive, like he's done a hundred times before. Him and his dive buddy and his powerful boat and all his wonderful equipment. Roger, Mr Experienced Diver.

But Faro's there. The Mer. All of it. The tiny bit of Ingo that I've seen, and everything else that lies hidden. It's hidden because it wants to be hidden. The Mer don't want Air People there. The Bawns mean something that I don't understand. Faro said so. It was when we were talking about the Bawns that he got so angry. Faro said that Roger would never go there. *All of Ingo will prevent it* – was that what he said? Or was it something about protecting the Bawns? *All of Ingo will protect them.* Whatever his exact words were, Faro meant every one of them. His face was like the sea when a storm's whipping up on it.

"Me and Saph'll go on down to the cove then, Mum, unless you need us here," says Conor. "Sure you'll be all right climbing down?"

"I can manage," says Mum. "It's not the climb down that worries me." She makes herself smile and I know how afraid of the sea she still is. How hard she's trying, because of Roger. "I've got to do it on my own."

"Be careful. The rocks are slippery," warns Conor. "Let me help you, Mum."

"Do you think I don't know by now what the sea can do?" asks Mum quietly. "You two go off now, and let me finish this in peace. I'll see you down there later. Roger'll be glad to show you the diving equipment, Con. He says there's a starter diving course you can take, at the dive school in St Pirans. It's just a week, to give you a taste of what diving's like. He's going to fix it up with that friend he told you about."

As soon as we are out of the cottage, we start to run.

"Conor, they hate divers. Faro told me—"

"I know. Air People with air on their backs—"

"Taking Air into Ingo. Did Elvira tell you that as well?"

"Yeah."

"And he's going to the Bawns. He doesn't know—"

"What about the Bawns? What doesn't Roger know?"

"I'm not sure. But it's something serious. Faro said there was something out at the Bawns so important that the whole of Ingo would defend it. He wouldn't tell me what it was."

"And Roger's going to dive there. That's all we need."

Down the track, down the path, over the lip of the cliff, and down, down, hearts pounding, hands slippery with sweat, stumbling on loose stones and catching hold of the rock. Down and down, sliding on seaweed, jumping from rock to rock, past limpets and mussels and dead dogfish and dark damp crevices where the sun never goes and there are piles of driftwood and bleached rope and plastic net buoys.

And down on to the firm white sand. Everything is calm and sunny and beautiful. The sea is like a piece of wrinkled silk. The beach is empty. Little waves curl and flop on to the shore. We shield our eyes from the light and squint towards the rocks at the entrance of the cove. Nothing. No sign of a boat.

"They must be out there."

"How long would it take to come round by boat from St Pirans?"

"I don't know. Not that long. Roger's boat has a power-ful engine."

"Maybe it'll break down," I say hopefully.

"It's new. Anyway, dive boats usually carry back-up parts," says Conor.

You can't see the Bawns from here. The rocks at the mouth of the cove hide them. Maybe Roger and Gray are out there now, preparing to dive. They don't know what the Bawns mean to the Mer. They'll trespass without knowing what they're doing, and all the force of Ingo will be against them.

"If only we had a boat," mutters Conor.

"We've got to get out there somehow, before they do!"

"We can't," says Conor. "We'll just have to wait. It'll be OK, Sapphy. Roger knows what he's doing. He's a dive leader."

"What's that mean?"

"He's got loads of experience. He's passed exams and stuff. He'll be all right."

But Conor doesn't sound as if he believes it, and nor do I.

"Conor, we can't just stand here waiting. We've got to do something."

"Swim?" asks Conor sarcastically. He knows as well as I do why we mustn't swim out of the cove. We know how dangerous it is. There's always the rip waiting to take you.

The water's deep and cold and wild, and a swimmer who gets swept away doesn't last long.

"But I've *got* to do something, Conor. It's my fault. It was me who told Faro about Roger."

"You didn't mean any harm."

"I did. You don't understand." I pause, and think. Maybe, at the same time that I was telling Faro about Roger diving near the Bawns, Roger was telling Mum that she ought to think about letting us have Sadie. "I *wanted* Roger to get hurt," I whisper. "Oh, Conor, why have I got so much badness in me?"

As I say these words a gull plunges, screaming, from the cliff. We both turn. It's coming straight for us, diving, wings sleek against the air currents. Its beak is open. Down it comes, crying out in its fierce gull voice. It swerves above our heads, so close that my hair lifts in the wake of its claws. Up it soars, high into the blue, then it turns and positions itself for a second dive. Again it screams out in its wild language as it balances on the air. And down it comes again, passing my ear with a shriek.

"It's trying to tell us something."

"What?"

"If only I could understand it."

But maybe... maybe... if I really try... I could make out what the gull is saying. It wants me to know, that's why it's diving so close. Here it comes again.

"I can't hear what you're saying," I shout above the gull's shrieks. "Please, please try to say it so that I can under-stand—"

The gull's screams batter my ears again, but all I get from it is noise.

"Please try, *please*. I know you're trying to tell me something important..."

And then it happens. I am through the skin of English, and into another language. Suddenly the new language is all around me. The jumble of wild shrieks changes to syllables, then words. The gull brakes in the air and hovers just above us. His wings beat furiously and his claws dig into the air for balance. He fixes me with a cold yellow eye.

"Go to Ingo. Go to Ingo NOW."

And he spreads his wings and swoops low over the water, out to sea.

"He was going crazy about something, wasn't he?" says Conor. "Wouldn't it be great if we could understand what birds are saying."

"He wants us to go into Ingo," I say.

Conor stares. "You're making it up."

"You know I'm not. Look at me. Am I lying?"

Conor scrutinises me. At last he says reluctantly, "No. But you could be crazy too."

"The gull said, *Go to Ingo now*."

"Then it's definitely mad. We can't go into Ingo on our own."

"I think we can. I think it's the same as understanding what the gulls say. If you want to enough, you can. And as soon as we're in Ingo we can get out to the Bawns. The rips won't hurt us. You can't drown when you're in Ingo."

"*You* could understand the gull, Saph. It just sounded

like a gull screeching to me. I've only ever been in Ingo with Elvira. Holding her wrist all the time."

"You mean... Do you mean that maybe I could get into Ingo without help from any of the Mer, but you couldn't?"

Conor's eyes flash with anger. "You don't think I'd let you go into danger on your own, do you? If you go, Saph, I'm going too."

Everything is turning around. All our lives it's been Conor who does everything first and best. Riding a bike, riding a horse, swimming, surfing, going out in the boat with Dad, climbing to the top of the cliffs. I've always been coming along behind, with Conor turning back to help me. And now, for the first time, there's something that's easier for me than it is for Conor.

Granny Carne said that inheritances don't come down equally, even to brother and sister. *Powerful Mer blood*, she said. I hope it's powerful enough for both of us. If Conor comes into Ingo with me, it's up to me to make sure that he's safe.

"We'll go together," I say. "We'll hold on to each other's wrists, like we do with Faro and Elvira. Then we'll be OK."

"Sapphire, don't be stupid," says Conor. "How do you think we're going to dive like that? You don't have to pretend. *I'm* the one who'll have to hold on. You could breathe on your own, couldn't you? You told me."

"Two are stronger than one," I say. It's what Mum always says, when she tells us to stick together. I know how hard it must be for Conor. He's the older brother, I'm the little sister. But now he's got to trust me. I've got to take us both into Ingo and bring us back safe. I think I can do it. I'm almost sure I can do it. But is "almost sure" good enough, when Conor's going to be depending on me? I've got to. We have no choice.

"Yeah, two are stronger than one," says Conor. "And if you let me drown, I'm telling Mum."

We both laugh and it breaks the tension. I take a deep breath.

"I suppose we'd better—"

"Let's go," says Conor.

We walk forward over the sand. There's the sea I've longed for, cool and transparent and calm. When I was up at Granny Carne's cottage I felt as if I'd die if I didn't get to the sea.

And here it is, and here I am. And I'm afraid. My hands are sticky with sweat and my heart bumps inside me so loudly that I'm sure Conor can hear it. I've been longing for Ingo so much, but now that I'm standing on the borderline I want to turn around and run until I'm back in the cottage with my duvet wrapped over my head. I feel sick and I can't breathe properly.

Give up, says a voice in my head. *Go back. You don't even like Roger. Why risk your life and Conor's to help him? You know how dangerous it is. Go home now. No one will blame you. No one will know. You're only a child. Roger's a grown man, he can take care of himself.*

Yes. It's true. It's Roger's fault for coming here. It's not my responsibility. I can tell Conor that it's too dangerous and I haven't got the power to take him into Ingo. Nobody will ever know if it's true or not.

But then I hear Granny Carne. Of course I can't really hear her, but I remember her words so strongly that it's like her voice speaking in my ear: "You've got Mer blood in you, Sapphire. It's come down to you from your ancestors. You can do it."

Granny Carne will know that I had a choice, and I went home. And Conor will know too. And most of all, I will always know, and I won't be able to pretend to myself. I can try to help Roger or I can abandon him, and let him blunder into the Bawns with all of Ingo against him.

Roger tried to help me. We talked about Sadie in the kitchen and Roger understood about her. He told Mum he thought we were old enough and responsible enough to have a dog. Maybe Mum won't ever let me have Sadie, but if she doesn't, it's not because Roger didn't try.

I can try to help Roger, or not. *The choice is mine.*

As soon as I say these words to myself, the noise of blood rushing in my ears doesn't frighten me so much. I'm not panicking any more. The choice is mine. I can make it.

I look around, and spot another gull on the rock where Faro sat the first time I saw him. The gull leans forward, watching us, neck outstretched and beak wide, the way gulls do when they're warning you off their territory. This time I understand straight away.

"NOW!" shrieks the gull. "Go to Ingo NOW."

CHAPTER TWENTY-ONE

ngo is angry. We know it as soon as we are beneath the skin of the water, as soon as the pain of entering Ingo fades enough for us to notice anything else. Currents twist around us like a nest of snakes. The sea boils and bubbles. Down and down we go, spiralling, while white sand whirls around us, beaten by the underwater storm. The rage of the sea catches us and blows us before it like leaves in the wind.

"Look out!" says Conor. "Rocks!"

We're being swept towards the black rocks that guard the entrance to the cove. Ingo can't drown us, but it has other ways of destroying us if it wants to.

"Don't hurt us," I plead under my breath. "We haven't come to harm you."

The wicked spikes of the rock shoot past, less than a metre away. This time, Ingo has let us escape. We plunge into deep dark water, dragged by a current that lashes like a switchback. Down, down, down, deep into Ingo. Suddenly the current throws us off.

We've got to swim. I peer through the surging water, looking for some sign of the Bawns. Has the current carried us past them already? The water's so dark and wild, so strong, that I don't know if I can swim against it. I kick with all my strength, then kick again, but it's like trying to swim in a dream. Conor tugs my wrist.

"Saph, you OK?"

I turn to him. "I'm fine," I start to say, then realise that it's Conor who doesn't look right. There are blue shadows around his eyes and mouth, and his face is twisted with pain. His legs move feebly. But Conor is a brilliant swimmer, much better than me. What's the matter with him? Why isn't he swimming?

And then I know. Conor is not getting enough oxygen. Ingo won't let him. He's getting some oxygen through me, but only a little. Not enough.

"Conor, hold on to me! Hold tight."

Conor's grip on my wrist is weak. In a flash of terror I realise that I'm all he's got, and I'm not strong enough. Not when Ingo is angry, and the waters are dark with danger. Not when we're being whirled through the deep water like human rags inside a giant washing machine. I catch hold of Conor's other wrist and try to find his pulse. It's there, but it's so hard to feel that I'm frightened. Conor's fingers are slipping off my wrist.

"Conor! You've got to hold on!"

"M'OK, Saph. Tired."

"Don't try to swim. I'll swim for both of us. Just keep still. Try to relax."

Try to relax. You idiot. You brought him down here. You thought you had enough strength for two, and he believed you. It's your fault, Sapphire, no one else's.

"Can't breathe," mutters Conor.

Oh God, he mustn't start trying to breathe. It's dangerous. There's no air here. Oxygen is flowing smoothly into my body, but not into Conor's. He's suffering, it's hurting him. We're so deep down, I'll never get him to the surface in time. And even if I do, once we're out of Ingo, the sea will drown us both—

"Conor, don't try to breathe! You mustn't!"

What can I do? How can I help him? We should never have come alone. If Faro was here – Faro would be strong enough to help—

"Faro!" I cry out with all my strength. "Faro!"

"Don't, Saph. Faro won't help. He's with the Mer. He's on their side."

Conor's eyes are dull, half shut. We cling to each other as the current spins us around and drags us through the wide mouth of our cove. Below us the floor of the sea falls away. Deep, dark, stormy water sweeps us along. I hold on to Conor with all my strength but he's barely grasping me. His head falls back.

"Faro! Help us!"

I am sure Faro can hear me. I am sure he is there, just out of sight behind the tumult of the water. I know it. How can Faro let Conor suffer like this? Why won't he come to us?

The cry of the gull flashes over my mind. He spoke to

me, and I understood. Maybe I am using the wrong language to call Faro. Faro is Mer, not Air. Maybe I can find that other language, buried deep inside me. I found words before. *Moryow... broder...*

My ancestors had powerful Mer blood, I think fiercely. They passed their power down to me. It comes down from generation to generation, and it doesn't weaken. I am human, but if Granny Carne's right, I am also partly Mer. I can make Faro hear me. I must help Conor. *Broder, broder...*

I grasp Conor as tightly as I can. He's not holding on to me any more. Maybe he can't feel where I am. I'm going to lose him. He's going to drift away, my Conor, down and down into Ingo until he's lost. And I said I'd bring him back safe.

No. I'm not going to let it happen. If I have any power in Ingo, I'll *make* Faro come to me.

I open my mouth. Strong salt water bubbles into it, stroking my tongue and my palate, filling my throat. If I can make words out of water, Faro will hear me.

In my head there are words I didn't know that I knew. *Say them, Sapphire. All you've got to do is speak.* They fill my mouth. They echo in my ears. They pour out in strange syllables that I've never spoken before. It's a new language that sounds like the oldest and most familiar language in the world, shaped out of salt and currents and tides.

"Faro, I ask you in the name of our ancestors to come to me now."

The words echo more and more loudly, booming in my head, making waves of sound that are picked up by the water and carried away. *Faro… in the name of our ancestors… Faro… Faro…*

And he is here. Suddenly there on the other side of Conor, swimming alongside us, his hand closed tight around Conor's wrist. As I watch, the blue fades from under Conor's eyes and from around his mouth. Warm brown floods back into Conor's skin. His eyes open, bright and alert. He looks around, as if he's just woken up.

"Wow! This is like being inside a fantastic jacuzzi, Saph!"

And suddenly it is. The violence of the sea isn't terrifying any more. It's like a huge, wild game. We twist and turn and plunge and dive. It's like bodysurfing, but a million times better because we are part of the waves and free to go with them wherever we want. Like surfing in a world where the wave never breaks.

"Roger," yells Conor as he balances with Faro on a surging rope of current. "We mustn't forget Roger."

"Roger? Who is Roger?" asks Faro, his voice smooth as silk. But I know he's only pretending. He knows full well who Roger is.

"He's a diver. I told you about him. But he

doesn't mean any harm. He doesn't know what he's doing."

"You are talking Air to me now," says Faro, his tail savagely slashing a cloud of bubbles. "It wasn't Air talk that brought me here to help you. If I remember our ancestors, then so must you."

"I do remember them."

"You remember them when you want to, Sapphire. When you need them. Not when Ingo needs you. Your head is full of Air."

"I wish you two would stop arguing," says Conor. "We must be close to the Bawns now."

"It's all right, Con. They would never dive in this," I say quickly. "It's much too wild."

"But it's not wild on the surface," says Faro. "It looks perfectly calm, up there. You'd never guess there was a storm in Ingo." He grins at me, his face bright with malice. "Perfect diving conditions."

"Don't, Faro!"

Faro rolls to face me. "You are going to see something, my little hwoer."

"I'm not your sister. Elvira's your sister."

"It's just a figure of speech. Mer speech, that is. Look ahead. There are the Bawns."

I would never have thought the Bawns would be so huge. They loom ahead of us like a mountain country. The part that you can see above the water is nothing compared to these underwater peaks and valleys. I thought the Bawns were just rocks, but that was an Air thought.

"You're going to see something," repeats Faro, pulling us forward.

We are in the shadow of the Bawns now. The surge of the sea is calmer. The water is clear and there is a strange light, like moonlight. Every detail shows: white glistening sand below us, scattered with shells and crab skeletons, sculptured rock, darting fish.

"This way. Quietly."

We swim around a broad shoulder of rock then suddenly stop dead as Faro back-fins.

"There," he says.

A plain of sand spreads out in front of us, protected by the mountain range of the Bawns. The wind dies. The surge of the sea fades to stillness. Here, the sea is as quiet as a garden at the end of a long summer day. And scattered on the plain of soft, glistening, rippled sand there are figures like ghosts, or dreams. I blink, believing they'll disappear like shadows, but when I open my eyes the figures are still there. Bowed, bent, their hair as silver as the sand, they rest, half lying, half drifting in the still water.

"They are our wise ones," says Faro. "They will die soon."

As I watch, a gentle current lifts a lock of silver hair from one of the figures, and lets it fall back, softly, against the bowed shoulders.

"Nothing can hurt them. Nothing comes near them," says Faro. "Look. The seals guard them."

It's true. Watchful and powerful, grey seals patrol the edges of the plain. They swim to and fro, along a borderline that's invisible to me, turning their heads to scan the water and the mountain range of rock that rises behind us.

"They've seen us," says Faro. He raises both hands, palms flat and outwards, saluting the seals. "We can come this far," he adds, "but if we tried to go down to the plain, the seals would attack us."

"But you're Mer. Why would they attack you?"

"I'm not ready to die yet. The seals know that. Only Mer who are ready to die will cross the borderline. Their families will come this far with them, but no farther."

"It's beautiful," says Conor under his breath. "But they're not all old, are they?"

I look where he's pointing. He's right. Among the old there are a few young Mer. One looks like a girl, younger than me.

"We get sick, just as you do. We have accidents, just as you do," says Faro. "Not everyone lives to be old."

"What's that music?" asks Conor suddenly.

I strain my ears. I haven't noticed any music.

"There it is again," says Conor. "Listen!" He looks at me, his face bright with pleasure, but I still can't hear anything. Faro looks at Conor with surprise, and something else which I can't identify.

"What kind of music can you hear?" he asks.

"I don't know," says Conor. "It's a bit like the sound you get when you hold a shell up to your ear. But it's much sweeter, and it's full of patterns. Listen, there it is again. Can't you hear it, Saph?"

"No," says Faro. "Neither of us can. It's rare to hear it, even for us. And you're human. Some Mer have the gift of hearing it all their lives, but most of us only hear it when we come to die. It's the song the seals sing to us when we come to Limina."

"This place is Limina?" asks Conor.

"Yes."

"Of course. You're right, that's what they're singing," says Conor, and for a strange moment it's as if he knows more about this place than Faro. "That's what they are singing about. Listen, Saph. Try to hear it. It's so beautiful."

"I can't hear it," I say.

"You will one day," says Faro. "Limina is where we all come, and the seals watch over us until we die. No Air Person has ever seen this."

"But—"

"Your ancestors came here too, when they were wise," says Faro. "This is where they left their bones. Do you think I could bring you here, if you weren't bound to it by your blood? You believe you belong only to Air, but I promise you, one day you'll cross into Limina alongside me."

I want to argue, but I don't, and as I stare out over the plain my arguments drift away. How beautiful it is. Ingo has given them birth, Ingo will receive them back in death. There's nothing to be afraid of here. But how strange it is that Conor can hear the music and I can't, even though I can swim alone in Ingo and Conor nearly died without Faro's help. I wonder why that is. It doesn't seem fair that only Conor can hear the seals' music.

It doesn't seem fair because you want to come first in Ingo, Sapphire, says a small inconvenient voice inside me. *You quite liked it that Conor couldn't keep up with you here in Ingo, didn't you? It made a nice change, didn't it?*

Yes, I have to admit it. That little voice inside me is

telling the truth. I was jealous. But how pathetic it would be, to be jealous of Conor, and the look on his face now as he listens to the song of the seals.

I belong here too. I am bound to it by my Mer blood. That's what Faro said. Conor and I are both part of Ingo.

The three of us float there in a dream, Conor holding my wrist, Faro holding Conor's. The grey seals patrol with their watchful eyes, and the Mer who have passed into Limina rest on the shimmering sand. Time seems to have disappeared. There is only now, and now might last for ever.

For ever. Never changing. No one ever coming to disturb it except families bringing those who are ready to cross the border into Limina—

No!

I jolt out of my dream. It's like being shocked out of my sleep in the sunwater when Roger's boat passed over.

This is the place where Roger is going to dive. This is where he wants to explore for wrecks. Where the Mer are resting, preparing to die, that's where he'll dive. In a place that's so important to the Mer that Faro says the seals would even kill him, to protect Limina. They'd kill Faro. What would they do to a human trespasser? A shudder of terror runs over my skin.

"He must never come here. No Air person must ever see this," I say aloud. Conor looks at me curiously. Faro nods approval.

But even while I'm speaking, the dream wraps itself round me again and my fear vanishes. Roger is far away, in another dimension. Let him stay there. Ingo is what's real. Can it really be true that this is the place where my ancestors died – mine and Conor's? But my ancestors are buried in Senara churchyard. When I was little I used to trace the stone writing on their gravestones and imagine what they looked like. What did Faro say? *Do you think I could bring you here, if you weren't bound to it by your blood?*

For the first time I feel as if the veil that hides most of Ingo from me is being lifted. There's a whole world here, waiting for me. Waiting until I'm ready to understand it – and then it'll reveal itself—

"No Air Person must see this. No divers in Ingo," I say aloud.

"I knew you'd understand, once you'd seen this place," says Faro, as if he's read my thoughts. We look at each other in agreement, on the same side.

"What do you mean?" breaks in Conor. He swings round to us, turning his back on Limina. He's not listening to any music now. His eyes are sharp on me and Faro. "Do you mean Roger? How are you going to keep him out? What are you going to do?"

"We won't *do* anything," says Faro. His gaze drifts towards the patrolling seals. Grey seals are formidable creatures, in their own element. It's not safe to anger them. The swipe of their tail, their powerful muscles, their huge shoulders, the gouge of their teeth, their claws—

"I see," says Conor. He looks at me, and then at Faro. His look is a challenge. "Oh yes, we will do something," says Conor quietly.

"What?" asks Faro.

"I'm not going to stand by and watch Roger get hurt. You think it's all right for Roger to have an accident, do you? Just because he's strayed into your world without meaning to? It's not Roger's fault. He doesn't know this place is here. This *Limina*. It doesn't mean anything to him, how could it? He's got to be warned, so he doesn't come here. He won't dive if he knows."

"Won't he?" asks Faro. "Look over there. No, *there*. That shape in the sand."

"I can't see anything—"

"Yes, you can. There."

But all I can see is a dark mound, covered in weed.

"Part of a ship's hull," says Faro. "That's what your diver is looking for. It's buried there in the sand."

"Wow," says Conor, suddenly focusing on it. "Maybe it was a treasure ship."

"Maybe it was," agrees Faro.

"Haven't you ever explored it?"

Faro shrugs. "What for?"

"Gold? Jewels?"

Faro shakes his head. "We don't bother with them."

"But I thought…" I say, "I mean, in pictures, Mer Kings always have crowns and jewels."

"That's because Air People are drawing the pictures. They draw the things they'd want themselves, if they were kings. But do you know how heavy gold is? Just think of trying to surf a current with a lump of gold dragging you down."

"Faro, people don't wear lumps of gold. It's far too expensive. They wear a chain or something like that."

"A chain! Really, Air People are strange. Why would they want to chain themselves up?"

"They don't, it's—"

"Air People are in love with metal, as far as I can see. They'll do anything to get it. We hear them sometimes, digging tunnels deep under Ingo, mining for tin."

"That can't be true," says Conor. "All the tin mines round here closed years ago. You can't hear miners digging these days."

Faro shrugs. "They mined here for thousands of years. They'll be back. Air People will do anything for metal."

He looks out over the quiet plain, at the drifting, silvery figures in the ghostly light. They look as if a puff of current will carry them away.

"Look!" exclaims Conor, under his breath, grabbing my shoulder. "Over there! What's wrong with the seals?"

He's right. They've stopped patrolling. They are massing on the borderline, about fifty metres from the farthest outcrop of the Bawns. Two seals – five – seven. More are swimming towards the group from the far side of Limina. How fast they swim. How strong they are.

"They've seen something," says Conor under his breath. Faro says nothing. He just watches.

"What is it? What's wrong? Do you know what's going on, Faro?"

Faro shrugs. "Can't be sure. It's too far away. It could be anything."

His voice is carefully casual, but his face is tense. Something is going on, and it's serious.

"You've got to tell us, Faro!"

"I did tell you. The seals are guards. If they sense a threat to Limina, they'll deal with it."

"What threat?" Conor's voice is harsh. "What can they see that we can't?"

But I'm watching the seals. They mass together, move apart, turn, raise their heads as if they're—

"They're listening!" I say. "They can hear something." And suddenly knowledge leaps into my head. They're listening to something that I've heard too. A noise that doesn't belong to Ingo. The throb of an engine. A boat's engine, far away up on the surface.

"Roger's boat," says Conor.

"They've come, then."

We stare at each other. The fear in Conor's face mirrors and doubles the fear I know must be in mine. Only Faro isn't afraid. He looks relaxed but his face is intent, like a cat's when it's watching, waiting...

"Faro, you can't let this happen!"

"I can, Sapphire," he says very quietly, but with complete determination. "They'd think nothing of destroying the Mer, your divers. Can't you see what will happen to Limina once divers get near that wreck? Once humans know there's gold there? We're nothing to them. They don't even see us. They'll destroy our world and they won't even know they're doing it. Why should I help them? I am Mer, Sapphire. I belong to Ingo, not Air. I've made my choice."

I feel as if Faro has claws which are tearing the two halves of me apart. I could never say what he's just said. I could never say, *I am Mer*, without betraying the part of me that is Air, and human. Faro knows what he is, and I don't. I half belong, but I'm half a stranger.

I don't even *like* Roger. I wanted him to disappear out of our lives. And now I'm terrified, because it could be about to happen.

"Faro can let it happen," says Conor, with a determination that sounds equal to Faro's. "But I can't. I'm going to stop the seals."

"Conor, they'll kill you!" Their teeth, their claws. One seal would be hard to stop, and there are dozens of them. I swallow the taste of fear. Can't Conor see? These grey seals are the guardians of Limina. They'll do whatever they have to do to protect it.

"I can't let it happen, Sapphire," repeats Conor. "I can't let them kill Roger." He isn't boasting. He just sounds quiet, and determined.

"But you've forgotten one small detail," says Faro in his silkiest voice. "You need to hold on to my wrist. Sapphire's strength isn't enough for you. And *I'm* not going anywhere."

CHAPTER TWENTY-TWO

or long seconds Faro and Conor stare at each other like enemies.

"I'm not going anywhere," Faro repeats..

"So you think you've won," says Conor. Slowly, deliberately, he unclasps his hand from Faro's wrist. "But you haven't," he says, looking straight into Faro's eyes, every word full of purpose.

"Conor! Don't let go of him!"

"I've already let go, Saph. I'm going."

"Conor, no, no, you can't—"

But he's turned away.

"Conor!" I plunge forward, forgetting Faro. "Wait for me!"

He's swimming slowly, and I catch up with him in a few seconds. We are side by side, and as he glances at me I see that already he's paler.

"Take my wrist, Conor!"

"I'm going to the seals, Sapphire. Don't think you can stop me."

274

It was instinct that made me rush after Conor. My brother, going into danger. I had to follow him, stop him. Nothing else mattered.

But something else matters to Conor.

"Got to warn Roger."

Roger. In Ingo everything human seems far away. Even Mum, even our home. They don't seem real. But when Conor says those words, Roger comes into my mind as clear as day. He's standing in our kitchen. He's telling me about his black Labrador, Rufie.

Rufie was the best thing in my life, after we came back from Australia.

Roger told Mum she should change her mind about us having a dog. He didn't have to do that, but he did. Maybe... just possibly Mum was telling the truth when she said Roger cared what happened to us...

"Don't try to stop me, Saph," says Conor.

"I won't. I swear I won't. I'll – I'll help you."

"Swear and promise?"

"Swear and promise."

It's the strangest swear and promise we've ever done. We slap hands though the water and press our way forwards, to where the sea is thrashing with the movement of the seals. We skirt the jagged edges of the Bawns, keeping well clear of the borderline we must not cross. On one side there's the calm of Limina. On the other the wildness of angry water. Through the churn of waves around the Bawns the bulk of a grey seal looms, then vanishes. I peer through the seethe of bubbles. A great bull seal shoots upwards towards the surface, then another seal follows, and another. We stare up at them. So many seals. Now they're so close together that there isn't a chink of light between them – I can't count them, but more are still arriving—

What are they doing?

A wall of seals, solid, shoulder to shoulder. And then it parts. They are separate creatures again, twisting and diving. One, two, seven, nine – they're leaving the surface, coming back into Ingo—

But surely that's not a seal? Not that one there, the thin spindly one? It looks puny and out of place next to the strong sleek seals. And that's not a seal either, that black, stick-like body, turning over and over as it sprawls through the water—

"Oh my God," says Conor. "They've got them."

I see what Conor's already seen. Those stick-like creatures are two divers in wetsuits with air on their backs. The seals have got them. The divers' limbs flail as the seals toss them high, then let them fall. As each diver falls, another seal butts his body upward. The divers' heads flop back like puppet heads.

"They're playing football with them." I can't believe what I'm seeing. I'm watching a game in a nightmare. The divers tumble in slow motion, and every time they fall the seals are ready for them. Up they go, booted by the lash of a seal's tail.

"They're playing with them! It's horrible!"

"No," says Conor grimly, through lips that are already

turning blue. "It's not a game. They're pushing them in one direction – look. They're taking them somewhere."

He's right. The seals aren't just tossing the divers randomly. Each fall has a purpose. Each fall brings the divers closer to us, each brutal shove is in our direction. The seals are coming towards us. They want the divers here. Why?

The jagged underwater peaks of the Bawns glint like teeth, ready to rip and tear. If a man fell on them – if a diver was thrown on to them—

"They're going to smash them against the rocks," says Conor.

"They'll be killed, Con!"

"Yes. Come on!"

He's holding my wrist, but now he's the one driving us. We shoot up through the thick churning water, towards the seals.

They sense us before they see us. They turn. For a moment they forget to toss the divers, whose bodies start to drift downwards. The bull seal faces us, his shoulders huge, glistening with muscle.

Every detail of him burns into my mind. His eyes and whiskers, the sleek fullness of his skin, the bunched muscle under it, the power. And the anger of a guardian. Anger beneath his skin like muscle, powering him.

The seal comes closer. He seems to swell in my sight until nothing else is there. The bull seal blocks out everything. His head lowers and he starts to measure the space between him and us, ready to charge.

Until the day I go to Limina I'll see that seal's face. Behind him Roger's body drifts slowly downward. I don't know how I know it, but I recognise Roger as clearly as I recognise the seal's power. Roger, drifting through the water like a broken toy. *Rufie... best thing in my life...*

And then I hear the strangest sound. Like music, but not music. Syllables that fit together in wonderful patterns, like a puzzle in four dimensions. A sound you'd want to listen to for ever, if you once heard it.

The bull's whiskers quiver. The focus of his eyes shifts. He looks away from me, towards Conor.

I look sideways at my brother. His bluish lips are open, but his eyes are already half-closed and dulling as they did before. His head falls back. He can hardly move, but he can sing. All the strength he has left is pouring out of him in song. Conor sings, and the seals listen. The bull seal and all his companions listen. Slowly, their heads lift. Their shoulders relax. The bull seal's eyes are so close to mine that I think I see them change and soften.

Conor, you have your own power that belongs to you, never doubt that. The time will come to use it.

It only takes a few seconds. Before Conor finishes singing another seal has dived beneath Roger and caught him. Her teeth grip his wetsuit, but even from this distance I can tell that she has made her mouth soft to catch him, just as Poppy used to make her mouth soft to pick up her pups. She isn't hurting Roger. Another seal has captured

the second diver, Gray. They bring them to the bull seal,
the divers' limp bodies dangling in the water. Their heads
loll. I think they must be unconscious.

But the bull seal doesn't look at what the other seals
have brought him. He won't take his eyes off Conor. He
opens his seal mouth and begins to sing back his own
long and patterned song, which is like the brother of the
song Conor has sung. And this time I can hear the seal's
song. Maybe it's the other half of that puzzle in four
dimensions that Conor was making. As the song ends,
the bull seal shakes his great shoulders. The other
guardian seals have fallen back, except for those who
hold the divers. The bull seal calls to them, and they rise
up towards the surface, taking the divers with them.
Their movements are gentle now, as if the divers are as
breakable as eggs.

The divers' wet-suited legs trail. Their bodies are lifeless,
and their heads have fallen back. Maybe it's too late.
Maybe Roger and Gray aren't unconscious, but already
dead.

"Boat's up there," gasps Conor. "Got to get them into
boat. Seals can't do it. Come on."

"Will they let us?"

"Yes."

It feels like a nightmare, slow and heavy and tangled. We
swim up and up, pushing against the weight of the water.
Conor is heavy against me, barely breathing now. If the

seals weren't supporting Roger and Gray, we'd never get them to the surface. The weight of the divers is terrible. We push them up but they sag down again. There is no way that we're ever going to get them into the boat by ourselves. Conor's growing weaker by the second. No matter how tight he grips me, he can't get enough oxygen.

The seals aren't hostile any longer, but they make it clear they think their job is done. They push Roger and Gray towards us as if saying they're our problem now. They've delivered the divers over to us. They have done their duty, and protected Limina. The bull seal calls through the water one last time, and the seals who were helping us turn and dive towards the Bawns, leaving us alone with the divers. Immediately, we start to sink under their weight. Conor surely can't go on much longer.

"It's time to get Conor out of Ingo," says a calm, familiar voice behind me. I turn, and there is Faro. And not only Faro. A girl as well, who is familiar even though I've only seen her at a distance before. A girl with long dark hair, almost the same colour as mine and Conor's. It floats around her as mine does, like seaweed, below her waist. She has the same cool green eyes as Faro.

"Elvira." The name comes out of Conor's throat in a sigh.

"Quick, Sapphire," says Faro, "push up with all your strength. You can do it. Get Conor up into the Air. Elvira and I will look after the divers."

"You won't hurt them?"

"After all your heroic efforts?" he asks with a glint of malice. "No, we won't hurt them. Ingo has defended herself."

The weight of Roger and Gray falls away from me. Conor's eyes are closed as I push upwards with all my strength, thrusting him towards Air. And there it is, just above us, like a glittering plate of light. Air.

We burst through the skin before I have time to know that I'm leaving Ingo. The first gasp of air is like a knife going down into my lungs. I'm out of Ingo, coughing and spluttering, and it hurts. It hurts, and it shouldn't hurt. I'm *human.* I take another breath and the knife goes in again, doubling me over. The taste of Air makes me retch. I want to go back – let me go back—

"Saph!" Conor grabs my arm. "You OK? Here, hold on to me."

Conor's colour is better already. He doggy paddles vigorously, shaking his head so the water flies off it.

"I'm OK now," I gasp, and it's nearly true, even though each breath of air rasps like sand. "Give me a minute." I don't want Conor to guess how much it hurt for me to come out of Ingo. He'll be afraid. Conor will know what it means, when the Air hurts me.

We've come up a few metres from the boat. There's the ladder. But I can barely swim. The short distance to the ladder looks impossibly far. My arms are heavy, and I float helplessly as air stabs in and out of my lungs.

"We've got to get in the boat, Saph. Come on, you can make it. Hold on to me."

"Roger?"

"They're coming. Don't talk. Swim."

I cough out a mouthful of salt water. I'm full of sea,

that's why the air hurts. I cough again, choking, and spit out more water. That's better. For the first time a long, easy breath of air goes into me. I tread water and wipe my hair out of my eyes. "Conor. The divers. Are Faro and Elvira bringing them?"

"Yeah. I forgot Elvira was here," he says. The colour in his face deepens. *Oh yeah, you forgot. I believe you*, I think, but I haven't got the breath to say any more. The sun's too bright. The air's too sharp.

"Look, there they are!"

I turn. But I see the pain on their Mer faces as they enter Air and it stabs into their lungs, and I look away. I know how much it hurts. Like a thousand knives inside you. Faro won't want me to see him weak and suffering.

"Elvira!" calls Conor, flipping over and starting to swim towards her. Conor's strong now, stronger than any of us. I can't really swim yet. Elvira coughs, wiping the tears that have sprung into her eyes. Her wet hair clings to her neck and shoulders. She's supporting Roger, and Faro holds Gray.

"Get them up the ladder."

Even with four of us it's a nightmare struggle. They are grown men, unconscious dead weights in their diving equipment. Faro and Elvira are out of their element, hurting with the shock of Air. Each time we raise the divers towards the ladder, they slither back into the water.

"We can't do it this way," pants Conor. "Get in the boat, Saph." Conor and I scramble up the ladder and into the boat. We kneel, leaning over the side, hauling on Roger's arms in his cold, slippery wetsuit, while Faro shoves him upwards and Elvira swims round to the other side of the boat, still supporting Gray. She grips the side of the boat and presses her weight down hard to balance it, so we won't capsize. Elvira's strong. Even out of Ingo, Faro and Elvira are much stronger than me.

Grunting and sweating, Conor and I drag Roger up the ladder, bumping him, maybe hurting him. It doesn't matter. Nothing matters except getting him into the boat. Our muscles burn with the effort.

Suddenly Roger's weight shifts and he slithers forward like a fish we've caught, topples over and then slides into the bottom of the boat. He's doubled over, but there's no time to help him until we've got Gray into the boat. Gray's lighter than Roger, but I'm shaking now, I'm so exhausted.

"Faro, push harder! I can't get a grip on him!"

Air rasps in Faro's chest but there's no time for pity.

"Get his foot on the rung! Push him over! Don't let him fall back!"

And we do it at last. Gray flops forward. His weight carries him down and he sprawls beside Roger.

I crouch on the deck, feeling for Roger's pulse. My fingers dig into his cold flesh, but I can't pick up a beat. Panicking, I press deeper.

"That's the wrong place. Here." Conor pushes me aside. "His cuff's getting in the way—"

Conor kneels down, rolls back the latex cuff of the wetsuit, and finds the pulse point. For the longest few seconds I've ever known, Conor's fingers and face are still, concentrating.

He can't find the pulse. Roger is dead. Roger is dead and I couldn't stop it. I didn't help in time. I tried to stop it but it was too late.

It's all my fault. Roger didn't know what he was doing. We let him come out to the Bawns.

My mind goes dark with the horror of it. I could have saved Roger, I could have warned him about Ingo and the Bawns. Even if he hadn't believed me, at least I'd have tried to save him. But I didn't. *Mum*—

"I've got it. It's beating."

"He's alive! He's alive, he's going to be all right, he isn't dead—"

"Shut up, Saph. Stop yelling in my ear. Try and lift Gray's arm for me. I can't get at his pulse."

Gray's arm is wedged under Roger's body. Conor hauls and I push and we get it free. Again, Conor searches for the pulse in the cold limp flesh.

"He's there. I've got the pulse. Quick, we should've checked the airways first."

I bend over Roger's face. Against my cheek there's a faint warm flutter. Air. Human breath.

"Now we've got to get them in the recovery position."

They are breathing, and their hearts are beating. We haul them into the closest we can get to the recovery position, and then sit back on our heels, our arms and backs burning. I feel sick with relief. At that moment Roger moans terribly, deep in his stomach, rolls over and opens his eyes. He doesn't seem to know who I am or where he is. His eyes stare for a few moments as if they can't take in what they see, and then they close.

"He looked at me! Conor, Roger opened his eyes."

"We must get all this stuff off them quick. Roger's got foil blankets in one of the lockers."

"What for?"

"Stops people getting hypothermia, Roger said. If something goes wrong during a dive."

"They're going to be all right, aren't they?"

"I think so. They're probably in shock. That's dangerous, we've got to get them warm."

We don't even think about Faro and Elvira until much later. We don't realise that they're still there, waiting in the shadow of the boat, staying in the Air for our sake.

All that matters is that Roger and Gray are breathing, even though their faces are greyish under their tans and their skin is cold. We get the diving equipment off them somehow. Conor knows a bit about how it works, because of going out with Roger. I think we damage some of it but we don't care. We struggle to strip off their wet-suits, and get the foil blankets wrapped around them. I remember hearing that people lose most heat from their heads, so we wrap the blankets right over, leaving only their faces clear. They are semiconscious now and Roger's shaking. I wrap the foil blanket tighter.

They look like creatures from outer space with the

foil glittering in the sun. But their colour's better, I'm sure of it. They're pale, but not grey now. There's a long, deep scratch across Gray's face, with blood oozing out of it. That scratch came from a seal's claw. Will he remember that? I think how close they came to death. I shiver, but not because I'm frightened this time. It's the sadness of it. Roger and Gray, blundering into Ingo, not knowing what they were doing or what the consequences might be. And us not knowing, either, not really knowing. Air and Ingo set against each other, like enemies. The seals' terrible vengeance. Baby gulls and guillemots bobbing on the tide, saturated with oil. Everything we've done to Ingo swims in my mind and sickens me.

"Don't cry, Saph. They're going to be all right. Look, Gray's trying to open his eyes!"

"I know. I'm not crying because of that."

"What is it then?"

"Do you think Ingo and Air will always hate each other?"

Conor sits back on his heels and frowns. "I don't know. They're so different. So separate. They can't understand each other, because they never meet. Humans stay in the Air – on Earth – and the Mer stay in Ingo."

"But *we* don't."

"What do you mean?"

"We do both. We live in the Air, and we can live in Ingo."

"*You* can."

"You can too. And maybe we're not the only ones. There might be other humans who can cross over, only we don't know about them. There might be Mer who can cross over too."

"Maybe," says Conor slowly. "But don't let's talk about it now, Saph. I've had enough of Ingo for today. I've got to get the anchor up and get the engine working. Lucky I went out with Roger that time, I think I can remember how it works."

"Look! Roger's hand! It's moving."

I put my hand under the foil blankets and touch Roger's cold fingers. They reach for mine. He clasps my hand feebly.

"It's all right," I say, bending over him. "You're going to be OK. There was an accident. Me and Conor are looking after you."

Roger struggles to lift his head, but it seems to hurt him. He groans and his head falls back. He must be bruised all over, like a boxer coming out of the ring.

"It's OK," I repeat. "You're going to be fine. Don't try to move. You're safe."

A splash of salt water comes over the side of the boat. Salt spray flicks in my face. I get up from where I'm crouching, and look over the side.

There they are. Faro, and Elvira. Elvira's beautiful dark hair swirls in the water around her. Faro's eyes fix on mine.

"Are they alive?" he asks.

"Yes, they're alive."

"Ah," says Faro. It's the faintest sigh of Air going out of him. I can't tell if it's a sigh of relief, or a sigh of regret. But even Faro – no, surely Faro couldn't want them to die?

Suddenly Faro does something I've seen before, but only deep under the water. Now he does it on the surface. He curls his body tight and with all the muscled power of his tail he spins into a somersault, half in the water and half out of it. One turn – two – three—

The sea thrashes and sparkles. Faro is a whirling circle. As he comes round for the third time he straightens, lifts his tail and with all its power he smacks it down on the water so it sends a wave of spray into my face.

I wipe it off, laughing. There's Faro, upright in the water again, tail sculling for balance. He's laughing too.

"Goodbye, little sister," he says casually, and slips beneath the sea. I wait, leaning over the bow. Surely he'll come up again? Surely he's not going to disappear just like that, without saying any more?

But the sea is flat. Nothing moves. Not even a bubble rises.

Elvira! Where's Elvira?

I turn. Halfway down the boat, Conor is leaning towards the water. Elvira has drawn herself right up. They aren't talking, just staring at each other, their faces so close they almost touch. As I watch, Elvira slowly drops in the water. Her shoulders slip beneath it, her neck, and then her face, hidden in the cloud of her hair.

She's gone. Conor and I are left, staring at the surface of the sea. We wait for a long moment, then we turn and meet each other's gaze.

Our boat rocks, very gently. High above, a gull drifts,

watching us, crying out the news. Telling Ingo everything that has happened. I could understand what the gull is saying, if I tried. But I'm too tired to try.

CHAPTER TWENTY-THREE

aro, I never even said thank you. You helped me to bring Conor to the surface. Without you and Elvira we'd never have got Roger and Gray on board. So you did save us, even if you didn't want to.

There was no time to thank you or say goodbye, and now you've gone. The sea has swallowed you. There are so many things I want to say to you, but I can't, because Roger and Gray are waking up. First, Conor and I have to find a convincing reason for them to be in the bottom of Roger's boat, wrapped in foil blankets, covered in bruises and with their equipment damaged. We also have to explain how it happens that when they wake up the first people they'll see will be Conor and me. They're well able to remember that their boat was way out by the Bawns when they dived. They're also well able to remember that we weren't in their boat when they set off from St Pirans. And so where did we come from, and how?

While Roger and Gray are still semiconscious, we make our plans about what to say to them. How to convince them.

"We don't really have to convince them, Saph," whispered Conor. "It doesn't matter how unlikely our story is, does it? If the alternative to believing something unlikely is believing something impossible, then they'll *have* to believe us."

"You mean, if it's a choice between believing that we rescued them from Ingo with the help of two Mer People, after a battle with guardian seals, or believing that we swam out to help because we thought they were in trouble, they'll believe that we're Olympic swimmers."

Conor nodded. "They'll go with the Olympic swimming option. They'll have to. Hush. Roger's opening his eyes again."

Gray and Roger recover more quickly than we'd dared believe they would. Half an hour after Roger was feebly clutching my hand, he's standing up and giving Conor instructions about managing the boat.

Roger can't work out what's happened. What went wrong with the dive? Where did we spring from? Roger and Gray are bruised and bleeding and bewildered, but they're recovering fast and they're full of questions. They want answers.

"Conor and I were out on the rocks by the mouth of the cove, Roger. You know how you can see the Bawns from there, though you can't see them from the beach? We spotted your boat out there – we had Dad's binoculars with us. We watched you dive. They're really good binoculars. Conor wanted to watch you come up from the dive, so we waited. You were gone for a long time. We got worried. People are always saying how dangerous it is around the Bawns. We thought maybe something had happened to you. So we decided – we decided to swim out."

"*Swim out?*" asks Roger, frowning in disbelief.

"Yes," says Conor. "We didn't think there was time to fetch help."

"You swam out from those rocks? All the way to the boat? But we were anchored way out by the Bawns. You *swam*?"

"Yes."

Roger looks from one of us to the other. He looks like a judge in his foil-blanket robes. Slowly he shakes his head. No judge would believe us. Roger doesn't, can't believe us.

"That's – that's unbelievable," says Roger. But I stare back at him without blinking. After all, it is true. We *did* swim all the way out to the Bawns. It wasn't exactly swimming as Roger understands it, but he doesn't need to know that.

"My God, you were so lucky," says Roger at last, shaking his head again. He believes us! He has to believe us. He has no choice. How else could we have reached the boat?

Now Roger's foil-blanket robes crackle around him as he looks from one of us to the other. "My God, you two have no idea how lucky you were. What a crazy thing to do. All that way – and in that cold water. You weren't even wearing wetsuits. The currents round this coast are lethal.

You should never have tried to swim. What if you'd been swept away? You *should* have been swept away. Your guardian angels must have been working overtime."

We know, Roger, we know, I think, keeping my face innocent. *You don't need to tell us that this is a dangerous coast. Much more dangerous than you realise.*

"Conor and I know where the rip is," I continue. I put on a serious expression, as if I understand just how risky it was, and I want Roger to know we were as careful as we could be. "We kept well clear of the rip. And we were lucky that it was such a calm day. The sea was flat. I know we shouldn't've risked it, but we thought there'd been an accident and we had to get to you. We're strong swimmers, aren't we, Con?"

Conor gives me a look that means, *Don't push it, Saph.*

"And when we got out to the boat, we saw you both clinging on to the ladder. Even though you were nearly unconscious, you were holding on. We didn't know what had happened, but it looked like there'd been a bad accident. So Conor pushed and I pulled until we got you into the boat. Then we got the foil blankets and checked your pulse and stuff."

"Jesus. You guys must be pretty strong," says Gray in his twanging Australian voice, looking from me to Con and back again. "Hauling two grown men up a ladder after swimming that distance. You deserve a medal."

I check to see if he's being sarcastic, but he isn't. Like Roger, he's got to believe the incredible, because there is no alternative.

"It was pretty tough," I say modestly. "But we sort of knew we had to keep going, didn't we, Con?"

"Yeah," Conor agrees reluctantly. He was hating this parade of lies, especially because it was making us look like heroes when we weren't.

"I'd give a lot to know what happened during that dive," says Gray. "I feel like a kangaroo's been jumping up and down on my belly."

"We were lucky," says Roger. "But all the same, never, ever take such a risk again, kids. Your mother would hang, draw and quarter me if she knew."

If she knew? Does this mean – can this possibly mean that Roger isn't going to tell Mum?

"Call the coastguard if you ever think something's gone wrong. Don't risk your own lives," goes on Roger, sounding like one of those safety posters on the beaches in St Pirans. I can't stop a little smile curling round my lips. Big mistake. Roger looks at me sharply.

"By the way, what happened to the binoculars?"

"Binoculars?"

"Yes. Your father's binoculars. The ones you were looking through when you saw us dive."

"Oh. Oh, *those* binoculars. We—"

"We left them there," interrupts Conor.

"On the rocks?"

"We put them up above the tide line for safety. We'll be able to find them again."

"Good," says Roger.

"But I'm too tired to look for them today," I say quickly,

in case he suggests that we pick up the binoculars when we bring the boat in. "We'll come down for them at low tide tomorrow, won't we, Conor?"

"You do that," says Roger.

Roger and Gray finally make up their minds not to tell Mum about me and Conor swimming out to their boat. They're reluctant to discuss this decision with us, in case we think they're cheating Mum in some way. But we both agree that it would be crazy to tell her. What use would it be for Mum to know about the danger, now that it's all over? She'd only have nightmares for months, because of what happened to Dad. She would never feel safe about us being near the sea again.

Roger doesn't want Mum to be frightened because of him. He knows Mum well enough to sense that her fear of the sea is a real thing, alive and active. He doesn't want her to start worrying every time he takes his boat out, the way she did with Dad.

"Your mum's had enough to bear," he says quietly. "And nothing so terrible happened this time. We're all safe. A bit bruised and battered, but it could have been so much worse."

So much worse than you know, I thought.

"And whatever happened out there – and we'll probably never know – it's thanks to you two that it turned out no worse," says Roger. "Not that I want you to think I'm encouraging you to take that sort of risk again."

"Don't thank us," says Conor abruptly. Roger glances at him, but asks no questions, and they both busy themselves with bringing the boat in.

Maybe somewhere in Gray and Roger's minds, in some buried place, they knew how much worse it could have been. They don't consciously remember the seals' attack, but it must have left a mark on their minds as well as their bodies. Just thinking about it makes me shudder. Maybe that's another reason they want to keep the events of today from Mum. They'd like to wipe away the memory, as if it never happened.

But I don't think you can do that. I think that everything that happens to you stays in you, even if it stays in a part of your mind where you can't find it. That's why you should never try to forget when people urge you to.

People want me to forget Dad. They don't say it as straight as that, but it's what they want, all the same.

"You must try to move on, Saph. You've got your life to live. You mustn't be trapped in the past. You've got to think of the future now."

How I hate those words. *Move on.* Dad isn't the past, and I'm not trapped. He's alive, I know it. I will never stop thinking about him and trying to find him. I believe Dad knows that. He knows that I would never forget him, or stop searching for him.

While we're heading the boat back towards our cove, Roger keeps glancing back at the Bawns. Each time he sees those black jagged rocks sticking out of the water, he frowns. Gray doesn't look back at all.

A tiny film keeps running over and over again through my mind. The black, stick-like figures of Roger and Gray sprawl through the water again, turning over and over in slow motion. They sink down to the sea bed and rest there, until the currents cover them with sand.

No. It didn't happen. Gray and Roger didn't die. Roger is safe beside me, and now he's going to come back to our cottage and play cards with Mum and tell her what a great cook she is and generally irritate me until I want to scream.

But maybe he doesn't irritate me all the time. Sometimes I quite like talking to Roger.

I squeeze my eyes shut, and the film stops. But it hasn't disappeared, I know that. It's waiting inside my head, like a warning.

We all agree the story we're going to tell Mum. Roger will say that Conor and I went out with them in the boat, to watch the dive. (Mum will be bound to see us coming back in the boat, because she'll be waiting with the picnic.) Picnic! Is it possible that it's still the same day, and that only a couple of hours have passed? It seems so. Roger's watch says quarter to four. Ingo time and human time have kept close together, today. I wonder why that is. Maybe because Roger and Gray were never in Ingo at all? Divers go down into the water, but they never go into Ingo. And because Roger and Gray were following human time, we had to as well, or we'd never have been able to rescue them.

But when we bring the boat into the cove, Mum isn't there, waiting on shore. She didn't come down to the cove at all, she tells us later. She changed her mind, because there was so much picnic food to carry, and she wasn't sure what time Roger and Gray would arrive in the boat. She thought it would be better to keep the food in the cool, and have the picnic up in our garden.

Roger and Gray agree enthusiastically that it's not worth taking the picnic back down to the cove now. Mum has spread a rug in the garden, and laid out the food with cloths to cover it against the flies.

But once the first flurry of greetings is over, Mum gets a proper look at Roger and Gray. She sees everything. She's horrified by the scratch across Gray's face, and the bruises that are starting to appear on Roger and Gray's arms and legs.

"What happened? Oh God, you should never have gone. I should have guessed something would happen."

Roger puts his arm around her shoulders. It's the first time I've seen him touch Mum.

"Take it easy, Jennie, nothing's happened. We took a bit of a battering against the rocks, that's all. The currents out there are stronger than I'd allowed for."

"It's dangerous," says Mum. Her voice cracks with tension. "This whole coast is dangerous. People don't realise."

"It's OK, Jennie." Roger's hand grips Mum's shoulder, rocking her gently. "You don't have to think about it any more. Put it out of your mind. We won't be diving around the Bawns again. There's nothing there."

Mum's face slowly relaxes.

"You promise?"

"Swear and promise," says Roger. Conor and I exchange startled glances. I can see how relieved Mum is. Before we eat the picnic, she cleans Gray's scratch carefully with boiled water and a pad of lint.

"Strange," she mutters. "This doesn't look like a cut from a rock. It looks almost like a cat scratch. And it's deep. I'm worried it's going to leave a scar."

"You have everything round here, even underwater cats," says Gray, wincing as Mum applies the antiseptic cream. It's a lame joke, but Mum smiles.

"But it *does* look like some sort of claw mark... we'll have to watch it doesn't turn septic."

"Give me dogs any day," says Roger. "You know where you are with a dog. That reminds me, Jennie. What do you say we walk up to the farm one day this week, and find out what the position is with Sadie?" ·

"Nothing's settled, Sapphy!" says Mum hastily. "We're making enquiries, that's all. Don't look like that."

"Like what?"

"As if you'll die if it doesn't happen, that's what she means," says Conor. "Take it easy, Saph."

I force myself to be calm. Jack's mum and dad might have changed their minds about selling Sadie. Who wouldn't want to keep a dog like Sadie? I can't imagine even thinking of giving her away, if she was mine.

"Don't look so desperate, Saph," says Roger. "We'll do what we can."

That night Roger sleeps on our sofa, and I hear him yelling out in the middle of the night. Mum goes padding downstairs, and I hear them talking, but I can't hear what they're saying. Their voices rise and fall for a long time. I ask Mum about it in the morning, once Roger has left.

"What happened last night, Mum?"

"Roger had a nightmare," Mum says.

"What was it about?"

"You know how it is. Nightmares never make sense. He dreamed he was being tossed by a herd of giant bulls. They were underwater and he couldn't escape. It must have been terrifying. He woke up drenched in sweat. Underwater bulls! Funny what our minds come up with when we're asleep."

"Poor Roger."

"It's nice the way you're trying to get on with him now," says Mum, smiling at me approvingly. "Do you know, when we were talking about his nightmare, he suddenly said he was very grateful to you. That was a strange thing for him to say, wasn't it? What's he got to be grateful to you for? You've only just stopped acting like a little madam with him... Sapphire, are you all right? You've gone very pale."

"It's OK, Mum. Just sometimes it hurts when I breathe."

"What sort of pain is it? Does your chest feel tight? Breathe in deeply now, Sapphy, let me hear if you're wheezing."

Mum wanted to be a nurse when she was young, but she didn't have the right qualifications. She's trained as a first-aider, but she always says she'd like to take it further. So far, the only place she has taken it further is in our house.

"Mum, I haven't had asthma since I was about six. It's not that sort of pain."

"All the same, you ought to have a quiet day for once, tomorrow. Watch a film, read a book. You and Conor are always in that sea. You'll turn into a fish if you're not careful."

"Oh, Mum."

"I mean it."

"If we had a dog," I say casually, glancing sideways at Mum, "it would be good to hang out around the house with her. When I wasn't taking her for walks."

I can almost see the thought crossing Mum's face. *It's true. If Sapphy had a dog to look after, she wouldn't be running off down to the cove all the time.*

I say nothing more. With Mum, it's best to let the thought settle, and sink in.

If Sadie was here now, I could tell her everything. I could whisper it into her soft ears and she'd strain to understand me. I think she would understand some of it. There are so many things I can't tell anyone, not even Conor, or Faro. So many questions I want to ask.

It's Conor that Roger ought to be grateful to, not me. Conor could barely breathe or move, but he faced the seals for Roger's sake. I don't know what magic was in Conor's song, but it must have been powerful, to stop the seals' attack. Granny Carne said that Conor had his own power, and he must never forget it. I believed that Conor was weak in Ingo, and I was strong, but it was Conor who saved Roger and Gray. Faro and I and Elvira only helped to finish what Conor began.

I've called for Faro twice now when I've needed him. Both times he's answered and come to help me. But he doesn't come because of any power I've got, I'm sure of that. I don't know why it is that there seems to be a bond between us. I feel as if I've known Faro much longer than I've really known him.

Faro called me 'little sister'. I said I wasn't his sister, and he looked as if he wanted to tell me something, but then he didn't. And then, when he was leaving us at the boat, he said it again. *Little sister*.

I wish I'd thanked him. And those somersaults were amazing. I'd love to learn to do somersaults like that. Maybe Faro would teach me one day.

No, don't think of Ingo now. Don't let Ingo get too strong in your heart, or it will crowd out everything. I've learned that now. It's what the first Mathew Trewhella did, when he followed the Zennor mermaid and left Annie behind to give birth to his son without him.

I used to think that when a child was born, a parent made a promise to stay with him. Or her. But if there's a promise, it can be broken. That first Mathew Trewhella broke his promises. I wonder if he ever forgot them, or did the torn edges of his promises hurt him to the end of his life?

When someone goes away from you suddenly, without warning, that's what it's like. A rip, a torn edge inside you. I have a torn edge in me, and Dad has a torn edge in him. I'm not sure if those edges will still fit together by the time I find him.

And I will find him. That's more than a promise. It's the next level up from a promise: it's a vow.

CHAPTER TWENTY-FOUR

I t's evening now. I've decided to clear the garden that's been neglected since Dad went. I've been digging up weeds, chopping back brambles and piling up the rubbish into a heap. Dad would be pleased. I'm hot and sweaty but it feels good. Conor's gone into St Pirans with Mum, but I'm all right on my own. Because... because something wonderful has happened. I have got someone with me. She's lying on the path, watching me intelligently. Sometimes she gets up and investigates one of the million smells of the garden that only dogs can recognise.

No, she's not my dog yet. But I'm working on it. She's visiting just for a week, while Jack's family is on holiday. We're going to see how she gets on here.

"Supper soon, Sadie," I tell her, and she thumps her tail. She understands every word I say.

"There now, Sadie, don't you think Dad would be pleased if he saw how much I've done?"

The bees are going home after working all day in the flowers. One of them brushes past me and I wonder if it's going home to Granny Carne's hive. It stops, and burrows into a snapdragon flower. I can hear it buzzing and bumbling around inside. Maybe it's stuck? No, slowly it emerges.

Suddenly an idea strikes me. Maybe, if Conor could talk to the hive, I could talk to one single bee?

"Um – listen, can you hear me?"

But as soon as I start talking to the bee, I know it's not going to work. I haven't any of the feeling in me that Conor described. To be honest I don't believe that I have any earth magic at all. Sure enough, the bee takes no notice of me, and flies off with its load of pollen.

At that moment, a shadow falls over me. I look up quickly. There's no one there, but Sadie is on her feet, bristling, a growl starting in the back of her throat. And the evening sun's not so bright. No, the light's changing. It's going a strange colour, greenish blue, like the colour of underwater. But the sea can't come here! Ingo is not allowed to break its bounds, I know that.

"Sadie!"

Sadie backs against me, growling loudly now, pressing herself against my body. She's terrified, although for some strange reason I'm not afraid. But something's about to happen, I know it is.

"Myrgh kerenza," says a voice. It is so close, so familiar, that I can't believe there is no one else in the garden. *"Myrgh kerenza…"*

My mind stretches, and discovers the meaning of the

words. *Dear daughter.* Only two people in the world can call me by that name. "Dad!" I whisper. "Is it really you?" Dad here, in his own garden, at home...

But no one answers. Slowly, the light begins to change. The green-blue tinge of the light fades to the warm gold of evening. Sadie moves away from me, shakes herself all over as if she's coming out of the water, and barks and barks and barks.

"Quiet, Sadie!"

I listen hard, but all that I can hear are the normal sounds of a summer evening. But I feel warm. It's a good feeling. I am Dad's *myrgh kerenza.* His dear daughter. Somewhere he knows it, and I know it too. After Conor talked to the bees, he knew that Dad was alive. I believed Conor, but I still didn't really *know* it.

But now I do.

COMING SOON, *THE TIDE KNOT,*
THE SECOND PART OF THE *INGO* TRILOGY